The Lonely Unicorn
A Novel

by

Alec Waugh

The Lonely Unicorn
A Novel
by Alec Waugh

Copyright © 2024

All Rights reserved.

ISBN: 978-93-63059-37-5

Published by

DOUBLE 9 BOOKS

2/13-B, Ansari Road
Daryaganj, New Delhi – 110002
info@double9books.com
www.double9books.com
Tel. 011-40042856

This book is under public domain

ABOUT THE AUTHOR

Alec Waugh was a British novelist, the elder brother of the more famous Evelyn Waugh, the uncle of Auberon Waugh, and the son of Arthur Waugh, an author, literary critic, and publisher. His first marriage was Barbara Jacobs (daughter of author William Wymark Jacobs), his second wife was Joan Chirnside, and his third wife was Virginia Sorenson, author of the Newbery Medal-winning Miracles on Maple Hill. Waugh was born in London to Arthur Waugh and Catherine Charlotte Raban, the great-granddaughter of Lord Cockburn (1779-1854), and attended Sherborne School, a public school in Dorset. As a result of his experiences, he wrote his first semi-autobiographical novel, The Loom of Youth (1917), which dramatized his school days. Waugh served in the British army in France during World War I, being commissioned in the Dorset Regiment in May 1917 and saw duty at Passchendaele. Captured by the Germans at Arras in March 1918, he spent the rest of the war in POW camps in Karlsruhe and the Mainz Citadel. Waugh married his first wife, Barbara Annis Jacobs (1900–1996), in 1919. He later became a successful author, albeit not as successful or original as his younger brother.

CONTENTS

PART I
THE OPENING ROUND

CHAPTER I
TWO HAPHAZARDS 7

CHAPTER II
THE OUTCOME 15

CHAPTER III
RALPH AND APRIL 21

CHAPTER IV
A KISS 29

CHAPTER V
A POTENTIAL DIPLOMAT 36

CHAPTER VI
APRIL'S LOOKING-GLASS 47

CHAPTER VII
A SORRY BUSINESS 52

PART II
THE RIVAL FORCES

CHAPTER VIII
A FORTUNATE MEETING 72

CHAPTER IX
HOGSTEAD 82

CHAPTER X
YOUNG LOVE 92

CHAPTER XI
THE ROMANCE OF VARNISH 108

CHAPTER XII
MARSTON & MARSTON 118

CHAPTER XIII
LILITH OF OLD 124

CHAPTER XIV
THE TWO CURRENTS 138

PART III
THE FIRST ENCOUNTERS

CHAPTER XV
SUCCESS... 145

CHAPTER XVI
LILITH AND MURIEL.. 170

PART IV
ONE WAY OR ANOTHER

CHAPTER XVII
THREE YEARS.. 175

CHAPTER XVIII
THREE DAYS.. 180

CHAPTER XIX
THE LONELY UNICORN 197

CHAPTER XX
THERE'S ROSEMARY 210

CHAPTER XXI
THE SHEDDING OF THE CHRYSALIS... 215

CHAPTER XXII
AN END AND A BEGINNING 228

PART I
THE OPENING ROUND

CHAPTER I
TWO HAPHAZARDS

It began, I suppose, on a certain September afternoon, when Roland Whately travelled back to school by the three-thirty train from Waterloo. There were two afternoon trains to Fernhurst: one left London at three-thirty and arrived at a quarter to six; the other left at four-eighteen, stopped at every station between Basingstoke and Salisbury, waited twenty-five minutes at Templecombe for a connection, and finally reached Fernhurst at eight-twenty-three. It is needless to state that by far the greater part of the school travelled down by the four-eighteen—who for the sake of a fast train and a comfortable journey would surrender forty-eight minutes of his holidays?—and usually, of course, Roland accompanied the many.

This term, however, the advantages of the fast train were considerable. He was particularly anxious to have the corner bed in his dormitory. There was a bracket above it where he could place a candle, by the light of which he would be able to learn his rep. after "lights out." If he were not there first someone else would be sure to collar it. And then there was the new study at the end of the passage; he wanted to get fresh curtains and probably a gas mantle: when once the school was back it was impossible, for at least a week, to persuade Charlie, the school custos, to attend to an odd job like that. And so he travelled back by a train that contained, of the three hundred boys who were on the Fernhurst roll, only a dozen fags and three timid Sixth-Formers who had distrusted the animal spirits of certain powerful and irreverent Fifth-Formers. On the first day, as on the last, privilege counts for little, and it is unpleasant to pass four hours under the seat of a dusty railway carriage.

It was the first time that Roland had been able to spend the first evening of a term in complete leisure. He walked quietly up to the house, went down to the matron's room and consulted the study and dormitory lists. He found that he was on the Sixth-Form table, had been given the study for which he had applied, and was in the right dormitory. He bagged the bed he wanted, and took his health certificate round to the Chief's study.

"Ah, Whately, this is very early. Had a good holiday?"

"Yes, thank you, sir."

"Feeling ready for football? They tell me you've an excellent chance of getting into the XV.?"

"I hope so, sir."

He went over to the studies and inspected the gas fittings. Yes, he would certainly need a new mantle, and he must try to see if Charlie couldn't fit him up with a new curtain. After a brief deliberation Charles decided that he could; a half-crown changed hands, and as Roland strolled back from the lodge the Abbey clock struck half-past six. Over two hours to prayers. He had done all his jobs, and there didn't seem to be a soul in the place. He began to wonder whether, after all, it had been worth his while to catch that early train: it had been a dull journey, two hours in the company of three frightened fags, outhouse fellows whom he didn't know, and who had huddled away in a corner of the carriage and talked in whispers. If, on the other hand, he had waited for the four-eighteen he would at that moment be sitting with five or six first-class fellows, talking of last year's rags, of the new prefects, and the probable composition of the XV. He would be much happier there. And as for the dormitory and study, well, he'd have probably been able to manage if he had hurried from the station. He had done so a good many times before. Altogether he had made a bit of an ass of himself. An impetuous fool, that was what he was.

And for want of anything better to do, he mouched down to Ruffer's, the unofficial tuck-shop. There was no one he knew in the front of the shop, so he walked into the inside room and found, sitting in a far corner, eating an ice, Howard, one of the senior men in Morgan's.

"Hullo!" he said. "So you've been ass enough to come down by the early train as well?"

"Yes, I was coming up from Cornwall, and it's the only way I could make the trains fit in. A bad business. There's nothing to do but eat: come and join me in an ice."

Howard was only a very casual acquaintance; he was no use at games; he had never been in the same form as Roland, and fellows in the School house usually kept pretty much to themselves. They had only met in groups outside the chapel, or at roll-call, or before a lecture. It was probably the first time they had ever been alone together.

"Right you are!" said Roland. "Mr Ruffer, bring me a large strawberry ice and a cup of coffee."

But the ice did not last long, and they were soon strolling up the High Street, with time heavy on their hands. Conversation flagged; they had very little in common.

"I know," said Howard. "Let's go down to the castle grounds; they'll probably have a band, and we can watch the dancing."

Half-way between the station and the school, opposite the Eversham Hotel, where parents stopped for "commem" and confirmation, was a public garden with a band-stand and well-kept lawns, and here on warm summer evenings dances would promote and encourage the rustic courtships of the youthful townsfolk. During the term these grounds were strictly out of bounds to the school; but on the first night rules did not exist, and besides, no one was likely to recognise them in the bowler hats and coloured ties that would have to be put away that night in favour of black poplin and broad white straw.

It was a warm night, and they leaned against the railing watching the girls in their light print dresses waltz in the clumsy arms of their selected.

"Looks awfully jolly," said Howard. "They don't have a bad time, those fellows. There are one or two rippingly pretty girls."

"And look at the fellows they're dancing with. I can't think how they can stand it. Now look there, at that couple by the stand. She's a really pretty girl, while her man is pimply, with a scraggy moustache and sweating forehead, and yet look how she's leaning over his shoulder; think of her being kissed by that."

"I suppose there's something about him."

"I suppose so."

There was a pause: Roland wished that difference of training and position did not hold them from the revel.

"By Jove!" said Roland, "it would be awful fun to join them."

"Well, I dare you to."

"Dare say you do. I'm not having any. I don't run risks in a place where I'm known."

As a matter of fact, Roland did not run risks anywhere, but he wanted Howard to think him something of a Don Juan. One is always ashamed of innocence, and Howard was one of those fellows who naturally bring out the worst side of their companions. His boisterous, assertive confidence was practically a challenge, and Roland did not enjoy the rôle of listener and disciple, especially as Howard was, by the school standards, socially his inferior.

At that moment two girls strolled past, turned, and giggled over their shoulders.

"Do you see that?" said Roland.

"What about it?"

"Well, I mean...."

The girls were coming back, and suddenly, to Roland's surprise, embarrassment and annoyance, Howard walked forward and raised his hat.

"Lonely?" he said.

"Same as you."

"Like a walk, then?"

"All right, if your friend's not too shy."

And before Roland could make any protest he was walking, tongue-tied and helpless, on the arm of a full-blown shop-girl.

"Well, you're a cheerful sort of chap, aren't you?" she said at last.

"Sorry, but you see I wasn't expecting you!"

"Oh, she didn't turn up, I suppose?"

"I didn't mean that."

"Oh, get along, I know you; you're all the same. Why, I was talking to a boy last week...."

To save her the indignity of a confession, Roland suggested that they should dance.

"All right, only don't hold me too tight—sister's looking."

There was no need to talk while they were dancing, and he was glad to be able to collect his thoughts. It was an awkward business. She wasn't on the whole a bad-looking girl; she was certainly too plump, but she had a nice smile and pretty hair; and he felt no end of a dog. But it was impossible to become romantic, for she giggled every time he tried to hold her a little closer, and once when his cheek brushed accidentally against hers she gave him a great push, and shouted, "Now then, naughty!" to the intense amusement of another couple. Still, he enjoyed dancing with her. It would be something to tell the fellows afterwards. They would be sitting in the big study. Gradually the talk would drift round to girls. He would sit in silence while the others would relate invented escapades, prefaced by, "My brother told me," or, "I saw in a French novel." He would wait for the lull, then himself would let fall—oh! so gently—into the conversation, "a girl that I danced with in the castle grounds...."

The final crash of the band recalled him to the requirements of the moment, and the need for conversation. They sat on a seat and discussed the weather, the suitability of grass as a dancing floor, the superiority of a band over a piano. He introduced subject after subject, bringing them up one after another, like the successive waves of infantry in an attack. It was not a success. The first bars of a waltz were a great relief.

He jumped up and offered her his arm.

"From the school, aren't you?" she said.

"How did you guess?" he asked. She answered him with a giggle.

It was a blow, admittedly a blow. He had not imagined himself a shining success, but he had not thought that he was giving himself away quite as badly as that. They got on a great deal better though after it. They knew where they were, and he found her a very jolly girl, a simple creature, whose one idea was to be admired and to enjoy herself, an ambition not so very different from Roland's. It was her sense of humour that beat him: she giggled most of the time; why he could not understand. It was annoying, because everyone stared at them, and Roland hated to be conspicuous. He was prepared to enjoy the illusion but not the reality in public. He was not therefore very sorry when the Abbey clock warned him that in a few minutes the four-eighteen would have arrived and that the best place for him was the School house dining-room.

On the way back he met Howard.

"I say, you rather let me in for it, you know," he said.

"Oh, rot, my dear chap; but even if I did, I'll bet you enjoyed yourself all right."

"Perhaps I did. But that makes no difference. After all, you didn't know I was going to. I'd never seen the girl before."

"But one never has on these occasions, has one? One's got to trust to luck: you know that as well as I do."

"Of course, of course, but still...."

They argued it out till they reached the cloisters leading to the School house studies, exchanged there a cheery good-night and went their way. Five minutes later the four-eighteen was in; the study passages were filled with shouts; Roland was running up and down stairs, greeting his old friends. The incident was closed, and in the normal course of things it would never have been reopened.

That it was reopened was due entirely, if indirectly, to Roland's laziness on a wet Sunday afternoon, half way through October. It was a really wet afternoon, the sort of afternoon when there is nothing to be done but to pack one's study full of really good chaps and get up a decent fug. Any small boy can be persuaded, with the aid of a shilling, to brew some tea, and there are few things better than to sit in the window-seat and watch the gravel courts turn to an enormous lake. Roland was peculiarly aware of the charm of an afternoon so spent as he walked across to his study after lunch, disquieted by the knowledge that his football boots wanted restudding and that the night before he had vowed solemnly that he would take them down to the professional before tea. It would be fatal to leave them any longer, and he knew it. The ground on Saturday had been too wet for football, and the whole house had gone for a run, during which Roland had worn down one of his studs on the hard roads, and driven a nail that uncomfortable hundredth of an inch through the sole of his boot. If he wore those boots again before they had been mended that hundredth of an inch would become a tenth of an inch, and make no small part of a crater in his foot. It was obviously up to him to put on a mackintosh and go down to the field at once. There was no room for argument, and Roland knew it, but....

It was very pleasant and warm inside the study and damnably unpleasant anywhere else. If only he were a prefect, and had a fag, how simple his life would become. His shoes would be cleaned for him, his shaving water would be boiled in the morning, his books would be carried down to his classroom, and on this rain-drenched afternoon he would only have to put his head outside the study door and yell "Fag!" and it would be settled. But he was not a prefect, and he had no fag. It was no use growling about it. He would have to go, of course he would have to go, then added as a corollary—yes, certainly, at three o'clock. By that time the weather might have cleared up.

But it had not cleared up by three o'clock, and Roland had become hopelessly intrigued by a novel by Wilkie Collins, called *The Moonstone*. He had just reached the place where Sergeant Cuff looks up at Rachel's window and whistles *The Last Rose of Summer*. He could not desert Sergeant Cuff at such a point for a pair of football boots, and at three o'clock, with the whole afternoon before him. At half-past there would be tons of time. But by half-past three it was raining in the true Fernhurst manner, fierce, driving rain that whipped across the courts, heavy gusts of wind that shrieked down the cloisters. Impossible weather, absolutely impossible weather. No one but a fool would go out in it. He would wait till four, it was certain to have stopped a bit by then.

And by four o'clock it certainly was raining a good deal less, but by four o'clock some eight persons had assembled in the study and a most exciting discussion was in progress. Someone from Morgan's had started a rumour to the effect that Fitzgerald, the vice-captain of the XV., was going to be dropped out of the side for the Tonwich match and his place given to Feversham, a reserve centre from James's. It was a startling piece of news, that had to be discussed from every point of view.

First of all, would the side be improved? A doubtful matter. Fitzgerald had certainly been out of form this season, and he had played miserably in the last two matches, but he had experience; he would not be likely to lose his head in a big game, and Feversham, well, it would be his first school match. Altogether a doubtful issue, and, granted even that Feversham was better than Fitzgerald, would it be worth while in the long run to leave out the vice-captain and head of Buxton's? Would it be doing a good service to Fernhurst football? Buxton's was the athletic house; it had six school colours. The prestige of Fernhurst depended a good deal on the prestige of Buxton's. Surely the prestige of Buxton's was more important than a problematic improvement in the three-quarter line.

They argued it out for a quarter of an hour and then, just when the last point had been brought forward, and Roland had begun to feel that he was left with no possible excuse for not going down to the field, the tea arrived; and after that what chance did he stand? By the time tea was over it was nearly five o'clock. Choir practice would have started in a quarter of an hour: if he wanted to, he could not have gone down then. A bad business. But it had been a pleasant afternoon; it was raining like blazes still; very likely the ground would be again too wet for play to-morrow, and he would cut the walk and get his boots mended. No doubt things would pan out all right.

Things, however, did not on this occasion adapt themselves to Roland's wishes. The rain stopped shortly after eight o'clock; a violent wind shrieked all night along the cloisters; next morning the violent wind was accompanied by bright sunshine; by half-past two the ground was almost dry. Roland played in his unstudded boots, and, as he had expected, the projecting hundredth of an inch sank deeply into his toe. Three days later he was sent up to the sanatorium with a poisoned foot.

And in the sanatorium he found himself in the same ward and alone with Howard, who was recovering from an attack of "flu" that had been incorrectly diagnosed as measles.

It was the first time they had met since the first evening of the term.

CHAPTER II
THE OUTCOME

When two people are left alone together all day, with no amusement except their own conversation, they naturally become intimate, and as the episode of the dance was the only bond of interest between Howard and Roland they turned to it at once. As soon as the matron had gone out of the room Howard asked if he had been forgiven.

"Oh, yes, a long time ago; it was a jolly rag."

"Seen anything of your girl since then?"

"Heavens! no. Have you?"

"I should jolly well think so; one doesn't let a thing like that slip through one's fingers in a hurry. I go out with her every Sunday, and as likely as not once or twice during the week."

Roland was struck with surprise and admiration.

"But how on earth do you manage it?"

"Oh, it's quite easy: in our house anyone can get out who wants to. The old man never spots anything. I just heave on a cap and mackintosh, meet her behind the Abbey and we go for a stroll along the Slopes."

Roland could not ask too many questions and Howard was only too ready to answer them. He had seldom enjoyed such a splendid audience. He was not thought much of in the school, and to tell the truth he was not much of a fellow. He had absorbed the worst characteristics of a bad house. He would probably after he had left spend his evenings hanging about private bars and the stage doors of second-class music halls. But he was an interesting companion in the sanatorium, and he and Roland discussed endlessly the eternally fascinating subject of girls.

"The one thing that you must never do with a girl is to be shy," Howard said. "That's the one fatal thing that she'll never forgive. You can do anything you like with any girl if only you go the right way about it. She doesn't care whether you are good-looking or rich or clever, but if she feels that you know more than she does, that she can trust herself in your hands.... It's all personality. If a girl tries to push you away when you kiss her, don't worry her, kiss her again; she only wants to be persuaded; she'd despise you if you stopped; girls are weak themselves, so they hate weakness. You can take it from me, Whately, that girls are an easy game when you know the way to treat them. It would surprise you if you could only know what they were thinking. You'll see them sitting at your father's table, so demure, with their 'Yes, Mr Howard,' and their 'No, Mr Howard.' You'd think they'd stepped out of the pages of a fairy book, and yet get those same girls alone, and in the right mood, my word...."

Inflammatory, suggestive stuff: the pimp in embryo.

And Roland was one of those on whom such persons thrive. He had always kept straight at school; he was not clever nor imaginative, but he was ambitious: and he had realised early that if he wanted to become a power in the school he must needs be a success at games. He had kept clear of anything that had seemed likely to impair his prowess on the field. But it was different for him here in the sanatorium, with no exercise and occupation. In a very little while he had become thoroughly roused. Howard had enjoyed a certain number of doubtful experiences; had read several of the books that appear in the advertisements of obscure French papers as "rare and curious." He had in addition a good imagination. Within two days Roland's one idea was to pick up at the first opportunity the threads of the romance he had so callously flung aside.

"There'll be no difficulty about that, my dear fellow," said Howard. "I can easily get Betty to arrange it. We meet every Sunday, and we have to walk right out beyond Cold Harbour. She says she feels a bit lonely going out all that way by herself. Now suppose she went out with your girl and you went out with me—that'ld be pretty simple, wouldn't it?"

"Oh, that would be splendid. Do you think you could fix it up?"

"As easy as laughing."

"But I shall feel an awful fool," Roland insisted. "I shan't know what to say or anything."

"Don't you worry about that, my dear fellow; you just look as if you did and keep your eyes open, and you'll soon learn; these girls know a lot more than you would think."

So it was arranged. Roland found by the time his foot was right again that he had let himself in for a pretty exacting programme. It had all seemed jolly enough up at the sanatorium, but when he was back in the house, and life re-established its old values, he began to regret it very heartily. He didn't mind going out with the girl—that would be quite exciting: besides it was an experience to which everyone had to come some time or other—but he did not look forward to a long walk with Howard every Sunday afternoon for the rest of the term.

"Whately, old son," he said to his reflection in the glass as he shaved himself on the next Sunday morning, "you've made a pretty sanguinary fool of yourself, but you can't clear out now. You've got to see it through."

It was very awkward though when Anderson ran up to him in the cloisters with "Hullo, Whately, going out for a stroll; well, just wait half-a-sec. while I fetch my hat." Roland had an infernal job getting rid of him.

"But, my dear man," Anderson had protested, "where on earth are you going? I've always thought you the piest man in the house. But if it's a smoke I'll watch you and if it's a drink I'll help you."

"Oh no, it's not that. I'm going out with a man in Morgan's."

Anderson's mouth emitted a long whistle of surprise.

"So our Whately has deserted his old friends? Ah, well, when one gets into the XV., I know."

Roland could see that Anderson was offended.

But it was even worse when he came back to find his study full of seven indignant sportsmen wanting to know why on earth he had taken to going out for walks with "a dirty tick in Morgan's, who was no use at anything and didn't even wash."

"He's quite a decent chap," said Roland weakly. "I met him in the san."

"I dare say you did," said Anderson; "we're not blaming you for that. You couldn't help it. But those sorts of things, one does try to live down."

For days he was ragged about it, so much so that he hadn't the face to say he had been going out with a girl. Such a statement should be a proud acknowledgment, not a confession. If ever he said he couldn't go anywhere, or do something, the invariable retort was, "I suppose you're going out for a walk with Howard."

The School house was exclusive; it was insular; it was prepared to allow the possibility of its members having friends in the outhouses; there were good men in the outhouses, even in Morgan's. But one had to be particular, and when it came to Whately, a man of whom the house was proud, deserting his friends for a greasy swine in Morgan's who didn't wash, well, the least one could do was to make the man realise that he had gone a little far.

It was a bad business, altogether a bad business, and Roland very much doubted whether the hour and a half he spent with Dolly was an adequate recompense. She was a nice girl, quite a nice girl, and they found themselves on kissing terms quickly enough. There were no signs of their getting any further, and, as a matter of fact, if there had been, Roland would have been extremely alarmed. He objected to awkward situations and intense emotions: he preferred to keep his life within the decent borders of routine. He wanted adventure certainly, but adventure bounded by the limits of the society in which he lived. He liked to feel that his day was tabulated and arranged; he hated that lost feeling of being unprepared; he liked to know exactly what he had to say to Dolly before he could hold her hand and exactly what he had to say before she would let him kiss her. It was a game that had to be rehearsed before one got it right; no actor enjoys his part before he has learnt his words; when he had learnt the rules it was great fun; kisses were pleasant things. He wrote a letter to his friend, Ralph Richmond, acquainting him of this fact.

> My Dear Ralph,—Why haven't you written to me, you lazy swine? I suppose you will say that you're awfully hard worked, getting ready for Smalls. But I don't believe it. I know how much I do myself.
>
> It's been quite a decent term. I got my colours and shall be captain of the house after the summer if the people I think are going to leave do leave. Think of me as a ruler of men. I'm having a pretty good slack in form and don't have to do any work, except in French, where a fellow called Carus-Evans, an awful swine, has his knife into me and puts me on whenever we get to a hard bit. However, as I never do much else I'm able to swot the French all right.
>
> The great bit of news, though, is that I've met a girl in the town who I go out for walks with. I'm not really keen on her, and I think I prefer her friend, Betty (we go in couples). Betty's much older and she's dark and she makes you blush when she looks at you. Still, Dolly's very jolly, and we go out for walks every Sunday and have great times. She lets me kiss her as much as I like. Now what do you think of it? Write and tell me at once. Yours ever,
>
> Roland.

Two days later Roland received the following reply:—

> My Dear Roland,—So glad to hear from you again, and many congratulations on your firsts. I had heard about them as a matter of fact, and had been meaning to write to

you, but I am very busy just now. April told me about it; she seemed awfully pleased. I must say she was looking jolly pretty; she thinks a lot of you. Sort of hero. If I were you I should think a bit more about her and a little less about your Bettys and Dollys.

I'm looking forward to the holidays. We must manage to have a few good rags somehow. The Saundersons are giving a dance, so that ought to be amusing. Ever yours,

Ralph.

Roland's comment on this letter was "Jealous little beast." He wished he hadn't written to him. And why drag April in? He and April were great friends; they always had been. Once they had imagined themselves sweethearts. When they went out to parties they had always sat next each other during tea and held hands under the table; in general post Roland had often been driven into the centre because of a brilliant failure to take the chair that was next to hers. They had kissed sometimes at dances in the shadow of a passage, and once at a party, when they had been pulling crackers, he had slipped on to the fourth finger of her left hand a brass ring that had fallen from the crumpled paper. She still kept that ring, although the days of courtship were over. Roland had altered since he had gone to Fernhurst. But they were great friends, and there was always an idea between the two families that the children might eventually marry. Mr Whately was, indeed, fond of prefacing some remote speculation about the future with, "By the time Roland and April are married — —"

There was no need, Roland felt, for Ralph to have dragged April into the business at all. He was aggrieved, and the whole business seemed again a waste and an encumbrance. Was it worth while? He got ragged in the house, and he had to spend an hour in Howard's company before he met Dolly at all. Howard was really rather terrible; so conceited, so familiar; and now that he had found an audience he indulged it the whole time. He was at his worst when he attempted sentiment. Once when they were walking back he turned to Roland, in the middle of a soliloquy, with a gesture of profound disdain and resignation.

"But what's all this after all?" he said. "It's nothing; it's pleasant; it passes the time, and we have to have some distractions in this place to keep us going. But it's not the real thing; there's all the difference in the world between this and the real thing. A kiss can be anything or nothing; it can raise one to—to any height, or it can be like eating chocolates. I'm not a chap, you know, who really cares for this sort of thing. I'm in love. I suppose you are too."

And Roland, who did not want to be outdone, confessed that there was someone, "a girl he had known all his life."

"But you don't want a girl you've known all your life; love's not a thing that we drift into; it must be sudden; it must be unexpected; it must hurt."

Howard was a sore trial, and it was with the most unutterable relief that Roland learned that he was leaving at Christmas to go to a crammer's.

"We must keep up with one another, old fellow," Howard said on their last Sunday. "You must come and lunch with me one day in town. Write and tell me all about it. We've had some jolly times."

Roland caught a glimpse of him on the last day, resplendent in an O.F. scarf, very loud and hearty, saying "good-bye" to people he had hardly spoken to before. "You'll write to me, won't you, old fellow? Come and lunch with me when you're up in town. The Regent Club. Good-bye." Since his first year, when the prefect for whom he had fagged, and by whom he had been beaten several times, had left, Roland had never been so heartily thankful to see any member of the school in old boys' colours.

CHAPTER III
RALPH AND APRIL

Ralph Richmond was the son of an emotional woman and he had read too many novels. He took himself seriously: without being religious, he considered that it was the duty of every man to leave the world better than he found it. Such a philosophy may be natural to a man of thirty-six who sees small prospect of realising his own ambition, and resorts to the consolation of a collective enthusiasm, but it is abnormal in a boy of seventeen, an age which usually sees itself in the stalls of a theatre waiting for the curtain to rise and reveal a stage set with limitless opportunities for self-development and self-indulgence.

But Ralph had been brought up in an atmosphere of ideals; at the age of seven he gave a performance of *Hamlet* in the nursery, and in the same year he visited a lenten performance of *Everyman*. At his preparatory school he came under the influence of an empire builder, who used to appeal to the emotions of his form. "The future of the country is in your hands," he would say. "One day you will be at the helm. You must prepare yourselves for that time. You must never forget." And Ralph did not. He thought of himself as the arbiter of destinies. He felt that till that day his life must be a vigil. Like the knights of Arthurian romance, he would watch beside his armour in the chapel. In the process he became a prig, and on his last day at Rycroft Lodge he became a prude. His headmaster gave all the boys who were leaving a long and serious address on the various temptations of the flesh to which they would be subjected at their Public Schools. Ralph had no clear idea of what these temptations might be. Their results, however, seemed sufficient reason for abstention. If he yielded to them, he gathered that he would lose in a short time his powers of thought, his strength, his moral stamina; a slow poison would devour him; in a few years he would be mad and blind and probably, though of this he was not quite certain, deaf as well. At any rate he would be in a condition when the ability of detecting sound would be of slight value. These threats were alarming: their effect, however, would not have been lasting in the case of Ralph, who was no coward and also, being no fool, would have soon observed that this process of disintegration was not universal in its application. No; it was not the threat that did the damage: it was the romantic appeal of the headmaster's peroration.

"After all," he said, after a dramatic pause, "how can any one of you who has been a filthy beast at school dare to propose marriage to some pure, clean woman?"

That told; that sentiment was within the range of his comprehension; it was a beautiful idea, a chivalrous idea, worthy, he inappropriately imagined, of Sir Lancelot. He could understand that a knight should come to his lady with glittering armour and an unstained sword. At the time he did not fully appreciate the application of this image: he soon learnt, however, that a night spent on one's knees on the stone floor of a draughty chapel is a cold and lonely prelude to enchantment: a discovery that did not make him the more charitable to those who preferred clean linen and soft down.

It was only to be supposed, therefore, that he would receive Roland's confidences with disgust. He had always felt a little jealous of April's obvious preference for his friend, but he had regarded it as the fortune of war and had taken what pleasure he might in the part of confidant. To this vicarious excitant their intimacy indeed owed its strength. His indignation, therefore, when he learnt of Roland's rustic courtship was only exceeded by his positive fury when, on the first evening of the holidays, he went round to see the Curtises and found there Roland and his father. It was the height of hypocrisy. He had supposed that Roland would at least have the decency to keep away from her. It had been bad enough to give up a decent girl for a shop assistant, but to come back and carry on as though nothing had happened.... It was monstrous, cruel, unthinkable. And there was April, so clean and calm, with her thick brown hair gathered up in a loop across her forehead; her eyes, deep and gentle, with subdued colours, brown and a shade of green, and that delicate smile of simple trust and innocence, smiling at him, ignorant of how she had been deceived.

It must be set down, however, to Roland's credit that he had felt a few qualms about going round at once to see the Curtises. Less than twenty-four hours had passed since he had held Dolly's hand and protested to her an undying loyalty. He did not love her; the words meant nothing, and they both knew it; they were merely part of the convention of the game. Nor for that matter was he in love with April—at least he did not think he was. He owed nothing to either of them. But conscience told him that, in view of the understanding that was supposed to exist between them, it would be more proper to wait a day or two. After all, one did not go to a theatre the day after one's father's funeral, however eagerly one's imagination had anticipated the event.

Things had, however, turned out otherwise. At a quarter to six Mr Whately returned from town. He was the manager of a bank, at a salary of seven hundred and fifty pounds a year, an income that allowed the family to visit the theatre, upper circle seats, at least once every holidays and provided Roland with as much pocket-money as he needed. Mr Whately walked into the drawing-room, greeted his son with the conventional joke about a holiday task, handed his wife a copy of *The Globe*, sat down in front of the fire and began to take off his boots.

"Nothing much in the papers to-day, my dear. Not much happening anywhere as a matter of fact. I had lunch to-day with Robinson and he called it the lull before the storm. I shouldn't be a bit surprised if he wasn't right. You can't trust these Radicals."

He was a scrubby little man: for thirty years he had worked in the same house: there had been no friction and no excitement in his life: he had by now lost any independence of thought and action.

"I've just found a splendid place, my dear, where you can get a really first-class lunch for one-and-sixpence."

"Have you, dear?"

"Yes; in Soho, just behind the Palace. I went there to-day with Robinson. We had four courses, and cheese to finish up with. Something like."

"And was it well cooked, dear?"

"Rather; the plaice was beautifully fried. Just beginning to brown."

His face flushed with a genuine animation. Change of food was the only adventure that life brought to him. He rose slowly.

"Well, I must go up and change, I suppose. I've one or two other things to tell you, dear, later on."

He did not ask his wife what she had been doing during the day; it was indeed doubtful whether he appreciated the existence of any life at 105 Hammerton Villas, Hammerton, during the hours when he was away from them. Himself was the central point.

Five minutes later he came down stairs in a light suit.

"Well, who's coming out with me for a constitutional?"

Roland got up, walked into the hall, picked up his hat and stick.

"Right you are, father; I'm ready."

It was the same thing every day. At eight-thirty-five Mr Whately caught a bus at the corner of the High Street. He had never been known to miss it.

On the rare occasions when he was a few seconds late the driver would wait till he saw the panting little figure come running round the corner, trying to look dignified in spite of the top hat that bobbed from one side of his head to the other. From nine o'clock till a quarter-past five Mr Whately worked at a desk, with an hour's interval for lunch. Every evening he went for an hour's walk; for half-an-hour before dinner he read the evening paper. After dinner he would play a game of patience and smoke his pipe. Occasionally a friend would drop in for a chat; very occasionally he would go out himself. At ten o'clock sharp he went to bed. Every Saturday afternoon he attended a public performance of either cricket or football according to the season. Roland often wondered how he could stand it. What had he to look forward to? What did he think about when he sat over the fire puffing at his pipe. And his mother. How monotonous her life appeared to him. Yet she seemed always happy enough: she never grumbled. Roland could not understand it. Whatever happened, he would take jolly good care that he never ran into a groove like that. They had loved each other well enough once, he supposed, but now—oh, well, love was the privilege of youth.

Father and son walked in silence. They were fond of each other; they liked being together; Mr Whately was very proud of his son's achievements; but their affection was never expressed in words. After a while they began to talk of indifferent things, guessing at each other's thoughts: a relationship of intuitions. They passed along the High Street and, turning behind the shops, walked down a long street of small red-brick villas with stucco fronts.

"Don't you think we ought to go in and see the Curtises?" Mr Whately asked.

"I don't know. I hadn't meant to. I thought...."

"I think you ought to, you know, your first day; they'd be rather offended if you didn't. April asked me when you were coming back."

And so Roland was bound to abandon his virtuous resolution.

It was not a particularly jolly evening before Ralph arrived. Afterwards it was a good deal worse.

In the old days, when father and son had paid an evening visit, Roland had run straight up to the nursery and enjoyed himself, but now he had to sit in the drawing-room, which was a very different matter. He did not like Mrs Curtis: he never had liked her, but she had not troubled him in the days when she had been a mere voice below the banisters. Now he had to sit in the small drawing-room, with its shut windows, and hear her voice cleave through the clammy atmosphere in languid, pathetic cadences; a sentimental voice, and under the sentiment a hard, cold cruelty. Her person was out of keeping with her voice; it should have been plump and comfortable-looking; instead it was tall, thin, angular, all over points, like a hat-rack in a restaurant: a terrible bedfellow. And she talked, heavens! how she talked. It was usually about her children.

"Dear Arthur, he's getting on so well at school. Do you know what his headmaster said about him in his report?"

"Oh, but, mother, please," Arthur would protest.

"No, dear, be quiet: I know Mr Whately would like to hear. The headmaster said, Mr Whately...." Then it was her daughter's turn. "And April too, Mr Whately, she's getting on so well with her drawing lessons. Mr Hamilton was only saying to me yesterday...."

It was not surprising that Roland was less keen now on going round there. It was little fun for him after all to sit and listen while she talked, to see his father so utterly complacent, with his "Yes, Mrs Curtis," and his "Really, Mrs Curtis," and to look at poor April huddled in the window-seat, so bored, so ashamed, her eyes meeting his with a look that said: "Don't worry about her, don't take any notice of what she says. I'm not like that." Once or twice he tried to talk to her, but it was no use: her mother would interrupt, would bring them back into the circle of her own egotism. In her own drawing-room she would tolerate nothing independent of herself.

"Yes, Roland; what was it you were saying? The Saundersons' dance? Of course April will be going. They're very old friends of ours, the Saundersons. Mr Saunderson thinks such a lot of Arthur too. You know, Mr Whately, I met him in the High Street the other afternoon and he said to me, 'How's that clever son of yours getting on, Mrs Curtis?'"

"Really, Mrs Curtis."

"Yes, really, Mr Whately."

It was at this point that Ralph arrived.

His look of surprised displeasure was obvious to everyone. But knowing Ralph, they mistook it for awkwardness. He did not like company, and his shyness was apparent as he stood in the doorway in an ill-fitting suit, with trousers that bagged at the knees, and with the front part of his hair smarmed across his forehead with one hurried sweep of a damp brush, at right angles to the rest of his hair, that fell perpendicularly from the crown of his head.

"Come along, Ralph," said April, and made room for him in the window-seat. She treated him with an amused condescension. He was so clumsy; a dear fellow, so easy to rag. "And how did your exam. go?" she asked.

"All right."

"No; but really, tell me about it. What were the maths like?"

"Not so bad."

"And the geography? You were so nervous about that."

"I didn't do badly."

"And the Latin and the Greek? I want to know all about it."

"You don't, really?"

"Yes, but I do."

"No, you don't," he said impatiently. "You'd much rather hear about Roland and all the things he does at Fernhurst."

There was a moment of difficult silence, then April said quite quietly:

"You are quite right, Ralph; as a matter of fact I should"; and she turned towards Roland, but before she could say anything, Mrs Curtis once more assumed her monopoly of the conversation.

"Yes, Roland, you've told us nothing about that, and how you got your firsts. We were so proud of you too. And you never wrote to tell us. If it hadn't been for your father we should never have known." And for the next half-hour her voice flowed on placidly, while Ralph sat in a frenzy of self-pity and self-contempt, and Roland longed for an opportunity to kick him, and April looked out between the half-drawn curtains towards the narrow line of sky that lay darkly over the long stretch of roofs and chimney-pots, happy that Roland's holidays had begun, regretting wistfully that childhood was finished for them, that they could no longer play their own games in the nursery, that they had become part of the ambitions of their parents.

When at last they rose to go, Ralph lingered for a moment in the doorway; he could not go home till April had forgiven him.

She stood on the top of the step, looking down the street to Roland, her heart still beating a little quickly, still disturbed by that pressure of the hand and that sudden uncomfortable meeting of the eyes when he had said "Good-bye." She did not notice Ralph till he began to speak to her.

"I am awfully sorry I was so rude to you, April. I'm rather tired. I didn't mean to offend you. I wouldn't have done it for worlds."

She turned to him with a quiet smile.

"Oh, don't worry about that," she said, "that's nothing."

And he could see that to her it was indeed nothing, that she had not thought twice about it. That nothing he said or did was of the least concern to her. He would much rather that she had been angry.

Next day Ralph came round to the Whatelys' soon after breakfast.

"Well, feeling more peaceful to-day, old friend?" Ralph looked at Roland in impotent annoyance. As he knew of old, Roland was an impossible person to have a row with. He simply would not fight. He either agreed to everything you said or else brushed away your arguments with a good-natured "All right, old man, all right!" On this occasion, however, he felt that he must make a stand.

"You're the limit," he said; "the absolute limit."

"I don't know about that, but I think you were last night."

"Oh, don't joke about it. You know what I mean. I think it's pretty rotten for a fellow like you to go about with a shop-assistant, but that's not really the thing. What's simply beastly is your coming back to April as though nothing had happened. What would she say if she knew?"

Roland refused to acknowledge omniscience. "I don't know," he said.

"She wouldn't be pleased, would she?" Ralph persisted.

"I don't suppose so."

"No; well then, there you are; you oughtn't to do anything you think she mightn't like."

Roland looked at him with a sad patience, as a preparatory schoolmaster at a refractory infant.

"But, my dear fellow, we're not married, and we're not engaged. Surely we can do more or less what we like."

"But would you be pleased if you learned that she'd been carrying on with someone else?"

Roland admitted that he would not.

"Then why should you think you owe nothing to her?"

"It's different, my dear Ralph; it's quite different."

"No, it isn't."

"Yes, it is. Boys can do things that girls can't. A flirtation means very little to a boy; it means a good deal to a girl—at least it ought to. If it doesn't, it means that she's had too much of it."

"But I don't see——" began Ralph.

"Come on, come on; don't let's go all over that again. We shall never agree. Let me go my way and you can go yours. We are too old friends to quarrel about a thing like this."

Most boys would have been annoyed by Ralph's attempt at interference, but it took a great deal to ruffle Roland's lazy, equable good nature. He did not believe in rows. He liked to keep things running smoothly. He could never understand the people who were always wanting to stir up trouble. He did not really care enough either way. His tolerance might have been called indifference, but it possessed, at any rate, a genuine charm. The other fellow always felt what a thundering good chap Roland was—so good-tempered, such a gentleman, never harbouring a grievance. People knew where they were with him; when he said a thing was over it was over.

"All right," said Ralph grudgingly. "I don't know that it's quite the game——"

"Don't worry. We're a long way from anything serious. A good deal's got to happen before we're come to the age when we can't do what we like."

And they talked of other things.

CHAPTER IV
A KISS

April sat for a long while before the looking-glass wondering whether to tie a blue or a white ribbon in her hair. She tried one and then the other and paused irresolute. It was the evening of the Saundersons' dance, to which for weeks she had been looking forward, and she was desperately anxious to look pretty. It would be a big affair: ices and claret-cup and a band, and Roland would be there. They had seen a lot of each other during the holidays—nearly every day. Often they had felt awkward in each other's company; there had been embarrassing silences, when their eyes would meet suddenly and quickly turn away; and then there would come an unexpected interlude of calm, harmonious friendship, when they would talk openly and naturally to each other and would sit afterwards for a long while silent, softened and tranquillised by the presence of some unknown influence—moments of rare gentleness and sympathy. April could not help feeling that they were on the edge of something definite, some incident of avowal. She did not know what, but she felt that something was about to happen. She was flustered and expectant and eager to look pretty for Roland on this great evening.

She had chosen a very simple dress, a white muslin frock, that left bare her arms and throat, and was trimmed with pale blue ribbon at the neck and elbow; her stockings, too, were white, but her shoes and her sash a vivid, unexpected scarlet. She turned round slowly before the glass and smiled happily at her clear, fresh girlhood, tossing back her head, so that her hair was shaken out over her shoulders. Surely he would think her beautiful to-night. With eager fingers she tied the blue ribbon in her hair, turned again slowly before the glass, smiled, shook out her hair, and laughed happily. Yes, she would wear the blue—a subdued, quiet colour, that faded naturally into the warm brown. She ran downstairs for her family's approval, stood before her mother and turned a slow circle.

"Well, mother?"

Mrs Curtis examined her critically.

"Of course, dear, I'm quite certain that you'll be the prettiest girl there whatever you wear."

"What do you mean, mother?"

"Well, April dear, of course I know you think you know best, but that white frock—it is so very simple."

"But simple things suit me, mother."

"I know they do, dear; you look sweet in anything; but at a big dance like this, where there'll be so many smart people, they might think—well, I don't know, dear, but it is very quiet, isn't it?"

The moment before April had been happy and excited, and now she was crushed and humiliated. She sat down on the edge of a chair, gazing with pathetic pity at her brilliant shoes.

"You've spoilt it all," she said.

"No, dear. I'm sure you'll be thankful to me when you get there. Now, why don't you run upstairs and put on that nice mauve frock of yours?"

April shook her shoulders.

"I don't like mauve."

"Well then, dear, there's the green and yellow; you always look nice in that."

It was a bright affair that her mother had seen at a sale in Brixton and bought at once because it was so cheap. It had never really suited April, whose delicate features needed a simple setting; but her mother did not like to feel that she had made a mistake, and having persuaded herself that the green and yellow was the right colour, and matched her daughter's eyes, had insisted on April's wearing it as often as possible.

"Yes, my dear, the green and yellow. I'm sure I'm right. Now hurry up; the cab will be here in ten minutes."

April walked upstairs slowly. She hated that green and yellow; she always had hated it. She took it down from the wardrobe and, holding the ends of the sleeves, stretched out her arms on either side so that the green and yellow dress covered her completely, and then she stood looking at it in the glass.

How blatant, how decorative it was, with its bows and ribbons and slashed sleeves. There were some girls whom it would suit—big girls with high complexions and full figures. But it wasn't her dress, it spoilt her. She let it slip from her fingers; it fell rustling to the floor, and once again the glass reflected her in a plain white frock, and once again she tossed back her head, and once again the slow smile of satisfaction played across her lips. And as she stood there with outstretched arms, for one inspired moment of revelation, during which the beating of her heart was stilled, she saw how beautiful she would one day be to the man for whom with such a gesture she would be delivered to his love. A deep flush coloured her neck and face, a flush of triumphant pride, of wakening womanhood. Then with a quick, impatient movement of her scarlet shoes she kicked the yellow dress away from her.

Why should she wear it? She dressed to please herself and not her mother. She knew best what suited her. What would happen if she disobeyed her? Would anyone ever know? She could manage to slip out when no one was looking. Annie would be sent to fetch her, but they would come back after everyone had gone to bed.

She sat on the edge of her bed and toyed with the thought of rebellion. It would be horribly exciting. It would be the naughtiest thing she had done in her life. She had never yet disobeyed deliberately anyone who had authority over her. She had lost her temper in the nursery; she had been insolent to her nurses; she had pretended not to hear when she had been called; but never this: never had she sat down and decided in cold blood to disregard authority.

There was a knock at the door.

"Yes. Who's that?"

"It's only me—mother. Can I help you, dear?"

"No thank you, mother, I'm all right."

"Quite sure?"

"Quite."

April heard her mother slowly descend the stairs, then heaved a sigh of half-proud, half-guilty relief. She was glad she had managed to get out of it without actually telling a lie. She sat still and waited, till at last she heard the crunch of a cab drawing up outside the house. She wrapped herself tightly in her coat, tiptoed to the door, opened it and listened. She could hear her mother's voice in the passage. Quietly she stole out on to the landing, quietly ran downstairs and across the hall, fumbled for the door handle, found it, turned it, and pulled it quickly behind her. It was done; she was

The Lonely Unicorn | 31

free. As she ran down the steps she heard a window open behind her and her mother's voice:

"Who's that? What is it? Oh, you, April. You might have come to see me before you went. A happy evening to you."

April could not trust herself to speak; she ran down the steps, jumped into the cab and sank back into the corner of the cushioned seat. Her breath came quickly and unevenly, her breasts heaved and fell. She could have almost cried with excitement.

It had been worth it, though. She knew that beyond doubt a quarter of an hour later, when she walked into the ballroom and saw the look of sudden admiration that came into Roland's eyes when he saw her for the first time across the room. He came straight over to her.

"How many dances may I have?" he asked.

"Well, there's No. 11."

"No. 11? Let me have a look at your card."

"No, of course you mustn't."

"Yes, of course. Why, I don't believe you have got one!"

"Yes, I have," she said, and held it up to him. In a second it was in his hand, as indeed she had intended that it should be.

"Well, now," said Roland, "as far as I can see you've got only Nos. 6, 7, 14 and 15 engaged; that leaves fourteen for me."

"Well, you can have the four," she laughed.

In the end she gave him six. "And if I've any over you shall have them," she promised.

"Well you know there won't be," and their eyes met in a moment of quiet intimacy.

As soon as he had gone other partners crowded round her. In a very short while her programme was filled right up, the five extras as well. She had left No. 17 vacant; it was the last waltz. She felt that she might like Roland to have it, but was not sure. She didn't quite know why, but she felt she would leave it open.

It was a splendid dance. As the evening passed, her face flushed and her eyes brightened, and it was delightful to slip from the heat of the ballroom on to the wide balcony and feel the cool of the air on her bare arms. She danced once with Ralph, and as they sat out afterwards she could almost feel the touch of his eyes on her. Poor Ralph; he was so clumsy. How absurd it was of him to be in love with her. As if she could ever care for him. She felt no pity. She accepted his admiration as a queen accepts a subject's loyalty; it was the right due to her beauty, to the eager flow of life that sustained her on this night of triumph.

And every dance with Roland seemed to bring her nearer to the wonderful moment to which she had so long looked forward. When she was dancing with Ralph, Roland's eyes would follow her all round the room, smiling when they met hers. And when they danced together they seemed to share a secret with one another, a secret still unrevealed.

Through the languid ecstasy of a waltz the words that he murmured into her ear had no relation with their accepted sense. He was not repeating a piece of trivial gossip, a pun, a story he had heard at school; he was wooing her in their own way, in their own time. And afterwards as they sat on the edge of the balcony, looking out over the roofs and lights of London, she began to tell him about her dress and the trouble that she had had with her mother. "She said I ought to wear a horrid thing with yellow and green stripes that doesn't suit me in the least. And I wouldn't. I stole out of the house when she wasn't looking."

"You look wonderful to-night," he said.

He leant forward and their hands touched; his little finger intertwined itself round hers. She felt his warm breath upon her face.

"Do I?" she whispered. "It's all for you."

In another moment he would have taken her in his arms and kissed her, and she would have responded naturally. They had reached that moment to which the course of the courtship had tended, that point when a kiss is involuntary, that point that can never come again. But just as his hands stretched out to her the band struck up; he rested his hand on hers and pressed it.

"We shall have to go," he whispered.

"Yes."

"But the next but one."

"No. 16."

But the magic of that one moment had passed; they had left behind them the possibility of spontaneous action. They were no longer part of the natural rhythm of their courtship. All through the next dance he kept saying to himself: "I shall have to kiss her the next time. I shall. I know I shall. I must pull myself together." He felt puzzled, frightened and excited, so that when the time came he was both nervous and self-conscious. The magic had gone, yet each felt that something was expected of them. Roland tried to pull himself together; to remind himself that if he didn't kiss her now she would never forgive him; that there was nothing in it; that he had kissed Dolly a hundred times and thought nothing of it. But it was not the same thing; that was shallow and trivial; this was genuine; real emotion was at stake. He did not know what to do. As they sat out after the dance he tried to make a bet with himself, to say, "I'll count ten and then I'll do it." He stretched out his hand to hers, and it lay in his limp and uninspired.

"April," he whispered, "April."

She turned her head from him. He leant forward, hesitated for a moment, then kissed her awkwardly upon the neck. She did not move. He felt he must do something. He put his arm round her, trying to turn her face to his, but she pulled away from him. He tried to kiss her, and his chin scratched the soft skin of her cheek, his nose struck hers, her mouth half opened, and her teeth jarred against his lips. It was a failure, a dismal failure.

She pushed him away angrily.

"Go away! go away!" she said. "What are you doing? What do you mean by it? I hate you; go away!"

All the excitement of the evening turned into violent hatred; she was half hysterical. She had been worked up to a point, and had been let down. She was not angry with him because he had tried to kiss her, but because he had chosen the wrong moment, because he had failed to move her.

"But, April, I'm sorry, April."

"Oh, go away; leave me alone, leave me alone."

"But, April." He put his hand upon her arm, and she swung round upon him fiercely.

"Didn't I tell you I wanted to be left alone. I don't know how you dared. Do leave me."

She walked quickly past him into the ballroom, and seeing Ralph at the far end of it went up and asked him, to that young gentleman's exhilarated amazement, whether he was free for No. 17, and if he was whether he would like to dance it with her. She wore a brave smile through the rest of the evening and danced all her five extras.

But when she was home again, had climbed the silent stairs, and turning up the light in her bedroom saw, lying on the floor, the discarded green and yellow dress, she broke down, and flinging herself upon the bed sobbed long and bitterly. She was not angry with Roland, nor her mother, nor even with herself, but with life, with that cruel force that had filled her with such eager boundless expectation, only in the end to fling her down, to trample on her happiness, to mock her disenchantment. Never as long as she lived would she forget the shame, the unspeakable shame, and degradation of that evening.

CHAPTER V
A POTENTIAL DIPLOMAT

Roland returned to school with the uncomfortable feeling that he had not made the most of his holidays. He had failed with April; he had not been on the best of terms with Ralph; and he had found the last week or so—after the Saundersons' dance—a little tedious. He was never sorry to go back to school; on this occasion he was positively glad.

In many ways the Easter term was the best of the three; it was agreeably short; there were the house matches, the steeplechases, the sports and then, at the end of it, spring; those wonderful mornings at the end of March when one woke to see the courts vivid with sunshine, the lindens trembling on the verge of green; when one thought of the summer and cricket and bathing and the long, cool evenings. And as Howard had now left, there was nothing to molest his enjoyment of these good things.

He decided, after careful deliberation, to keep it up with Dolly. There had been moments during the holidays when he had sworn to break with her; it would be quite easy now that Howard had left. And often during an afternoon in April's company the idea of embracing Dolly had been repulsive to him. But he had been piqued by April's behaviour at the dance, and his conduct was not ordered by a carefully-thought-out code of morals. He responded to the atmosphere of the moment; his emotion, while the moment that inspired it lasted, was sincere.

And so every Sunday afternoon he used to bicycle out towards Yeovil and meet Dolly on the edge of a little wood. They would wheel their machines inside and sit together in the shelter of the hedge. They did not talk much; there was not much for them to discuss. But she would take off her hat and lean her head against his shoulder and let him kiss her as much as he wanted. She was not responsive, but then Roland hardly expected it. His small experience of the one-sided romances of school life had led him to believe that love was a thing of male desire and gracious, womanly compliance. He never thought that anyone would want to kiss him. He would look at his reflection in the glass and marvel at the inelegance of his features—an ordinary face with ordinary eyes, ordinary nose, ordinary mouth. Of his hair certainly he was proud; it was a triumph. But he doubted whether Dolly appreciated the care with which he had trained it to lie back from his forehead in one immaculate wave. She had, indeed, asked him to give up brilliantine.

"It's so hard and smarmy," she complained; "I can't run my fingers through it."

The one good point about him was certainly lost on Dolly. He wondered whether April liked it. April and Dolly! It was hard to think of the two together. What would April say if she were to hear about Dolly? It was the theme Ralph was always driving at him like a nail, with heavy, ponderous blows. An interesting point. What would April say? He considered the question, not as a possible criticism of his own conduct, but as the material for an intriguing, dramatic situation. It would be hard to make her see the difference. "I'm a girl and she's a girl and you want to kiss us both." That was how she would look at it, probably—so illogical. One might as well say that water was the same thing and had the same effect as champagne. Ridiculous! But it would be hard to make April see it.

And there was a difference, a big difference; he felt it before a fortnight of the new term had passed. In spite of the kisses he was never moved by Dolly's presence as he was by April's. His blood was calm—calmer, far calmer, than it had been last term. He never felt now that excitement, that dryness of the throat that used to assail him in morning chapel towards the end of the Litany. Something had passed, and it was not solely April, though, no doubt, she had formed a standard in his mind and had her share in this disenchantment. It was more than that. In a subtle way, although he had hardly exchanged a dozen words with her in his life, he missed Betty. He had enjoyed more than he had realised at the time those moments of meeting and parting, when the four of them had stood together, awkward, embarrassed, waiting for someone to suggest a separation. It had always been Betty who had done it, with a toss of her head: "Come on, Dolly, time to be getting on"; or else: "Now then, Dolly, isn't it time you were taking your Roland away with you?" And what a provocative, infinitely suggestive charm that slow smile of hers had held for him. The thrill of it had borne him triumphantly over the preliminaries of courtship. He missed it now, and often he found himself talking of her to Dolly.

"Did she really like Howard?" he asked her once.

"Yes, I think so; in fact, I know she did. Though I couldn't see what she saw in him myself. I suppose there was something about him. She misses him quite a lot, so she says."

This statement Roland considered an excellent cue for an exchange of gallantries.

"But wouldn't you miss me if I went?"

Dolly, however, was interested in her own subject.

"Yes," she went on, "she seems really worried. Only the other day she said to me: 'Dolly, I can't get on without that boy. There's nothing to look forward to of a Sunday now, and I get so tired of my work.' And when I said to her: 'But, my dear Betty, there's hundreds more fish in the sea. What about young Rogers at the post office?' she answers: 'Oh, him! my boy's spoilt me for all that. I can't bear the sight of young Rogers any more.' Funny, isn't it?"

Roland agreed with her. To him it was amazing.

"Well," Dolly went on, "I saw quite clearly that there was nothing for it but that she must get hold of another young chap like your friend. And I asked her if there was anyone else up at the school she fancied, and she said, yes, there was; a boy she's seen you talking to once or twice; a young, fair-haired fellow with a blue and yellow hat ribbon. That's the best I can do. Is that any help to you? Would you know him?"

A blue and yellow hat ribbon limited the selection to members of the School XI., and there was only one old colour who answered to that description—Brewster in Carus Evans'.

"Oh, yes, I know him."

"Well, now, don't you think you could arrange it? Do, for my sake."

"But I don't know him well enough. I don't see how I could."

"Oh, yes, you do. Haven't I seen you talking together, and he would be only too pleased. I am sure he would. Betty's such a nice girl. Now, do try."

Roland promised that he would do his best, though it was not a job he particularly fancied. Brewster was the youngest member of the XI. He had been playing on lower side games all the season without attracting any attention and had then surprised everyone by making a century in an important house match. He was immediately transplanted to the first, and though he played in only two matches he was considered to have earned his colours. He was not, however, in any sense of the word a blood. He was hardly known by men of Roland's standing in other houses. He was low in form and not particularly brilliant at football. Roland knew next to nothing about him. Still it was a fascinating situation—a girl like Betty, who must be a good three years older than Dolly, getting keen on such a kid. Was she in love, he wondered. He had never met anyone who had enjoyed the privilege of having a girl in love with him. For towards the end he had believed very little that Howard had told him. It was an intriguing affair. And so he set himself to his task.

The difficulty, of course, was to find the auspicious moment. He hardly ever saw Brewster except when there were a lot of other people about, and he didn't want to ask him across to his study. People would talk; and, besides, it would not do to spring this business on him suddenly. He would have to lead up to it carefully. For a whole week he sought, unsuccessfully, for an opportunity, and on the Sunday he had to confess to Dolly that he was no nearer the attainment of her friend's desires.

"It's not as easy as you seem to think it is. We are not in the same house, we are not in the same form, and we don't play footer on the same ground. In fact, except that we happen to be in the same school——"

"Now! now! now! Haven't I seen you talking to him alone twice before I even mentioned him to you? And if you could be alone with him then, when you had no particular reason to, surely you can manage to be now, when you have."

"But, my dear Dolly——"

"There've not got to be any buts. Either you bring along your friend or it's all over between us."

It was not a very serious threat, and at any other stage of their relationship Roland, considering the bother that the affair involved, might have been glad enough to accept it as an excuse for his dismissal. But he had determined to bring this thing off. He thought of Betty, large, black-haired, bright-eyed, highly coloured, her full lips moistened by the red tongue that slipped continually between them, and Brewster, fair-haired and slim and shy. It would be amusing to see what they would make of one another. He would carry the business through, and as a reward for this determination luck, two days later, came his way. He drew Brewster in the second round of the Open Fives.

On the first wet day they played it off, and as Roland was a poor performer and Brewster a tolerably efficient one the game ended in under half-an-hour. They had, therefore, the whole afternoon before them, and Roland suggested that as soon as they had changed they should have tea together in his study.

For Roland it was an exciting afternoon; he was playing, for the first time in his life, the part of a diplomat. He had read a good many novels in which the motive was introduced, but there it had been a very different matter. The stage had been set skilfully; each knew the other's thoughts without being sure of his intention; there was a rapier duel of thrust and parry. But here the stage was set for nothing in particular. Brewster was unaware of dramatic tension; his main idea was to eat as much as possible.

With infinite care Roland led the conversation to a discussion of the mentality of women. He enlarged on a favourite theme of his—the fact that girls often fell in love with really ugly men. "I can't understand it," he said. "Girls are such delicate, refined creatures. They want the right coloured curtains in their bedrooms and the right coloured cushion for their sofas; they spend hours discussing the right shade of ribbon for their hair, and then they go and fall in love with a ridiculous-looking man. Look at Morgan, now. He's plain and he's bald and he's got an absurd, stubby moustache, and yet his wife is frightfully pretty, and she seems really keen on him. I don't understand it."

Brewster agreed that it was curious, and helped himself to another cake.

"I suppose," said Roland, "that a fellow like you knows a good deal about girls?"

Brewster shook his head. The subject presented few attractions to him.

"No," he said, "I don't really know anything at all about them. I haven't got a sister."

"But you don't learn about girls from your sister."

"Perhaps not. But if you haven't got a sister you don't run much chance of seeing anyone else's. We don't know any decent ones. A few of my friends have sisters, but they seem pretty fair asses. I keep out of their way."

"That's rather funny, you know, because you're the sort of fellow that girls run after."

As Roland had been discussing for some time the ugliness of the type of man that appealed most to girls, this was hardly a compliment. Brewster did not notice it, however. Indeed, he evinced no great interest in the conversation. He was enjoying his tea.

"Oh, I don't think I am," he said. "At any rate none of them have run after me, so far."

"That's all you know," said Roland, and his voice assumed a tone that made Brewster look up quickly.

"What do you mean?" he asked.

"Well, I know someone who is doing their best to."

Brewster flushed; the hand that was carrying a cream cake to his mouth paused in mid air.

"A girl! Who?"

"That's asking."

Roland had at last succeeded in arousing Brewster's curiosity, and he was wise enough to refrain from satisfying it at once. If he were to tell him that a girl down town had wanted to go for a walk with him, Brewster would have laughed and probably thought no more about it. He would have to fan his interest till Brewster's imagination had had time to play upon the idea.

"She's very pretty," Roland said, "and she asked me who you were. She was awfully keen to meet you, but I told her that it was no good and that you wouldn't care for that sort of thing. She was very disappointed."

"Yes, but who is she?"

"I'm not going to tell you that. Why should I give her away?"

"Oh, but do tell me."

Roland was firm.

"No; I'm jolly well not going to. It's her secret. You don't want to meet her, do you?"

"No," Brewster grudgingly admitted; "but I'd like to know."

"I daresay you would, but I'm not going to give away a confidence. Suppose you told me that you were keen on a girl and that you'd heard she wouldn't have anything to do with anyone, you wouldn't like me to go and tell her who you were, would you?"

"No."

"Of course you wouldn't. That's the sort of thing one keeps to oneself."

"Yes; but as I shall never see her— —"

Roland adopted in reply the stern tone of admonition, "Of course not; but if I told you, you'd take jolly good care that you did see her, and then you'd tell someone else. You'd point her out and say, 'That girl wanted me to come out for a walk with her.' You know you would, and of course the other fellow would promise not to tell anyone and of course he would. It would be round the whole place in a week, and think how the poor girl would feel being laughed at by everyone because a fellow four years younger than herself wouldn't have anything to do with her."

"What! Four years older than me."

"About that."

"And she's pretty, you say?"

"Jolly."

There was a pause.

"You know, Whately," he began, "I'd rather ..." then broke off. "Oh, look here, do tell me."

Roland shook his head.

"I don't give away secrets."

"But why did you tell me anything about it at all?"

"I don't know; it just cropped up, didn't it? I thought it might amuse you."

"Well, I think it's rotten of you. I shan't be able to think of anything else until I know."

Which was, of course, exactly what Roland wanted. He knew how Brewster's imagination would play with the idea. Betty would become for him strange, wistful, passionate. Four years older than himself he would picture her as the Lilith of old, the eternal temptress. In herself she was nothing. If he had met her in the streets two days earlier he would have hardly noticed her. "A pleasant, country girl," he would have said, and let her pass out of his thoughts. But now the imagination that colours all things would make her irresistible, and when he met her she would be identified with his dream.

Next morning Brewster ran across to him during break.

"I say, Whately, do tell me who she is."

"No; I told you I wasn't going to."

"Well, then. Oh, look here! Is it Dorothy Jones?"

Dorothy Jones was the daughter of the owner of a cycle shop and was much admired in the school.

"Would you like it to be?" Roland asked.

"I don't know. Perhaps. But is it, though?"

"Perhaps."

"It is Dorothy Jones, isn't it? It is her?"

"If you know, why do you ask me?"

"Oh, don't be a fool! Is it Dorothy Jones?"

"Perhaps."

"Well, if it isn't her, is it Mary Gardiner?"

"It is Mary Gardiner," Roland mocked. "It is she, isn't it?"

"Oh, you're awful," said Brewster, and walked away.

But that evening he came over to the School house studies and, just before Hall, a small boy ran across to the reading-room to tell Roland that Brewster was in the cloisters and would like to speak to him.

"Well," said Roland, "and what is it?"

"It's about the girl."

Roland affected a weary impatience.

"Oh, Lord, but I thought we'd finished with all that. I told you that I wasn't going to give her away."

"Yes, I know; but ... ah, well, look here, I must know who the girl is. No, don't interrupt. Will you tell me if I promise to come out with her once?"

Roland thought for a moment. He had his man now, but it would not do to hurry things. He must play for safety a little longer.

"Oh, yes, I know that game," he said. "I shall tell you her name and then you'll wish you hadn't promised and you'll get frightened, and when the time comes you will have sprained an ankle in a house match and won't be able to come for a walk. That won't do at all."

"But I swear I wouldn't do that," Brewster protested. "Really, I wouldn't."

"Yes, and I promised that I wasn't going to tell."

"But that's so silly. Suppose now that I was really keen on her. For all you know, or I, for that matter, I may have seen her walking about the town and thought her jolly pretty without knowing who she was."

"And I'm damned certain you haven't. You told me that you didn't take any interest in girls."

"No, but really, honest, man, I may have seen her. Only this morning as I was going down to Fort's after breakfast I saw an absolutely ripping girl, and I believe it was me she smiled at. It's very likely her."

"Yes, yes, I dare say, but— —"

"Oh, come on, do tell me, and I promise you I'll come and see her; honest, I will."

But at that moment the roll-bell issued its cracked summons.

"If you don't run like sin you'll be late for roll-call, and that'll finish everything," Roland said, and Brewster turned and sprinted across the courts.

Roland walked back to his study in a mood of deep self-satisfaction. He was carrying an extremely difficult job to a triumphant close. It did not occur to him that the rôle he filled was not a particularly noble one and that an unpleasantly worded label could be discovered for it. He was living in the days of unreflecting action. He did, or refrained from doing, the things he wanted to do, without a minute analysis of motive, but in accordance with a definite code of rules. He lived his life as he played cricket. There were rewards and there were penalties. If you hit across a straight long hop you ran a chance of being leg before, and if the ball hit your pad you went straight back to the pavilion. You played to win, but you played the game, provided that you played it according to the rules. It did not matter to Roland what the game was. And the affair of Betty and Brewster was a game that he was winning fairly and squarely.

Next morning he achieved victory. He met Brewster during break and presented his ultimatum.

"I won't tell you her name," he said. "I promised not to. It wouldn't be the game. But I tell you what I will do, though. If you'll promise to come out for a walk with me on Sunday I'll arrange for her to meet us somewhere, and then you can see what you think of each other. Now, what do you say to that?"

Brewster's curiosity was so roused that he accepted eagerly, and next Sunday they set out together towards Cold Harbour.

About a mile and a half from the school a sunken lane ran down the side of a steep hill towards the railway. The lane could be approached from two sides, and from the shelter of a thick hedge it was possible to observe the whole country-side without being seen. It was here that they had arranged their meeting.

They found the two girls waiting when they arrived. Betty looked very smart in a dark blue coat and skirt and a small hat that fitted tightly over her head. She smiled at Roland, and the sight, after months, of her fresh-coloured face, with its bright eyes and wide, moist mouth, sent a sudden thrill through him—half fear, half excitement.

"So you've managed to arrange it," said Dolly. "How clever of you."

"Very nice of him to come," said Betty, her eyes fixed on Brewster, who stood awkwardly, his hands in his pockets, kicking one heel against the other.

For a few minutes they talked together, stupid, inconsequent badinage, punctuated by giggles, till Betty, as usual, reminded them that they would only have an hour together.

"About time we paired off, isn't it?"

"I suppose so," said Roland. "Come along, Dolly," and they began to walk down the lane. At the corner they turned and saw the other two standing together—Betty, taller, confident and all-powerful; Brewster, looking up at her, scared and timid, his hands clasped behind him.

"He looks a bit shy, doesn't he?" said Dolly.

Roland laughed.

"He won't be for long, I expect."

"Rather not. He'll soon get used to her. Betty doesn't let her boys stop shy with her for long. She makes them do as she wants them."

And when they returned an hour later they saw the two sitting side by side chatting happily. But as soon as they reached them Brewster became silent and shy, and looked neither of them in the face.

"Had a good time?" asked Dolly.

"Ask him," she answered.

And they laughed, all except Brewster, and made arrangements to meet again, only a little earlier the next week.

"Well," said Roland, as soon as they were out of earshot, "and how did you enjoy yourself?"

Brewster admitted that it had been pretty good.

"Only pretty good?"

"Well, I don't know," he said, "it was all right. Yes, it was ripping, really; but it was so different from what I had expected."

"How do you mean?"

"Oh, well, you know. I felt so awkward; she started everything. I didn't have any say in it at all. I had thought it was up to me to do all that."

"Betty's not that sort."

"No, but it's a funny business."

"You are coming out next week, though?"

"Rather!"

And next week Dolly, as soon as she was alone with Roland, began to ask him questions about Brewster: "What did he say to you? What did he think of her? Was she nice to him? You must tell me all about it."

"Oh, I think he enjoyed himself all right. She startled him a bit."

"Did she? What did he say? Do tell me."

She asked him question after question, and he had to repeat to her every word he could remember of Brewster's conversation. Did he still feel shy? Did he think Betty beautiful? Was he at all in love with her? And then Roland began to ask what Betty had thought of Brewster. Had she preferred him to Howard? She wasn't disappointed in him? Did she like him better than the other boys? They talked eagerly.

"Wouldn't it be fun to go back and have a look at them?" said Dolly. "I'd give anything to see them together."

Their eyes met, and suddenly, with a fervour they had never reached before, they kissed.

CHAPTER VI
APRIL'S LOOKING-GLASS

For April the term which brought Roland so much excitement was slow in passing. In spite of the disastrous evening at the ball, Roland's return to school left a void in her life. When she woke in the morning and stretched herself in bed before getting up she would ask herself what good thing she could expect that day to bring her. When she felt happy she would demand the reason of herself. "Over what are you happy?" she would ask herself. "In five minutes' time you will get up. You will put on your dressing-gown and hurry down the corridor to the bathroom. You will dress hurriedly, but come down all the same a little late for breakfast. You will find that your father has eaten, as is his wont, more than his share of toast, which will mean that you, being the last down, will have to go without it. You will rush down to school saying over to yourself the dates of your history lesson. You will hang your hat and coat on the fourth row of pegs and on the seventh peg from the right. From nine o'clock to ten you will be heard your history lesson. From ten o'clock till eleven you will take down notes on chemistry. From eleven to a quarter past there will be an interval, during which you will try to find a friend to help you with the Latin translation, of which you prepared only the first thirty lines last night. From a quarter-past eleven till a quarter-past twelve you will be heard that lesson. At a quarter-past twelve you will attend a lecture on English literature, which will last till one o'clock. You will then have lunch, and as to-day is Tuesday you know that your lunch will consist of boiled mutton and caper sauce, followed by apple dumpling. In the afternoon you will have gymnastics and a music lesson, after which there will be an hour of Mademoiselle's French conversation class. You will then come home. You will hurry your tea in the hope of being able to finish your preparation before your father comes back from the office at twenty minutes to seven, because when once he is back your mother will begin to talk, and when she begins to talk work becomes impossible. You will then dine with your parents at half-past seven. You will sit perfectly quiet at the table and not say a word, while your mother talks and talks and father listens and occasionally says, 'Yes, mother,' or 'No, mother.' After dinner you will read a book in the drawing-room till your mother reminds you that it is nine o'clock and time that you were in bed. You have, in fact, before you a day similar in every detail to yesterday, and similar in every detail to to-morrow. If you think anything different is going to happen to you then you are a little fool." And April would have to confess that this self-catechism was true. "Nothing happens," she would say. "One day is like another, and I am a little fool to wake up in the morning excited about nothing at all."

But all the same she was excited and she did feel, in spite of reason, that something was bound to happen soon. "Things cannot go on like this for ever," she told herself. And, looking into the future, she came gradually to look upon the day of Roland's return from school as the event which would alter, in a way she could not discern, the whole tenor of her life. It was not in these words that the idea was presented to her. "It may be different during the holidays when Roland is here." That was her first thought, from which the words "when Roland is here" detached themselves, starting another train of thought, that "Life when Roland is here is always different"; and she began to look forward to the holidays, counting the days till his return. "Things will be different then."

It was not love, it was not friendship; it was simply the belief that Roland's presence would be a key to that world other than this, of which shadowy intimations haunted her continually. Roland became the focus for her disquiet, her longing, her vague appreciation of the eternal essence made manifest for her in the passing phenomena of life.

"When Roland comes back ..." And though she marked on the calendar that hung in her bedroom April 2, the last day of her own term, with a big red cross, it was April 5 that she regarded as the real beginning of her holidays. And when she came down to breakfast and her father said to her, "Only seven more days now, April," she would answer gaily, "Yes, only a week. Isn't it lovely?" But to herself she would add, "Ten days, only ten days more!"

And so she missed altogether the usual last day excitement. She did not wake on that first morning happy with the delicious thought that she could lie in bed for an extra ten minutes if she liked. She had not yet begun her holidays.

But two days later she was in a fever of expectation. In twenty-four hours' time Roland would be home. How slowly the day passed. In the evening she said she was tired and went to bed before dinner, so that the next day might come quickly for her. But when she got to bed she found that she could not sleep, and though she repeated the word "abracadabra" many hundred times and counted innumerable sheep passing through innumerable gates, she lay awake till after midnight, hearing hour after hour strike. And when at last sleep came to her it was light and fitful and she woke often.

Next day she did not know what to do with herself. She tried to read and could not. She tried to sew and could not. She ran up and down stairs on trifling errands in order to pass the time. In vain she tried to calm herself. "What are you getting so excited about? What do you think is going to happen? What can happen? The most that can happen is that he will come round with his father in the evening, and you know well enough by now what that will mean. Your mother will talk and his father will say, 'Yes, Mrs Curtis,' and 'Really, Mrs Curtis,' and you and Roland will hardly exchange a word with one another. You are absurdly excited over nothing."

But logic was of no avail, and all the afternoon she fidgeted with impatience. By tea-time she was in a state of repressed hysteria. She sat in the window-seat looking down the road in the direction from which he would have to come. "I wonder if he will come without his father. It would be so dear of him if he would, but I don't suppose he will. No, of course he won't. It's silly of me to think of it. He'll have to wait for his father; he always does. That means he won't be here at the earliest till after six. And it's only ten minutes to five now."

And to make things worse, seldom had she found her mother more annoying.

"Now, why don't you go for a walk, April, dear?" she said. "It's such a lovely evening and you've been indoors nearly all day. It isn't good, and I was saying to your father only the other day, 'Father, dear, I'm sure April isn't up to the mark. She looks so pale nowadays.'"

"I'm all right, mother."

"No, but are you, dear? You're looking really pale. I'm sure I ought to ask Dr Dunkin to come and see you."

"But I'm all right—really, I'm all right, mother. I know when anything is wrong with me."

"But you don't, April, dear. That's just the point. Don't you remember that time when you insisted on going to the tennis party and assured us that you were quite well, and when you came back we found you had a temperature of 101° and that you were sickening for measles? I was saying to Dr Dunkin only this morning: 'Dr Dunkin, I'm really not satisfied about our little April. I think I shall have to ask you to give her a tonic'; and he said to me: 'Yes, that's right, Mrs Curtis; you bring me along to her and I'll set her straight.'"

April put her hands up to her head and tried not to listen, but her mother's voice flowed on:

"And now, dear, do go out for a walk—just a little one."

"But, mother, dear, I don't want to, really, and I'm feeling so tired."

"There, what did I say? You're feeling tired and you've done nothing all day. There must be something wrong with you. I shall certainly ask Dr Dunkin to come and see you to-morrow."

"Oh, yes, yes, yes, mother. I'll do anything you like to-morrow. If you'll only leave me alone to-night."

But Mrs Curtis went on talking, and April grew more and more exasperated, and the minutes went past and Roland did not come. Six struck and half-past six, and a few minutes later she heard her father's latch-key in the door. And then the whole question of her health was dragged out again.

"I was saying to you only yesterday, father, that our little April wasn't as well as she ought to be. She has overworked, I think. Last night she went to bed early and to-day she looks quite pale, and she says that she feels tired although she hasn't really done anything. I must send for Dr Dunkin to-morrow."

It seemed to April that the voice would never stop. It beat and beat upon her brain, like the ticking of the watch that reminded her of the flying moments. "He won't come now," she said; "he won't come now." Seven o'clock had struck, the lamps were lit, evening had descended upon the street. He had never come as late as this before. But she still sat at the window, gazing down the street towards the figures, that became distinct for a moment in the lamplight. "He will not come now," she said, and suddenly she felt limp, tired, incapable of resistance. She put her head upon her knees and began to sob.

In a moment her mother's arms were round her. "But, darling, what is it, April, dear?"

She could not speak. She shook her head, tried desperately to make a sign that she was all right, that she would rather be left alone; but it was no use. She felt too bitterly the need for human sympathy. She turned, flung her arms about her mother's neck, and began to sob and sob.

"Oh, mother, mother," she cried. "I'm so miserable. I don't know what to do. I don't know what to do."

Next morning Dr Dunkin felt her pulse, prescribed a tonic and told her not to stay too much indoors.

"Now, you'll be all right, dear," her mother said. "Dr Dunkin's medicines are splendid."

April smiled quietly. "Yes, I expect that was what was wanted. I think I worked a little too hard last term."

"I'm sure you did, my dear. I shall write to Mrs Clarke about it. I can't have my little girl getting run down."

And that afternoon April met Roland in the High Street. It was the first time that she had seen him alone since the evening of the dance, and she found him awkward and embarrassed. They said a few things of no importance—about the holidays, the weather and their acquaintances. Then April said that she must be going home, and Roland made no effort to detain her—did not even make any suggestion about coming round to see her.

"So that is what you have been looking forward to for over a month," she said to herself, as he passed out of sight behind an angle of the road. "This is the date you wanted to mark upon your calendar with a red cross. Little fool. What did you think you were doing? And what has it turned out to be in the end? Five minutes' discussion of indifferent things. A fine event to make such a fuss about; and what else did you expect?"

She was not bitter. It was one of those mild days that in early spring surprise us with a promise of summer, on which the heart is stirred with the crowded glory of life and the sense of widening horizons. The long stretch of roofs and chimney stacks became beautiful in the subdued sunlight. It was an hour that in the strong might have quickened the hunger for adventure, but that to April brought a mood of chastened, quiet resignation. She appreciated, as she had not done before, the tether by which her scope was measured. For the last month she had made Roland's return a focus for the ambitions and desires and yearnings towards an intenser way of living, for which of herself she had been unable to find expression. This, in a confused manner, she understood. "I can do nothing by myself. I have to live in other people. And what I am now I shall be always. All my life I shall be dependent on someone else, or on some interest that is outside myself. And whether I am happy or unhappy depends upon some other person. That is my nature, and I cannot go beyond my nature." When she reached home she sat for a long time in the window-seat, her hands folded in her lap. "This will be my whole life," she said. "I am not of those who may go out in search of happiness." And she thought that if romance did not come to her, she would remain all her life sitting at a window. "Of myself I can do nothing."

CHAPTER VII
A SORRY BUSINESS

April did not see very much of Roland during the holidays, and was not, on the whole, sorry. Now that the hysterical excitement over his return had passed, she judged it better to let their friendship lapse. She did not want any repetition of that disastrous evening, and thought that it would be easier to resume their friendship on its old basis after the long interval of the summer term. Roland was still a little piqued by what he considered her absurd behaviour, and had resolved to let the first step come from her.

This estrangement was a disappointment to his people.

"Have you noticed, my dear, that Roland's hardly been round to the Curtises' at all these holidays?" Mr Whately said to his wife one evening. "I hope there has not been a row or anything. I rather wish you'd try and find out."

And so next day Mrs Whately made a guarded remark to her son about April's appearance: "What a big girl she's getting. And she's prettier every day. If you're not careful you'll have all the boys in the place running after her and cutting you out."

Roland answered in an off-hand manner, "They can for all I care, mother."

"Oh, but, Roland, you shouldn't say that; I thought you were getting on so well together last holidays. We were even saying— —"

But Roland never allowed himself to be forced into a confidence.

"Oh, please, mother, don't. There was nothing in it; really, there wasn't."

"You haven't had a row, have you, Roland?"

"Of course not, mother. What should we have a row about?"

"I don't know, dear. I only thought— —"

"Well, you needn't worry about us, mother; we're all right."

Roland was by no means pleased at what seemed to him a distinct case of interference. It arrived, too, at a most inopportune moment, for he had been just then wondering whether he ought not to forget about his high-minded resolves and try to make it up with April. His mother's inquiries, however, decided him. He was not going to have others arranging that sort of thing for him. "And for all I know," he said to himself, "Mrs Curtis may be at the back of this. I shan't go round there again these holidays." And this was the more unfortunate, because if the intimacy between Roland and April had been resumed, it is more than likely that Roland, at the beginning of the summer term, would have decided to give up Dolly altogether. Both he and Brewster were a little tired of it; the first interest had passed, and they had actually discussed the wisdom of dropping the whole business.

"After all," said Brewster, "it can't go on for ever. It'll have to stop some time, and next term we shall both be fairly high in the school, house prefects and all that, and we shall have to be pretty careful what we do."

Roland was inclined to agree with him, but his curiosity was still awake.

"It's not so easy to break a thing like this. Let's wait till the end of the term. The summer holidays are a long time, and by the time we come back they'll very likely have picked up someone else."

"All right," said Brewster, "I don't mind. And it does add an interest to things."

And so the affair went on smoothly and comfortably, a pleasant interlude among the many good gifts of a summer term—cricket and swimming and the long, lazy evenings. Nothing, indeed, occurred to ruffle the complete happiness of Roland's life, till one Monday morning during break Brewster came running across to the School house studies with the disastrous news that his house master had found out all about it. It had happened thus:

On the previous Saturday Roland had sent up a note in break altering the time of an appointment. It was the morning of a school match and Brewster received the note on his way down to the field. He was a little late, and as soon as he had read the note he shoved it into his pocket and thought no more about it. During the afternoon he slipped, trying to bring off a one-handed catch in the slips, and tore the knee of his trousers. The game ended late and he had only just time to change and take his trousers round to the matron to be mended before lock-up. In the right-hand pocket the matron discovered Roland's note, and, judging its contents singular, placed it before Mr Carus Evans.

As Roland walked back with Brewster from the tuck-shop a small boy ran up to tell him that Mr Carus Evans would like to see him directly after lunch.

Roland was quite calm as he walked up the hill three hours later. One is only frightened when one is uncertain of one's fate. When a big row is on, in which one may possibly be implicated, one endures agonies, wondering whether or not one will be found out. But when it is settled, when one is found out, what is there to do? One must let things take their course; nothing can alter it. There is no need for fret or fever. Roland was able to consider his position with detached interest.

He had been a fool to send that note. Notes always got lost or dropped and the wrong people picked them up. How many fellows had not got themselves bunked that way, notes and confirmation? They were the two great menaces, the two hidden rocks. Probably confirmation was the more dangerous. On the whole, more fellows had got the sack through confirmation, but notes were not much better. What an ass he had been. He would never send a note again, never; he swore it to himself, and then reflected a little dismally that he might very likely never have the opportunity.

Still, that was rather a gloomy view to take. And he stood more chance with Carus Evans than he would have done with any other master. Carus Evans had always hated him, and because he hated him would be desperately anxious to treat him fairly. As a result he would be sure to underpunish him. It is always safer to have a big row with a master who dislikes you than with one who is your friend. And from this reflection Roland drew what comfort he might.

Mr Carus Evans sat writing at his desk when Roland came in. He looked up and then went on with his letter. It was an attempt to make Roland feel uncomfortable and to place him at the start at a disadvantage. It was a characteristic action, for Carus Evans was a weak man. His house was probably the slackest in the school. It had no one in the XV., Brewster was its sole representative in the XI. and it did not possess one school prefect. This should not have been, for Carus Evans was a bachelor and all his energies were available. He had no second interest to attract him, but he was weak when he should have been strong; he chose the wrong prefects and placed too much confidence in them. He was not a natural leader.

For a good two minutes he went on writing, then put down his pen.

"Ah, yes, yes, Whately. Sit down, will you? Now then, I've been talking to one of the boys in my house and it seems that you and he have been going out together and meeting some girls in the town. Is that so?"

"Yes, sir."

"And the suggestion came from you, I gather?"

"Yes, sir."

"This is a very serious thing, Whately. I suppose you realise that?"

"I suppose so, sir."

"Of course it is, and especially so for a boy in your position. Now, I don't know what attitude the headmaster will adopt, but of this I am quite certain. A great deal will depend on whether you tell me the truth. I shall know if you tell me a lie. You've got to tell me the whole story. Now, how did this thing start?"

"On the first night of the Christmas term, sir."

"How?"

"I met them at a dance in the pageant grounds."

"The pageant grounds are out of bounds. You ought to know that."

"It was the first night, sir."

"Don't quibble with me. They're out of bounds. Well, what happened next?"

"I danced with her, sir."

"Were you alone?"

"No, sir."

"Who was with you?"

"I can't tell you, sir."

"If you don't tell me——"

"He's left now, sir. It wouldn't be fair."

They looked each other in the face and in that moment Carus Evans realised that, in spite of their positions, Roland was the stronger.

"Oh, well, never mind that; we can leave it till later on. And I suppose you made an appointment?"

"No, sir."

"What?"

"You asked me if I made an appointment, sir. I answered I didn't."

Roland was not going to give him the least assistance. Indeed, in the joy of being able to play once again the old game of baiting masters, that had delighted him so much when he had been in the middle school and that he had to abandon so reluctantly when he attained the dignity of the Fifths and Sixths, he had almost forgotten that he was in a singularly difficult situation.

He would make "old Carus" ask him a question for every answer that he gave. And he saw that for the moment Carus had lost his length.

"Well, then, let me see. Yes, well—er—well, where did you meet her next?"

"In a lane beyond Cold Harbour, sir."

"Did you go there alone?"

"No, sir."

"You were with this other fellow?"

"Yes, sir."

"And what did you do?"

"Do, sir?"

"Yes, do. Didn't you hear me?"

"Yes, sir, but, Do? I don't quite understand you. What exactly do you mean by the word 'do'?"

"You know perfectly well what I mean, Whately. You flirted, I suppose?"

"Yes, sir. I suppose that's what I did do. I flirted."

"I mean you held her hand?"

"Yes, sir."

"And you kissed her?"

"Yes, sir."

"Disgusting! Simply disgusting! Is this place a heathen brothel or a Christian school?" Carus' face was red, and he drove his fingers through the hair at the back of his neck. "You go out on a Sunday afternoon and kiss a shop-girl. What a hobby for a boy in the XV. and Sixth!" And he began to stamp backwards and forwards up and down the room.

This fine indignation did not, however, impress Roland in the least. Carus appeared to him to be less disgusted than interested—pruriently interested—and that he was angry with himself rather than with Roland, because he knew instinctively that he was not feeling as a master should feel when confronted with such a scandal. It was a forced emotion that was inspiring the fierce flow of words.

"Do you know what this sort of thing leads to?" he was saying. "But, of course, you do. I could trust you to know anything like that. Your whole life may be ruined by it."

"But I didn't do anything wrong."

"Perhaps you didn't, not this time, though I've only your word for it; but you would have, sooner or later, under different conditions. There's only one end to that sort of thing. And even if you were all right yourself, how did you know that Brewster was going to be? That's the beastly part of it. That's what sickens me with you. Your own life is your own to do what you like with, but you've no right to contaminate others. You encourage this young fellow to go about with a girl four years older than himself, about whom you know nothing. How could you tell what might be happening to him? He may not have your self-control. He'd never have started this game but for you, and now that he's once begun he may be unable to break himself of it. You may have ruined his whole life, mayn't you?"

Roland considered the question.

"I suppose so, but I didn't look at it that way."

"Of course, you didn't. But it's the results that count. That's what you've got to keep in mind; actions are judged by their results. And now, what do you imagine is going to happen to you? I suppose you know that if I go across and report you to the headmaster that it'll mean the next train back to London?"

"Yes, sir."

"And if I did, you'd have no cause for complaint. It would be what you'd deserved, wouldn't it?"

"Yes, sir."

There was a pause. They looked at each other. Carus Evans hoped that he had frightened Roland, but he had not. Roland knew that Carus did not intend to get him expelled. He would not have talked like that if he had. He was trying to make Roland feel that he was conferring a favour on him in allowing him to stop on.

"There's no reason why I should feel kindly disposed towards you," Carus said. "We've never got on well together. You've worked badly in my form. I've never regarded you as a credit to the school. When you were a small boy you were rowdy and bumptious, and now that you have reached a position of authority you have become superior and conceited. There's no reason why I, personally, should wish to see you remain a member of the school. As regards my own house, I cannot yet judge what harm you may have done me. You've started the poison here. Brewster will have told his friends. One bad apple will corrupt a cask. I don't know what trouble you may have laid up for me."

"No, sir."

"But all the same, I know what it means to expel a boy. He's a marked man for life. I'm going to give you another chance."

"Thank you, sir."

"But you've got to make this thing good first. You've got to go to the headmaster yourself and tell him all about it—now, at once. Do you see?"

"Yes, sir."

It was going to be an awkward business, and Roland made no attempt to conceal it from himself. It was just on the half-hour as he walked across the courts. Afternoon school was beginning. Groups had collected round the classrooms, waiting for the master to let them in. Johnson waved to him from a study window and told him to hurry up and help them with the con.

"Don't wait for me," Roland called back. "I've got one or two things to do. I shall be a little late."

"Slacker," Johnson laughed.

It was funny to see the machine revolving so smoothly, with himself, to all outward appearance, a complacently efficient cog in it. He supposed that a criminal must feel like this when he watched people hurry past him in the streets; all of them so intent upon their own affairs and himself seemingly one with them, but actually so much apart.

He knocked at the headmaster's door.

"Come in."

The headmaster was surprised to see Roland at such an hour.

"Yes, Whately?" he said, and then appeared to remember something, and began to fumble among some papers on his desk. "One moment, Whately; I knew there was something I wanted to speak to you about. Ah, yes, here it is. Your essay on Milton. Will you just come over here a minute? I wanted to have a few words with you about it. Sit down, won't you? Now, let me see, where is it? Ah, yes, here it is: now you say, 'Milton was a Puritan in spite of himself. Satan is the hero of the poem.' Now I want to be quite certain what you mean by that. I'm not going to say that you are wrong. But I want you to be quite certain in your own mind as to what you mean yourself."

And Roland began to explain how Milton had let himself be carried away by his theme, that his nature was so impregnated by the sense of defeat that defeat seemed to him a nobler thing than victory. Satan had become the focus for his emotions on the overthrow of the Commonwealth.

"Yes, yes, I see that, but surely, Whately, the Commonwealth was the Puritan party. If Milton was so distressed by the return of the Royalists, how do you square this view with your statement, 'Milton was a Puritan in spite of himself'? Surely if his puritanism was only imposed, he would have welcomed the return of the drama and a more highly coloured life."

Roland made a gallant effort to explain, but all the time he kept saying to himself, "I came here for a confessional, and yet here I am sitting down in the Chief's best arm-chair, enjoying a friendly chat. I must stop it somehow." But it was excessively difficult. He began to lose the thread of his argument and contradicted himself; and the Chief was so patient, listening to him so attentively, waiting till he had finished.

"But, my dear Whately," the Chief said, "you've just said that *Comus* is a proof of his love of colour and display, and yet you say in the same breath...."

Would it never cease? And how on earth was he at the end going to introduce the subject of his miserable amours? He had never anticipated anything like this. But at last it was finished.

"You see what you've done, Whately? You've picked up a phrase somewhere or other about the paganism of Milton and the nobility of Satan and you have not taken the trouble to think it out. You've just accepted it. I don't say that your statement could not be justified. But it's you who should be able to justify it, not I. You should never make any statement in an essay that you can't substantiate with facts. It's a good essay, though, quite good." And he returned to his papers. He had forgotten altogether that Roland had come unasked to see him.

It was one of the worst moments of Roland's life. He stood silent in the middle of the room while the Chief continued his letter, thinking the interview was at an end.

"Sir," he said at last.

The headmaster looked up quickly and said a little impatiently, for he was a busy man and resented interruption, "Well, Whately? Yes; what is it?"

"I came to see you, sir."

"Oh, yes, of course you did. I forgot. Well, what is it?"

"Sir, I've come to tell you that Mr Carus Evans told me to come and report myself to you and say that—well, sir—that I've been going out for walks with a girl in the town."

"What!"

"Yes, sir, a girl in the town, and that I'd asked a boy in his house to come with me, sir."

The Chief rose from his chair and walked across to the mantelpiece. There was a long pause.

"But I don't quite understand, Whately. You've been going out with some girl in the town?"

"Yes, sir."

"And you've encouraged some boy in Mr Carus Evans' house to accompany you?"

"Yes, sir."

"And he, I suppose, has been going for walks with a girl as well?"

"Yes, sir."

There was another long pause, during which Roland realised that he had chosen the worst possible moment for his confession. Whatever decision the Chief might arrive at would be influenced, not only by his inevitable disappointment at the failure of a boy in whom he had trusted, but by its violent contrast with the friendly discussion over the essay and the natural annoyance of a busy man who has been interrupted in an important piece of work to discuss an unpleasant situation that has arisen unexpectedly. When the Chief at last began to speak there was an impatience in his voice that would have been absent if Roland had tackled him after dinner.

"I don't know," he said. "I am tempted sometimes to give up faith in you fellows altogether. I never know where I am with any of you. I feel as though I were sitting upon a volcano. Everything seems quiet and satisfactory and then suddenly the volcano breaks out and I find that the boys in whom I have placed, or am thinking of placing, responsibility have deceived me. Do you realise the hypocrisy of your behaviour during the last year? You have been meeting Mr Carus Evans and myself on friendly, straightforward terms, with an open look on your face, and all the time, behind our backs, you've been philandering with girls in the town. I haven't asked you for any details and I am not going to; that doesn't enter into the question at all. You've been false and doublefaced. You've been acting a lie for a year. It's the sort of thing that makes me sick of the whole lot of you. You can go."

Roland walked back to the studies, perplexed and miserable. The word "deceit" had cut hard into him. He loathed crookedness and he had always considered himself dead straight. It was a boast of his that he had never told a lie, at least not to a boy; masters were different. Of course they were, and it was absurd to pretend they weren't. Everyone did things that they wouldn't care to tell the Chief. There was a barrier between. The relationship was not open like friendship. He saw the Chief's point of view, but he did not consider it a sound one. He disliked these fine gradations of conduct, this talk of acting a lie: things were either black or white. He remembered how the Chief had once come round the upper dormitories and had endeavoured to persuade him that it was acting a lie to get into bed without cleaning his teeth. He had never understood why. An unclean act, perhaps, but acting a lie! oh, no, it wouldn't do. It was an unfair method of tackling the problem. It was hitting a man in the back, this appeal to a better nature. Life should be played like cricket, according to rules. You could either play for safety and score slowly, or you could run risks and hit across straight half-volleys. If one missed it one was out and that was the end of it. One didn't talk about acting a lie to the bowler because one played at the ball as though it were outside the leg stump. Why couldn't the Chief play the game like an umpire? Roland knew that he had done a thing which, in the eyes of authority, was wrong. He admitted that. He had known it was wrong all the time. He had been found out; he was prepared for punishment. That was the process of life. One took risks and paid the penalty. The issue was to Roland childishly simple, and he could not see why all these good people should complicate it so unnecessarily with their talk of hypocrisy and deceit.

That evening the headmaster wrote to Roland's father:

Dear Mr Whately, — I write to inform you of a matter that will cause you, I fear, a good deal of pain. I have discovered that for the last year Roland has been in the habit of going out for walks on Sunday afternoons with a young girl in the town, and that he has encouraged another and younger boy to accompany him. These walks resulted, I am sure, in nothing beyond a little harmless flirtation, and I do not regard the actual issue as important. I do consider, however, and I think that in this you will agree with me, that Roland's conduct in the matter is most reprehensible. It has involved a calculated and prolonged deception of you, his parent, and of us, his schoolmasters, and he has proved himself, I fear, unworthy of the responsibility of prefectship that I had hoped to place in him next term. If he were a younger boy the obvious course would be a sound thrashing. But Roland is too old for that. Perhaps he is too old to be at school at all. The leaving age of nineteen is arbitrary. Boys develop at such different ages; and though I should not myself have thought so before this affair arose, it may very well be that Roland has already passed beyond the age at which it is wise and, indeed, safe to keep him any longer at a school. For all we know, this trouble may prove to have been a blessing in disguise, and will have protected him from more serious difficulties. At any rate, I do not feel that I should be doing my duty by you or by the other parents who place the welfare of their boys in my hands if I were to keep Roland here after the summer. There is, of course, in this not the least suggestion of expulsion. Roland will leave at the end of the term with many of his contemporaries in the ordinary course of events. And he will become, if he wishes, as I hope he will wish, a member of the old Fernhurstian Society. Perhaps you may yourself decide to come down and have a talk with Roland. If so, perhaps we might discuss his future together. I do not myself see why this should prejudice in any way his going up to the University in a year's time. Of course he could not go up now as he has not yet passed responsions.

I very much hope that you will come down and that we shall be able to discuss the whole matter from every point of view. Sincerely yours,

J. F. Harrison.

This letter arrived at Hammerton by the evening post. Mr Whately had that morning received a letter from Roland, written before the row, with an account of a house game in which he had made 59 runs and taken 3 wickets. Mr Whately was most excited.

"He's really doing remarkably well," he said, after dinner. "He says that he's pretty certain for his second XI. colours, and I can't think why they don't give him a trial for the first. I know that Fernhurst have a pretty strong side this year, but they ought to try all the men they've got."

"He ought to get in next year at any rate," said his wife.

"Next year! Of course there should be no doubt about that at all. But I should like to see him get in this. It will make a big difference to his last term if he knows he's safe for his place. It's always a little worrying having to play for one's colours, and I should like him to have a really good last term. He's deserved it; he's worked hard; he's been a real success at Fernhurst."

His soliloquy was at this point interrupted by the double knock of the postman. Mr Whately jumped up at once.

"The Fernhurst postmark, my dear," he said. "I wonder what this can be about. The headmaster's writing!"

He tore open the envelope eagerly and began to read.

"Well, dear?" said his wife.

He said nothing, but handed the letter across to her. She read it through and then sat forward in her chair, her hands lying on her knees.

"Poor darling," she said. "So that's why he saw so little of April last holidays."

"Yes, I suppose that's the reason."

"Do you think he was in love with her?"

"With April?"

"No, of course not, dear. With this girl at Fernhurst?"

"I don't know. How could I tell?"

And again they sat in silence. It was such a long while since they had been called upon to face a serious situation. For many years now they had lived upon the agreeable surface of an ordered life. They were unprepared for this disquieting intrusion.

"And what's going to happen now?" she said at last. "I suppose you'll have to go down and see him."

"Yes, I think so. Yes, certainly. I ought to go down to-morrow."

"And what will you say to him?"

"I don't know. What is it the headmaster says?"

She handed him the letter and he fumbled with it. "Here it is. 'I do not see myself why this should prejudice in any way his going up to the University.' That's what the headmaster says. But I don't really see how we could manage it. After all, what would happen? He would have to go to a crammer's and everyone would ask questions. We have always said how good the Fernhurst education is, and now they'll begin to wonder why we've changed our minds. If we take Roland away and send him to a crammer's they would be sure to think something was up. You know what people are. It would never do."

"No, I suppose not. But it seems rather hard on Roland if he's got to give up Oxford."

"Well, it will be his own fault, won't it?"

"We haven't heard the whole story yet."

"I know; but what's the good of discussing it. He knew he was doing something he ought not to be doing. He can't expect not to have to pay for it."

And there was another pause.

"He was doing so well, too," she said.

"He would have been a prefect after the summer. He would have been captain of his house. We should have been so proud of him."

"And it's all over now."

They did not discuss the actual trouble. He knew that on the next day he would have to go over the whole thing with Roland, and he wanted to be able to think it out in quiet. They were practical people, who had spent the last fifteen years discussing the practical affairs of ways and means. They had come nearest to each other when they had sat before their account-books in the evening, balancing one column with another, and at the end of it looking each other in the face, agreeing that they would have to "cut down this expense," and that they could "save a little there." The love of the senses had died out quickly between them, but its place had been taken by a deep affection, by the steady accumulation of small incidents of loyalty and unselfishness, of difficulties faced and fought together. They had never ventured upon first principles. They had fixed their attention upon the immediate necessities of the moment.

And now, although Roland's moral welfare was a deep responsibility to them, they spoke only of his career and of how they must shape it to fit the new requirements. Mr Whately thought that he might be able to find a post for him in the bank. But his wife was very much against it.

"Oh, no, dear, that would be terrible. Roland could never stand it; he's such an open-air person. I can't bear to think of him cooped up at a desk all his days."

"That's what my life's been."

"I know; but, Roland. Surely we can find something better for him than that."

"I'll try. I don't know. Things like the Civil Service are impossible for him now, and the Army's no use, and I've got no influence in the City."

"But you must try, really, dear. It's awful to think of him committed to a bank for the rest of his life just when he was doing so well."

"All right. I'll do my best."

A few minutes later he said that he was tired and would go to bed. At the door he paused, walked back into the room and stood behind his wife. He wanted to say something to show that he appreciated her sympathy, that he was glad she was beside him in this disappointment, this hour of trouble. But he did not know what to say. He stretched out a hand timidly and touched her hair. She turned and looked up at him, and without a word said put her arms slowly about his neck, drew his hand down to her and kissed him. For a full minute he was pressed against her. "Dear," he murmured, and though he mounted the stairs sadly, he felt strengthened by that embrace of mutual disappointment.

He set off very early next morning, for he would have to go down to the bank and make arrangements for his absence. He had hoped that Roland would have written to them, but the post brought only a circular from a turf accountant.

"Have you decided what you are going to say to him?" his wife asked.

"Not yet. I shall think it out in the train. I shall be able to say the right thing when the time comes."

"You won't be hard to him. I expect he's very miserable."

It was a bad day for Mr Whately. During the long train journey through fields and villages, vivid in the bright June sunlight, he wondered in what spirit he should receive his son. Roland would be no doubt waiting for him at the station. What would they say to each other? How would they begin? He would have lunch, of course, at the Eversham Hotel, and then, he supposed, he would have to see the headmaster. That would be very difficult. He always felt shy in the headmaster's presence. The headmaster was such an aristocrat; he was stamped with the hall-mark of Eton and Balliol, while he himself was the manager of a bank in London. He was always aware of his social inferiority in that book-lined study, with the five austere reproductions of Greek sculpture. The interview would be very difficult. But the headmaster would at least do most of the talking; whereas with Roland.... Mr Whately shifted uneasily in his corner seat. What on earth was he going to say? Something, surely, about the moral significance of the act. Roland must realise that he was guilty of really immoral conduct, and yet how was he to be made to realise it? What arguments must be produced? Wherein lay the harm of calf love? And looking back over his own life Mr Whately could not see that there was any particular vice attached to it. It was absurd and preposterous, but it was very pleasant. He remembered how he had once fancied himself in love with his grandmother's housemaid. He used to get up early in the morning so that he could sit with her while she laid the grate, and he had knelt down beside her and joined his breath with hers in a fierce attempt to kindle the timid flame. He had never kissed her, but she had let him hold her hand, and the summer holidays had passed in delicious reveries. He remembered also how, a little later, he had fallen desperately in love with the girl at the tobacconist's, and he could still recall the breathless excitement of that morning when he had come into the shop and found it empty. For a second she had listened at the door leading to the private part of the house and had then leant forward over the counter: "Quick," she had whispered.

Mr Whately smiled at the recollection and then remembered suddenly for what cause he was travelling down to Fernhurst. "I must say something to him. What shall I say?" And for want of any better argument he began to adapt a speech that he had heard spoken a few weeks earlier in a melodrama at the Aldwich. The hero, a soldier, had come home from the war to find his betrothed in the arms of another, and she had protested that it was him alone she loved, and that she was playing with the other; but the returned warrior had delivered himself of an oration on the eternal sanctity of love. "Love cannot be divided like a worm and continue to exist. It is not a game." There was something in that argument, and Mr Whately decided to tell Roland that love came only once in a man's life, and that he must reserve himself for that one occasion. "If you make love to every girl you meet, you will spoil yourself for the real love affair. It will be the removal of a shovelful of gravel from a large pile. One shovelful appears to make no difference, but in the end the pile of gravel disappears." That is what he would say to Roland. And because the idea seemed suitable, he did not pause to consider whether or not it was founded upon truth. He lay back in his corner seat and began to arrange his ideas according to that line of persuasion.

But all this fine flow of wit and logic was dispelled when the train drew up at Fernhurst station and Mr Whately descended from the carriage to find Roland waiting for him on the platform.

"Hullo! father," he said, and the two of them walked in silence out of the station, and turned into the Eversham Rooms.

"I've booked a table at the hotel," said Roland.

"Good."

"I expect you're feeling a bit hungry after your journey, aren't you, father?"

"Yes, I am a bit."

"Not a bad day for travelling, though?"

"No, it was very jolly. The country was beautiful all the way down. It's such a relief to be able to get out of London for a bit."

"I expect it must be."

"It's quite a treat to be able to come here"; and so nervous was he that he failed to appreciate the irony of his last statement.

By this time they had reached the hotel. Roland walked with a cheerful confidence into the entrance, nodded to the porter, hung his straw hat upon the rack, and suggested a wash.

Mr Whately looked at himself in the glass as he dried his hands. It was a withered face that looked back at him; the face of a bank clerk who had risen with some industry and much privation to a position of authority; a face that was lined and marked and undistinguished; the face of a man who had never asserted himself. Mr Whately turned from his own reflection and looked at his son, so strong, and fresh and eager; unmarked as yet by trouble and adversity. Who was he, a scrubby, middle-aged little man, emptied of energy and faith, with his life behind him—who was he to impose his will on anyone?

"Finished, father?"

He followed his son into the dining-room and picked up the menu; but he did not know what to choose, and handed the card across to Roland. Roland ordered the meal; the waiter rubbed his hands, and father and son sat opposite each other, oppressed by a situation that was new to them. Roland waited for his father to begin. During the last thirty-six hours he had been interviewed by three different masters, all of whom had, in their way, tried to impress upon him the enormity of his offence. He was by now a little tired of the subject. He wanted to know what punishment had been fixed for him. He had heard enough of the moral aspect of the case. "These people treat me as though I were a fool," he had said to Brewster. "To hear the way they talked one would imagine that I had never thought about the damnable business at all. They seem to expect me to fall down, like St Paul before Damascus, and exclaim: 'Now, all is clear to me!' But, damn it all, I knew what I was doing. I'd thought it all out. I'm not going to do the conversion stunt just because I've been found out." He expected his father to go over the old ground—influence, position, responsibility. He prepared himself to listen. But as his father did not begin, and as the soup did not arrive, Roland felt it was incumbent upon him to say something.

"A great game that against Yorkshire?" he said.

"What! Which game?"

"Don't you remember, about a fortnight ago, the Middlesex and Yorkshire match? Middlesex had over two hundred to get and only three hours to get them in. They're a fine side this year."

And within two minutes they were discussing cricket as they had discussed it so often before. At first they talked to cover their embarrassment, but soon they had become really interested in the subject.

"And what chance do you think you have of getting in the XI.? Surely they ought to give you a trial soon."

"Oh, I don't know, father; I'm not much class, and there are several old colours. I ought to get my seconds all right, and next season...."

He stopped, realising suddenly that he did not as yet know whether there would be any next season for him, and quickly changed the conversation, telling his father of a splendid rag that the Lower Fourth had organised for the last Saturday of the term.

Sooner or later the all-important question had to be tackled, but by the time lunch had finished, son and father had established their old intimacy of quiet conversation, and they were ready to face and, if need be, to dismiss the violent intrusion of the trouble. They walked up and down the hotel grounds, Mr Whately wondering at what exact point he should dab in his carefully constructed argument. There was a pause, into which his voice broke suddenly:

"You know, Roland, about this business...."

"Yes, father."

"Well, I mean, going out with a girl in the town. Do you think it's...." He paused. After all, he did not know what to say.

"I know, father. I know." And looking at each other they realised that it would be impossible for them to discuss it. Their relationship was at stake. It had no technique to deal with the situation. And Roland asked, as his mother had asked, "What's going to happen, father?"

For answer, Mr Whately put his hand into his pocket, took out the headmaster's letter and gave it to Roland. Roland read it through and then handed it back. "Not a bad fellow, the Chief," he said, and they walked up and down the path in silence.

"It's a disappointment," said Roland.

"For all of us."

"I suppose so."

And after another pause: "What's going to happen to me at the end of the term?"

"That's what I've got to decide. I suggested a bank, but your mother was very much against it."

"Oh, not the bank, father!"

"Well, I'll do my best for you, but it'll be difficult. Oxford's out of the question. You can see that, can't you? I should have to send you to a crammer, and everyone would talk. It would be sure to leak out. And we don't want anything like that to happen, because they would be sure to think it was something worse than it really was. I'm afraid Oxford's got to go. Your mother agreed with me about that."

"I'm sure you're right, father."

"But I don't know what else there is, Roland. I shall have to ask the headmaster."

But the headmaster was not very helpful. He was kind and sympathetic. He spoke of the moral significance of the situation and the eventual service that this trouble might prove to have been. He wished Roland the very best of luck. He didn't agree with Mr Whately about the impossibility of Oxford, but he appreciated Mr Whately's point of view. After all, Mr Whately knew his own son better than he did. Was there anything more Mr Whately would wish to ask him? He would be always very glad to give Mr Whately any advice or help that lay within him. He hoped Mr Whately would have a pleasant journey back to town.

"Dorset's at its best in June," he said, as he escorted Mr Whately to the door.

There was an hour to put in before the departure of the London train, and Roland and his father walked down to the cricket field. They sat on the grass in the shade of the trees that cluster round the pavilion, and watched the lazy progress of the various games that were scattered round the large high-walled ground. It was a pretty sight—the green fields, the white flannels, the mild sunshine of early summer. It was bitter to Mr Whately that he would never again see Fernhurst. For that was what Roland's trouble meant to him. And the reflection saddened his last hour with his son.

When Roland had left him at the station he walked up and down the platform in the grip of a deep melancholy. On such an afternoon, five years ago, he had seen Fernhurst for the first time. He had brought Roland down to try for a scholarship and they had stayed for three days together at the Eversham Hotel. Fernhurst had been full of promise for them then. He had not been to a public school himself. When he was a boy the public school system had indeed hardly begun to impose its autocracy on the lower middle classes, and he had always felt himself at a disadvantage because he had been educated at Burstock Grammar School. He had been desperately anxious for Roland to make a success of Fernhurst. He had looked forward to the day when his son would be an important figure in the school, and when he himself would become important as Whately's father. How proud he would feel when he would walk down to the field in the company of a double first. He would come down to "commem" and give a luncheon party at the Eversham Hotel, and the masters would come and speak to him and congratulate him on his son's performance: "A wonderful game of his last week against Tonwich." And during the last eighteen months it had indeed seemed that these dreams were to be realised. Roland had his colours at football, he was in the Sixth, a certainty for his seconds at cricket: after the summer he would be a prefect and captain of games in the house. And now it was all over. As far as he was concerned, Fernhurst was finished. His life would be empty now without the letter every Monday morning telling of Roland's place in form, of his scores during the week, and all the latest news of a vivid communal life. That was over. And as Mr Whately mounted the train, closed the door and sat back against the carriage, he felt as though he were undergoing an operation; a part of his being was being wrenched from him.

Roland felt none of this despondency. After saying good-bye to his father he walked gaily up the Eversham Road. The brown stone of the Abbey tower was turning to gold in the late sunlight, a cool wind was blowing, the sky was blue. What did this trouble matter to him? Had he not strength and faith and time in plenty to repair it? He had wearied of school, he reminded himself. He had felt caged this last year; he had wanted freedom; he had outgrown the narrow discipline of the field and classroom. Next term he would be a man and not a schoolboy. He flung back his shoulders as though he were ridding them of a burden.

There was still three-quarters of an hour to put in before lock-up, and he walked up past the big school towards the hill. He thought he would like to tell Brewster what had happened. He found him in his study, and with him an old boy, Gerald Marston, who had been playing against the school that afternoon.

"Hullo!" he said. "So here's the criminal. I've just been hearing all about you. Come along and sit down."

Roland was flattered at Marston's interest in his escapade. He had hardly known him at all when he had been at Fernhurst. Marston had been in another house, was two years his senior, and, in addition, a double first. Probably it was the first time they had even spoken to each other.

"Oh, yes, we've been having an exciting time," laughed Roland.

"And what's going to be the end of it?"

"Well, as far as I can gather, the school will meet without me next September."

"The sack?"

"Well, hardly that; the embroidered bag."

They talked and laughed. Marston was very jolly; he gave himself no airs, and Roland could hardly realise that three years ago he had been frightened of him, that when Marston had passed him in the cloister he had lowered his voice, and as often as not had stopped speaking till he had gone by.

"And what's going to happen to you now?" asked Marston.

"That's just what I don't know. My pater talked about my going into a bank."

"But you'd hate that, wouldn't you?"

"I'm not too keen on it."

"Lord, no! I should think not. And there's no real future in it. You ought to go into the City. There's excitement there, and big business. You don't want to waste your life like that."

It happens sometimes that we meet a person whom we seem to have known all our life, and by the time the clock began to strike the quarter, Roland felt that he and Marston were old friends.

"A good fellow that," said Marston, after he had gone, "and a bit of a sport too, by all accounts. I must try and see more of him."

And in his study Roland had picked up a calendar and was counting the days that lay between him and Freedom.

PART II
THE RIVAL FORCES

CHAPTER VIII
A FORTUNATE MEETING

Mr Whately's one idea on his return to Hammerton was to hide the fact that Roland's sudden leaving was the result of a scandal. He wished the decision in no way to seem unpremeditated. Two days later, therefore, he went round to the Curtises' and prepared the way by a discussion of the value of university training.

"Really, you know, Mrs Curtis," he said, "I very much doubt whether Oxford is as useful as we sometimes think it is. What will Roland be able to do afterwards? If I know Roland he will do precious little work. He is not very clever; I doubt if he will get into the Civil Service, and what else is there open to him? Nothing, perhaps, except schoolmastering, and he would not be much use at that. I am not at all certain that it is not wiser, on the whole, to take a boy away at about seventeen or eighteen, send him abroad for a couple of months and then put him into business."

Mrs Curtis was not a little surprised. For a good sixteen years Mr Whately had refused to consider the possibility of any education for Roland other than Fernhurst and Brasenose.

"But you are not thinking of taking him away from Fernhurst and not sending him to Brasenose?" she said.

"Oh, no, Mrs Curtis, but I have been thinking that if we could do things all over again I am not at all sure but that's not the way I should have arranged his education."

That was the first step.

A few nights later he came round again, and again talked of the value of two or three months in France.

"What does Roland think about it, Mr Whately?" she asked.

"As a matter of fact, I only heard from Roland on the subject to-day; he seems quite keen on it. I just threw it out as a suggestion to him. I pointed out that most of his friends will have left at the end of the term, that next year he would be rather lonely, and that there would not be anything very much for him to do when he came down from Oxford. He seemed to agree with me."

Mrs Curtis, however, was no fool. She had spent the greater part of her middle age sitting in front of a fire watching life drift past her, and her one amusement had been the examination of the motives and actions of her friends.

"There is something rather curious here," she said that evening to her husband. "As long as we have known the Whatelys they have insisted on the value of public school and university education. Now, quite suddenly, they have turned round, and they are talking about business and commerce and the value of French."

Mr Curtis, who was a credulous creature, saw no reason why they should not change their minds if they wanted to.

"After all," he said, "it is quite true that Latin and Greek are of very little use to anyone in the City."

But Mrs Curtis refused to be convinced.

"I do not care what you say," she said. "You just wait and see."

And, sure enough, within a week Mr Whately had confessed his intention of taking Roland away from Fernhurst at the end of the term.

"And you are going to send him to France?" said Mrs Curtis.

"I am not quite certain about that," he said. "I am going to look round first to see if I can't get him a job at once. We both agree that another year at Fernhurst would be a waste of time."

Mrs Curtis smiled pleasantly. As soon as he had gone she expressed herself forcibly.

"I do not believe for a moment," she insisted, "that Mr Whately has changed his mind without some pretty strong reason. He was frightfully anxious to see Roland captain of his house. He was so proud of everything he did at Fernhurst. There must be a row or something; unless, of course, he has lost his money."

But that idea Mr Curtis pooh-poohed.

"My dear Edith," he said, "that is quite impossible. You know that Whately's got a good salaried post in the bank. He has got no private means to lose and he is not the sort of man to live above his income. It is certainly not money. I don't see why a man should not change his mind if he wants to."

Mrs Curtis again refused to be convinced.

"You wouldn't," she said.

April was of the same opinion. She knew perfectly well that Roland, of his own free will, would never have agreed to such a plan. There must be trouble of some sort or other, she said to herself, and Roland instantly became more interesting in her eyes. She wondered what he had done. Her knowledge of school life was based mainly upon the stories of Talbot Baines Reid, and she began to picture some adventure in which he had taken the blame upon his own shoulders. A friend of his had contracted liabilities at the Eversham Arms and Roland had become involved; or perhaps someone had endeavoured to steal the papers of a Scholarship examination and Roland had been falsely accused. She could not imagine that Roland had himself done anything dishonourable, and she could not be expected to know the usual cause for which boys are suddenly removed from their school. Ralph Richmond was the only person who was likely to know the true story, and to him she went.

Now, there is in the Latin Grammar a morality contained in an example of a conditional sentence which runs in the following words:—"Even though they are silent they say enough." In spite of Ralph's desperate efforts to assume ignorance it was quite obvious to April that he knew all about it, also that it was something that Roland would not want her to know. She was puzzled and distressed. If there had been no embarrassment between them during the holidays she would probably have written to Roland and asked him about it, but under the conditions she felt that this was impossible.

"I shall have to wait till he returns," she said. "Perhaps he will tell me of his own accord."

But when Roland came home he showed not the slightest inclination to tell her anything. If he were acting a part he was acting it extraordinarily well. He told her how glad he was that he was leaving Fernhurst. "One outgrows school," he said. "It is all right for a bit. It is great fun when you are a fag and when you are half-way up; but it is not worth it when you have got responsibilities. And as I went there at thirteen—a year earlier than most people—nearly all my friends will have left. I should have been very lonely next term. I think I am well out of it."

April reminded him of his eagerness to go to Oxford. That objection, too, he managed to brush aside.

"Oxford," he said; "that is nothing but school over again. It is masters and work and regulations. I am very glad it is over."

For a while she was almost tempted to believe he was telling her the truth, but as August passed she noticed that Roland seemed less satisfied with his prospects. He spoke with diminishing enthusiasm of the freedom of an office. Indeed, whenever she introduced the subject he changed it quickly.

"I expect father will find me something decent soon," he would say, and began to talk of cricket or of some rag that he remembered.

But Mr Whately was not finding it easy to procure a post for his son. Roland, after all, possessed no special qualifications. He had been in the Sixth Form of a public school, but he had not been a particularly brilliant member of it. He had passed no standard examinations. He was too young for any important competitive work and Mr Whately had very few influential friends. Roland began to see before him the prospect of long days spent in a bank—a dismal prospect. "What will it lead to, father?" he used to ask, and Mr Whately had not been able to hold out very much encouragement.

"Well, I suppose in time if you work well you would become a manager. If you do anything brilliant you might be given some post of central organisation."

"But it is not very likely, is it, father?" said Roland.

"Not very likely; no."

The years seemed mapped out before him and he found it difficult to maintain his pose of complacent satisfaction, so that one evening, when he felt more than ordinarily depressed, and when the need of sympathy became irresistible, he found himself telling April the story of his trouble.

She listened to him quietly, sitting huddled up in the window-seat, her knees drawn up towards her, her hands clasped beneath them. She said nothing for a while after he had finished.

"Well," he said at last, "that's the story. You know all about it now."

She looked up at him. There was in her eyes neither annoyance nor repulsion nor contempt, but only interest and sympathy.

"Why did you do it, Roland?" she asked.

"I don't know," he said. And because this happened to be the real reason, and because he felt it to be inadequate, he searched his memory for some more plausible account.

"I don't know," he said. "It seemed to happen this way. Things were awfully dull at school, and then, during the Christmas holidays, we had that row. If it hadn't been for that I think I should have chucked it up altogether. But you didn't seem to care for me; it didn't seem to matter much either way; and—well one drifts into these things."

There was another pause.

"But I don't understand, Roland. Do you mean to say if we hadn't had that row at Christmas nothing of this would have happened?"

Because their disagreement had not been without its influence on Roland's general attitude towards his school romance, and because Roland was always at the mercy of the immediate influence, and in the presence of April was unable to think that anything but April could have influenced him, he mistook the part for the whole, and assured her that if they had not had that quarrel at the dance he would have given up Dolly altogether. And because the situation was one they had often met in plays and stories they accepted it as the truth.

"It's all my fault," she said, "really all my fault." And turning her head away from him she allowed her thoughts to travel back to that ineffectual hour of loneliness and resignation. "I can do nothing, nothing myself," she said. "I can only spoil things for other people."

At the time Roland was disappointed, but two hours later he decided that he was, on the whole, relieved that Mrs Curtis should have chosen that particular moment to return from her afternoon call. In another moment he would have been saying things that would have complicated life most confoundedly. April had been very near to tears; he disliked heroics. He would have had to do something to console her. He would probably have said to her a great many things that at the time would have seemed to him true, but which afterwards he would have regretted. He had sufficient worries of his own already.

At home life was not made easy for Roland. He received little sympathy. Ralph told him that he deserved all he had got and had been lucky to get off so cheaply. His father repeated a number of moral platitudes, the source of which Roland was able to recognise.

"After all," said Mr Whately, "I have been in a bank all my life; I have not done badly in it, and you, with your education and advantages, should be able to do much better."

This was a line of argument which did not appeal to Roland. He was very fond of his father, but he had always regarded his manner of life as a fate, at all costs, to be avoided. And though his mother in his presence endeavoured to make him believe that all was for the best in the best of all possible worlds, when she was alone with her husband she saw only her son's point of view.

"If this is all we have got to offer him," she said, "all the money and time we have spent will be wasted. If a desk at a bank is going to be the end of it, he might just as well have gone to a day school, and all the extra money we have spent could have been put away for him in a bank."

Mr Whately reminded her that the change in their plans was due entirely to Roland.

"Oh, yes, yes, yes," she said, "that is all very well. But it is a cruel shame that a boy's whole life should depend on a thing he does when he is seventeen years old."

Mr Whately murmured something about it being the way of the world, adding he himself had been in a bank now for thirty years.

"Which is the very reason," said Mrs Whately, "that I don't want my son to go into one" — an argument that did not touch her husband.

But talk how they might, and whatever philosophic attitude they might adopt, the practical position remained unchanged. Roland had been offered a post in a bank, which he could take up at the beginning of October. Three weeks were left him in which he might try to find something better for himself; but of this there seemed little prospect.

And as he sat in the free seats at the Oval, on an afternoon of late September, Roland had to face his position honestly, and own to himself there was no alternative to the bank.

He was lonely as he sat there in the mild sunshine watching the white figures move across the grass. That evening school would be going back and he would not be with them. It was hard to realise that in four hours' time the cloisters would be alive with voices, that feet would be clattering up and down the study steps, that the eight-fifteen would have just arrived and the rush to the hall would have begun.

The play became slow; two professionals were wearing down the bowling. He began to feel sleepy in the languid atmosphere of this late summer afternoon. He could not concentrate his attention upon the cricket. He could think only of himself, and the river that was bearing him without his knowledge to a country he did not know.

It was not merely that he had left school, that he had exchanged one discipline for another; he had altered entirely his mode of life, and for this new life a new technique would be required. Up till now everything had been marked out clearly in definite stages; he had been working in definite lines. It was not merely that the year was divided into terms, but his career also was so divided. There had been a gradation in everything. It had been his ambition to get his firsts at football, and the path was marked out clearly for him—house cap., seconds, firsts: in form he had wanted to get into the Sixth, and here again the course had been clear—Fourth, Fifth, Sixth: he had wanted to become a house prefect; the process was the same—day room table, Lower Fourth table, Fifth Form table, Sixth Form table. He had known exactly what he was doing; everything had been made simple for him. His ambitions had been protected. It was quite different now: nothing was clearly defined. He would have to spend a certain number of hours a day in an office. Outside of that office he would be free to do what he liked. He could choose his own ambition, but as yet he could not decide what that would be. He was as dazed by the imminence of this freedom as a mortal man whose World is ordered by the limits of time and space when confronted suddenly with the problem of infinity. Roland could not come to terms with a world in which he would not be tethered to one spot by periods of three months. His reverie was interrupted by a hand that descended heavily on his shoulder and a voice he recognised, that addressed him by his name. He turned and saw Gerald Marston standing behind him.

"So you are a free man at last," he said. "How did the rest of the term go?"

It was a pleasant surprise; and Roland welcomed the prospect of a cheery afternoon with a companion who would soon dispel his melancholy.

"Oh, not so badly," he said. "I lay pretty quiet and saw as little of Carus Evans as I could."

"And how is the amiable Brewster?" asked Marston.

"He's all right, I suppose. He won't have much of a time this year, though, I should think. He ought to have been captain of the XI., but they say now he is not responsible enough, and Jenkins, a man he absolutely hates, is going to run it instead."

"So you're not sorry you have left?"

Roland shrugged his shoulders.

"In a way not; if there hadn't been a row, though, I should have had a pretty good time this term."

"Well, you can't have things both ways. What's going to happen to you now?"

With most people Roland would have preferred to pass the matter off with some casual remark about his father having got him a good job in the City. He liked sympathy, but was afraid of sympathy when it became pity. He did not want the acquaintances who, six months ago, had been talking of him as "that lucky little beast, Whately," to speak of him now as "poor old Whately; rotten luck on him; have you heard about it?" But it is always easier to make a confession to a stranger than to a person with whom one is brought into daily contact. Marston was a person with whom he felt intimate although he knew him so little; and so he found himself telling Marston about the bank and of the dismal future that awaited him.

Marston was highly indignant.

"What a beastly shame," he said. "You will simply hate it. Cannot your father get you something better?"

"I don't think so. He has always lived a very quiet life; he has not got any influential friends—but really, what's the good of talking about it? Something may turn up. Let's watch the cricket."

"Oh, rot, man!" expostulated Marston. "You can't let the thing drop like this. After all, my father is rather a big pot in the varnish world; he may be able to do something."

"But I don't know anything about varnish."

"You don't need to, my dear fellow. The less you know about it the better. All you've got to do is to believe that our kind of varnish is the best." And as they walked round the ground during the tea interval a happy idea occurred to Marston.

"I've got it," he said. "We have got a cricket match on Saturday against the village; we're quite likely to be a man short; at any rate we can always play twelve-a-side. You come down and stay the week-end with us. The pater's frightfully keen on cricket. If you can manage to make a few he's sure to be impressed, and then I'll tell him all about you. You will get a pleasant week-end and I expect quite a good game of cricket."

Roland naturally accepted this proposal eagerly. He did not, however, tell his people of the prospect of a job in Marston & Marston, Limited; he preferred to wait till things were settled one way or another. If he were to be disappointed, he would prefer to be disappointed alone. He did not need any sympathy at such a time.

But when he went round to the Curtises' April could tell, from the glow in his face, that he was unusually excited about something. She did not have a chance to speak to him when he was in the drawing-room. Her mother talked and talked. Arthur had just gone back to school and she was garrulous about his outfit.

"It is so absurd, you know, Mr Whately," she said, "the way people say women care more about clothes than men. There is Arthur to-day; he insisted on having linen shirts instead of woollen ones, although woollen shirts are much nicer and much warmer. 'My dear Arthur,' I said, 'no one can see your shirt; your waistcoat hides most of it and your tie the rest.' But he said that all the boys wore linen shirts instead of flannel. 'But, my dear Arthur,' I said, 'who is going to see what kind of a shirt you are wearing if it is covered by your waistcoat and tie? And I can cut your sleeves shorter so that they would not be seen beneath your coat.' And do you know what he said, Mr Whately? He said, 'You don't understand, mother; the boys would see that I was wearing a flannel shirt when I changed for football, and I would be ragged for it.' Well, now, Mr Whately, isn't that absurd?"

She went on talking and talking about every garment she had bought for her son—his ties, his boots, his socks, his coat.

Roland hardly talked at all. His father mentioned that he was going down for the week-end to stay with some friends and take part in a cricket match.

"So that is what you are so excited about!" April had interposed. And Roland had laughed and said that that was it.

But she would not believe that he could be so excited about a game of cricket, and in the hall she had pulled him by his coat sleeve.

"What is it?" she had whispered. "Something has happened. It is not only a cricket match."

And because he wanted to share his enthusiasm with someone, and because April looked so pretty, and because he felt that courage would flow to him from her faith in him, he confided in her his hope.

"Oh, that would be lovely," she said. "I do hope things will turn out all right. I've felt so guilty all along about it; if it hadn't been for me none of this would ever have happened."

"Don't worry about that," said Roland. "Things are beginning to turn right now."

There was no time for further conversation; Mrs Curtis had completed her doorstep homily to Mr Whately. April pressed Roland's hand eagerly as she said good-bye to him.

"Good luck!" she whispered.

CHAPTER IX
HOGSTEAD

It was a glorious week, and through Thursday and Friday Roland watched in nervous anticipation every cloud that crossed the pale blue sky. Sooner or later the weather must break, he felt; and it would be fatal for his prospects if it rained now. It is miserable to sit in a pavilion and watch the wicket slowly become a bog: cheeriness under such conditions is anti-social. Mr Marston would be unable to work up any sympathy for him, and would remember him as "that fellow who came down for the cricket match that was such a fiasco"—an unfortunate association.

Everything went well, however. Roland travelled down on the Friday night, and as he got out of the train at Hogstead station he saw the spire of the church black against a green and scarlet sky. "With such a sky it can hardly be wet to-morrow," he said.

The Marstons were a rich family and it was the first time Roland had seen anything of the life of really wealthy people. He was met at the station and was driven up through a long, curving drive to a Georgian house surrounded by well-kept lawns. Marston received him in a large, oak-panelled hall, and although at first Roland was a little embarrassed by the attentions of the footman, who took his hat and coat and bag, within five minutes he found himself completely at his ease, sitting in a deep arm-chair discussing with Mr Marston the prospects of a certain young cricketer who had made his first appearance that summer at the Oval.

Mr Marston was a fine healthy man, in the autumn of life. The enthusiasm of his early years had been spent in a bitter struggle to build up his business and he had had very little time for amusement. During the long hours at his desk and the long evenings with ledgers and account-books piled before him he had looked forward to the days when he would be able to delegate his authority and spend most of his time in the country, within the sound of bat and ball. Having had little coaching he was himself a poor performer; for which reason he was the more kindly disposed to anyone who showed promise. It was a rule of his estate that, winter as well as summer, every gardener, groom and servant should spend ten minutes each morning bowling at the nets. He lived in the hope that one day an under-gardener would be deemed worthy of transportation to the county ground.

"My son tells me you are a great performer," he said to Roland.

"Oh, no, sir; only very moderate. I did not get into the first XI. at Fernhurst."

"They had an awfully strong XI.," interposed Marston. "And he had a blooming good average for the second. Didn't you make a century against the town?"

Roland confessed that he had, but remarked that with such bowling it was very hard to do anything else.

"Well, ten other people managed to," said Marston.

"And a century is a century whoever makes it," said his father, who had never made as many as fifty in his life. "You've got to make a lot of good shots to make a hundred."

"At any rate," said Marston, "I don't mind betting he gets a few to-morrow."

And for half-an-hour they exchanged memories of the greatest of all games.

Roland found his evening clothes neatly laid out on his bed when he went up to change for dinner; and when he came down the whole family was assembled in the drawing-room. There were Mrs Marston, a large rather plump woman of about fifty years old; her daughter Muriel, a small and pretty girl, with her light hair scattered over her shoulders; and two or three other members of the next day's side. There was an intimate atmosphere of comfort and well-being to which Roland was unaccustomed. At home they had only one servant, and had to wait a good deal upon themselves. He enjoyed the silent, unobtrusive methods of the two men who waited on them. He never needed to ask for anything; as soon as he had finished his bread another piece was offered him; his glass was filled as it began to empty; and the conversation was like the meal—calm, leisured, polished.

Roland sat next to Muriel and found her a delightful companion. She was at an age when school and games filled her life completely. She told Roland of a rag that they had perpetrated on their French mistress, and he recounted her the exploits of one Foster, who used to dress up at night, go down to the Eversham Arms, sing songs and afterwards pass round the hat.

Roland had his doubts as to the existence of Foster; he had become at Fernhurst one of those mythical creatures which every school possesses—a fellow who took part in one or two amusing escapades, and around whose name had accumulated the legends of many generations. His story was worth telling, none the less.

After dinner they walked out into the garden, with the chill of the autumn night in the air. It reminded Roland that his sojourn in that warmly coloured life was only temporary, and that outside it was the cold, cheerless struggle for existence.

"It is so ripping this," he said to Muriel, "and it is so rotten to think that in a few weeks I shall be sitting down in front of a desk and adding up figures." He told her, though she was already acquainted with the facts, of how he had left Fernhurst at the end of the term, and in a few weeks would be going into a bank.

"Oh, how beastly," she said. "I suppose you will have rotten short holidays?"

"A fortnight a year."

"I think it is a shame," she said. "I am sure a boy like you ought to be leading an open-air life somewhere."

And that night, before he fell asleep, Roland thought wistfully of the company he had met that day. It was marvellous how money smoothed everything. It was the oil that made the cogs in the social machine revolve; without it there was no rhythm or harmony, but only a broken, jarring movement. Without money he felt life must be always in a degree squalid. He remembered his own home and the numerous worries about small accounts and small expenses; he knew how it had worn down the energy of his father. He knew that such worries would never touch a girl like Muriel. How easy and good-natured all these people were; they were flowers that had been grown in a fertile soil. Everything depended upon the soil in which one was planted; the finest plants would wither if they grew far from the sunshine in a damp corner of a field.

Next day Roland awoke to a world heavy with a dripping golden mist, that heralded a bright hot day. There had been a heavy dew, and after breakfast they all walked down to the ground to look at the wicket.

"If we win the toss to-day, Gerald," said Mr Marston to his son, "I think we had better put them in first. It is bound to play a bit trickily for the first hour or so."

There was no need for such subtlety, however, for the village won the toss, and, as is the way with villagers, decided to go in first.

"Good," said Mr Marston, "and if we have not got eight of them out by lunch I shall be very surprised."

And, sure enough, eight of the village were out by lunch, but the score had reached one hundred and five. This was largely due to three erratic overs that had been sent down by an ecclesiastical student from Wells who had bowled, perhaps in earnest of future compromise, on the leg theory, with his field placed upon the off.

The local butcher had collected some thirty runs off these three overs, and thirty runs in a village match when the whole score of a side does not usually reach more than fifty or sixty is a serious consideration.

At lunch-time Mr Marston was most apologetic. "I had heard he was a good bowler," he said to Roland, "and I thought it would be a good thing to give him a chance to bowl early on; and then when I saw him getting hit all over the place I imagined he was probably angling for a catch or something; and then after he had been hit about in the first two overs I had to give him a third for luck."

"An expensive courtesy," said Roland.

"Perhaps it was; but, after all, a hundred and five is not a great deal, and we have a good many bats on our side."

Within half-an-hour's time a hundred and five for eight had become a hundred and fifty. Under the kindly influence of his excellent champagne-cup Mr Marston had decided to give the ecclesiastical student another opportunity of justifying his reputation. He did not redeem that reputation. He sent down two overs, which resulted—in addition to three wides and a "no ball"—in twenty-five runs; and a hundred and fifty would take a lot of getting. Indeed, Mr Marston's XI. never looked at all like getting them.

Roland, who was sent in first, was caught at short leg in the second over; it was off a bad ball and a worse stroke—a slow, long hop that he hit right across, and skied. He was bitterly disappointed. He did not mind making ducks; it was all in the run of a game, and he never minded if he was got out by a good ball. But it was hard on such a day to throw away one's wicket.

"Very bad luck indeed," said Muriel, as he reached the pavilion.

"Not bad luck, bad play!" he remarked good-humouredly. Having taken off his pads he sat down beside her and watched the game. It was not particularly exciting; wickets fell with great regularity. Mr Marston made a few big hits, and his son stayed in for a little while without doing anything much more than keep his end up. In the end the total reached a hundred and thirteen, and in a one-day match a first innings result was usually final.

But Mr Marston was not at all despondent. He refused to wait for the tea interval and led his side straight on to the field.

"We don't want any rest," he said. "Most of us have rested the whole afternoon, and those of the other side who are not batting can have tea."

It was now four-thirty; two hours remained before the drawing of stumps, and from now on the game became really exciting. Marston took two wickets in his first over, and at the other end a man was run out. Three wickets were down for two runs: a panic descended upon the villagers. The cobbler was sent in to join the doctor, with strict instructions not to hit on any account. The cobbler was not used to passive resistance; he played carefully for a couple of overs, then a faster ball from Marston found the edge of the bat. Short slip was for him, providentially, asleep, and the umpire signalled a four. This seemed to throw him off his balance.

"It is no good," he said. "If I start mucking about like that I don't stand the foggiest chance of sticking in. I'm going to have a hit."

At the next ball he did have a hit—right across it, and his middle stump fell flat.

After this there was no serious attempt to wear down the bowling. Rustic performers—each with a style more curious than the last—drove length balls on the off stump in the direction of long on. Wickets fell quickly. The score rose; and by the time the innings was over only an hour was left for play, and ninety-two runs were required to win—ninety-two runs against time in a fading light, on a wicket that had been torn up by hob-nailed boots, was not the easiest of tasks.

"Still, we must have a shot for it," Mr Marston said. "We cannot be more than beaten, and we are that already."

And so Gerald Marston and Roland went in to open the innings with the firm intention of getting on or getting out.

The start was sensational. Marston had few pretensions to style; and indeed his unorthodox, firm-footed drive had been the despair of the Fernhurst Professional. The ball, when he hit it, went into the air far more often than along the ground. And probably no one was more surprised than he was when he hit the first two balls that he received right along the ground to the boundary, past cover-point. The third ball was well up: he took a terrific drive at it, missed it, and was very nearly bowled. Roland, who was backing up closely, called him for a run, and if surprise at so unparalleled an example of impertinence had not rendered the wicket-keeper impotent, nothing could have saved him from being run out. A fever entered into Roland's brain. He knew quite well that he ought to play carefully for a few balls to get his eye in, but that short run had flung him off his balance. The first ball he received he hit at with a horizontal bat, and it sailed, fortunately for him, over cover-point's head for two. He attempted a similar stroke at the next ball, was less fortunate, and saw cover-point prepare himself for an apparently easy catch. But there is a kindly Providence which guards the reckless.

Cover-point was the doctor, and probably the safest man in the whole field to whom to send a catch. He was not, however, proof against the impetuous ardour of mid-off. Mid-off saw the ball in the air and saw nothing else. He rushed to where it was about to fall. He arrived at the spot just when the doctor's hands were preparing a comfortable nest for the ball, and the doctor and mid-off fell in a heap together, with the ball beneath them!

Twelve runs had been scored in the first five balls; there had been a possible run out; a catch had been missed at cover-point. It was a worthy start to a great innings.

After that everything went right with Roland. He attempted and brought off some remarkably audacious shots. He let fly at everything that was at all pitched up to him. Sometimes he hit the ball in the centre of the bat, and it sailed far into the long field; but even his mishits were powerful enough to lift the ball out of reach of the instanding fieldsman: and fortune was kind. By the time Marston was caught at the wicket the score had reached fifty-seven, and there were still twenty-five minutes left for play. At the present rate of scoring there would be no difficulty in getting the runs. At this point, however, a misfortune befell them.

In the first innings the ecclesiastical student had made a duck; he had not, indeed, received a single ball. His predecessor had been bowled by the last ball of an over, and off the first ball of the next over the man at the other end had called him for an impossible run and he had been run out. To recompense him for this ill luck Mr Marston had put him in first wicket down. "After all," he had said, "we ought to let the man have a show, and if he does make a duck it won't make any difference." He was not prepared, however, for what did occur. The ecclesiastical student was a left-handed batsman, and a sigh of relief seemed to go up from the fielding side at the revelation. They were sportsmen; they were prepared to run across in the middle of the over; but even so, the preparation of a field for a left-hander was a lengthy business.

A grey gloom descended on the pavilion.

"Well, I declare!" said Mr Marston. "First of all he bowls on the leg theory, with his field placed on the off, and then at a moment like this he doesn't let us know that he's a left-hander!"

And the prospective divine appeared to be quite unconscious of the situation. He had come out to enjoy himself; so far he had not enjoyed himself greatly. He had taken no wickets, and had been responsible for the loss of some fifty runs. This was his last chance, and he was not going to hurry himself. He played his first three balls carefully, and placed the last ball of the over in front of short leg for a single. During the next four overs only eight runs were scored; four of these were from carefully placed singles, off the fifth and sixth balls in the over. Roland only had three balls altogether, and off one of these he managed to get a square leg boundary.

The total had now reached sixty-five, twenty-eight runs were still wanted, and only a quarter of an hour remained. Unless the left-hander were got out at once there seemed to be no chance of winning; this fact the village appreciated.

One would not say, of course, that the bowlers did not do their best to dismiss the ecclesiastical student; they were conscientious men. But it is very hard to bowl one's best if one knows that one's success will be to the eventual disadvantage of one's side; a certain limpness is bound to creep into the attack. And if Roland had received the balls that were being sent down to his partner, there is little doubt that a couple of overs would have seen the end of the match.

Roland realised that something desperate must be done. Either the left-hander must get out, or he himself must get down to the other end; and so off the first ball of the next over Roland backed up closely. He was half-way down the pitch by the time the ball reached the batsman. It was a straight half-volley, which was met with a motionless, if perpendicular, bat. The ball trickled into the hands of mid-off.

"Come on!" yelled Roland.

It was an impossible run, and the left-hander stood, in startled dismay, a few steps outside the crease.

"Run!" yelled Roland. His partner ran a few steps, saw the ball was in the hands of mid-off, and prepared to walk back to the pavilion. Mid-off, however, was in a highly electric state. He had already imperilled severely the prospects of his side by colliding with cover-point, and was resolved, at any rate, not to make a second blunder. He had the ball in his hands. There was a chance of running a batsman out; he must get the ball to the unprotected wicket as soon as possible, and so, taking careful aim, he flung the ball at the wicket with the greatest possible violence. It missed the wicket; and a student of the score-book would infer that, after having played himself in carefully and scoring four singles, F. R. Armitage opened his shoulders in fine form. He might very well remain in this illusion, for there is no further entry in the score-book against that gentleman's name. There are just four singles and a five. He did not receive another ball.

Off the next four balls of the over Roland hit two fours and a two; off the last ball he got another dangerously close single. Only ten more runs were needed: there was now ample time in which to get them. Roland got them indeed off the first four balls of the next over.

At the end of the match there was a scene of real enthusiasm, in which Mr Armitage was the only person who took no part. He was still wondering what had induced Roland to call him for those absurd singles. He indeed took Mr Marston aside after dinner and pointed out to him that that young man should really be given a few lessons in backing up.

"My dear sir," he said, "it was only the merest fluke that saved my wicket—another inch and I should have been run out."

"Well, he managed to win the match for us," replied Mr Marston.

"Perhaps, perhaps, but he nearly ran me out."

Mr Armitage was, however, the only one of the party at all alarmed by Roland's daring. That evening Roland was a small hero. Mr Marston could find no words too good for him.

"A splendid fellow," he said to Gerald afterwards. "A really splendid fellow—the sort of friend I have always wanted you to make—a first-class, open, straight fellow."

Marston thought this a good opportunity to drop a hint about Roland's position.

"Yes—a first-class fellow," he said. "Isn't it rotten to think a chap like that will have to spend the whole of his life in a bank, with only a fortnight's holiday a year, and no chance to develop his game!"

Mr Marston's rubicund face expressed appropriate disapproval.

"That fellow going to spend all his life in a bank? Preposterous! He will be simply ruined there—a fellow who can play cricket like that!"

Mr Marston, having spent his own life at a desk, was anxious to save anyone else from a similar fate, especially a cricketer.

"Well, it seems the only thing for him to do, father; his people haven't got much money and have no influence. I know they have tried to get him something better, but they haven't been able to."

"My dear Gerald, why didn't you tell me about it? If I had known a fellow like that was being tied up in a bank I'd have tried to do something to help him."

"Well, it's not too late now, is it?"

"No, but it's rather short notice, isn't it? What could he do?"

"Pretty well anything you could give him, father. He is jolly keen."

"Um!" said Mr Marston; and Gerald, who knew his father well, recognised that he was about to immerse himself in deep thought, and that it would be wiser to leave him alone.

By next morning the deep thought had crystallised into an idea.

"Look here, Gerald," said Mr Marston. "I don't know what this young man is worth to me from a business point of view—probably precious little at present. But he is a good fellow, the sort of young chap we really want in the business. None of us are any younger than we were. As far as I know, you are the only person under thirty in the whole show. Now, what we do want badly just now are a few more foreign connections. We have got the English market pretty well, but that is not enough. We want the French and Belgian and German markets, and later on we shall want the South American markets. Now, what I suggest is this: that when you go out to France in November you should take young Whately with you, show him round, and see what he is worth generally; and then we will send him off on a tour of his own and see how many clients he brings us. He is just the sort of fellow I want for that job. We don't want the commercial traveller type at all; he is very good at small accounts, but he does not do for the big financiers. I want a man who is good enough to mix in society abroad— whom big men like Bertram can ask to their houses. A man like that would always have a pull over a purely business man. Now, if your young friend would care to have a shot at that, he can; and if he makes good at it he will be making more at twenty-five with us than he would be at a bank by the time he was fifty."

Marston carried the news at once to Roland.

"My lad," he said, "that innings of yours is about the most useful thing that has ever happened to you in your life. The old man thinks so much of you he is prepared to cut me out of his will almost; at any rate, as far as I can make out, he is going to offer you a job in our business."

"What?"

"You will have to fix it up with him, of course, but he suggested to me that you and I should go out together to France in November, and you will be able to see the sort of way we do things, and then he will give you a shot on your own as representative. If you do well at it—well, my lad, you will be pretty well made for life!"

It was wonderful news for Roland. Life, at the very moment when it had appeared to be closing in on him, had marvellously broadened out. He returned home on the Monday morning, not only excited by the prospect of a new and attractive job, but moved irresistibly by this sudden vision of a world to which he was unaccustomed—by the charm, the elegance and the direct good-naturedness of this family life.

CHAPTER X
YOUNG LOVE

Roland said nothing to his people of Mr Marston's conversation with Gerald. He disliked scenes and an atmosphere of expectation. When everything was settled finally he would tell them, but he would not risk the exposure of his hope to the chill of disappointment. He could not, however, resist the temptation to confide in April. She was young; she could share his failures as his successes. Life was before them both.

No sooner had he turned the corner of the road than he saw the door of the Curtises' house open. April was in the porch waiting for him. "She must have been looking for me," he thought. "Sitting in the window-seat, hoping that I should come." His pride as well as his affection was touched by this clear proof of her interest in him.

"Well?" she said.

"I made a duck," he answered; and his vanity noted that her brown eyes clouded suddenly with disappointment. "But that was only in the first innings," he added.

"Oh, you pig!" she said, "and I thought that after all it had come to nothing."

Roland laughed at the quick change to relief.

"But how do you know that I did do anything in the second innings?"

"You must have."

"But why?"

"'Cos—oh, I don't know. It's not fair to tease me, Roland; tell me what happened." They had passed into the hall, shutting the door behind them, and she pulled impatiently at his sleeve: "Come on, tell me."

"Well, as a matter of fact, I made forty-eight not out."

"Oh, how ripping, how ripping! Come and tell me all about it," and catching him by the hand she led him to the window-seat, from which, on that miserable afternoon, she had gazed for over an hour down the darkening street. "Come on, tell me everything."

And though he at first endeavoured to assume an attitude of superior indifference, he soon found himself telling the story of the match eagerly, dramatically. Reticence was well enough in the presence of the old and middle-aged—parents, relatives and schoolmasters—for all those who had put behind them the thrill of wakening confidence and were prepared to patronise it in others, from whose scrutiny the young had to protect their emotions with the shield of "it is no matter." But April's enthusiasm was fresh, unquestioning and freely given; he could not but respond to it.

She listened to the story with alert, admiring eyes. "And were they awfully pleased with you?" she said when he had finished.

"Well, it was pretty exciting."

"And did Mr Marston say anything to you?"

"Rather! Quite a lot. He was more excited than anyone."

"Oh, yes, but I didn't mean the cricket. Did he say anything about the business?"

Roland nodded.

"Oh, but, Roland, what?"

"Well, I'm not quite certain what, but I think he's going to let me have a shot at some sort of foreign representative affair."

"But, how splendid!" She felt that she shared, in a measure, in his success. It was in her that he had confided his hopes; it was to her that he had brought the news of his good fortune. Her face was flushed and eager, its expression softened by her faith in him. And Roland who, up till then, had regarded her as little more than a friend, her charm as a delicate, elusive fragrance, was unprepared for this simple joy in his achievement. The surprise placed in his mouth ardent, unconsidered words.

"But I shouldn't have been able to do anything without you," he said.

"What do you mean?" she asked, feeling herself grow nervous, taut, expectant.

"You encouraged me when I was depressed," he said. "You believed in me. You told me that things would come right. And because of your belief they have come right. If it hadn't been for you I shouldn't have worried; I should have resigned myself to the bank. As likely as not I shouldn't have gone down to the Marstons' at all. It's all you."

There was a pause. And when at last she spoke, the intonation of her voice was tender.

"Is that true, Roland, really true?"

And as she looked at him, with her clear brown eyes, he believed implicitly that it was true. He was not play-acting. His whole being was softened and made tender by her beauty, by the sight of her calm, oval face and quiet colour, her hair swept in a wide curve across her forehead, gathered under the smooth skin of her neck. His manhood grew strong through her belief in him. She was the key that would open for him the gate of adventure. He leant forward, took her hands in his, and the touch of her fingers brought to his lips an immediate avowal.

"It's quite true, April, every word of it. I shouldn't have done anything but for you." Her brown eyes clouded with a mute gratitude. Gently he drew her by the hand towards him, and she made no effort to resist him. "April," he murmured, "April."

It was the first real kiss of his life. His mouth did not meet hers as it had met Dolly's, in a hungry fierceness; he did not hold her in his arms as he had held Dolly; did not press her to him till she was forced, as Dolly had, to fling her head back and gasp for breath. For an instant April's cheek was against his and his mouth touched hers: nothing more. But in that cool contact of her lips he found for the first time the romance, poetry, ecstasy, what you will, of love. And when his arms released her and she leant back, her hand in his, a deep tenderness remained with them. He said nothing. There was no need for words. They sat silent in face of the mystery they had discovered.

Roland walked home in harmony with himself, with nature; one with the rhythm of life that was made manifest in the changing seasons of the year; the green leaf and the bud; the flower and the fruit; the warm days of harvesting. Hammerton was stretched languid beneath the September sunshine. The sky was blue, a pale blue, that whitened where it was cut by the sharp outline of roof and chimney-stack. The leaves that had been fresh and green in May, but had grown dull in the heat and dust of summer, were once more beautiful. The dirty green had changed to a shrivelled, metallic copper. A few mornings of golden mist would break into a day of sultry splendour; then would come the first warning of frost—the chill air at sundown, the grey dawn that held no promise of sunshine. Oh, soon enough the boughs would be leafless, the streets bare and wintersome. But who could be sad on this day of suspended decadence, this afternoon laden with the heavy autumn scents. Were not the year's decay, the lengthening evenings, part of the eternal law of nature—birth and death, spring and winter, and an awakening after sleep? The falling leaves suggested to him no analogy with the elusive enchantments of the senses.

Two days later he received a letter from Mr Marston offering him a post of a hundred and fifty pounds a year, with all expenses found.

"You will understand, of course," the letter ran, "that at present you are on probation. Our work is personal and requires special gifts. These gifts, however, I believe you to possess. For both our sakes I hope that you will make a success of this. Gerald is sailing for Brussels at the end of October, and I expect that you will be able to arrange to accompany him. He will tell you what you will need to take out with you. We usually make our representative an allowance of fifteen pounds for personal expenses, but I daresay that we could in your case, if it is necessary, increase this sum."

Roland handed the letter to his father.

Mr Whately, as usual in the morning, was in a state of nervous excitement. He was always a considerable trial to his family at breakfast. And as often as possible Roland delayed his own appearance till he had heard the slam of the front door. It is not easy to enjoy a meal when someone is bouncing from table to sideboard, reading extracts from the morning paper, opening letters, running up and down stairs, forgetting things in the hall. Mr Whately had never been able to face the first hour of the morning with dignity and composure. When Roland handed him Mr Marston's letter he received it with the impatience of a busy man, who objects to being worried by an absurd trifle.

"Yes, what is it? What is it?"

"A letter from Mr Marston, father, that I thought you might like to read."

"Oh, yes, of course; well, wait a minute," and he projected himself out of the door and up the stairs. He returned within a minute, panting and flustered.

"Yes; now what's the time? Twenty-five past eight. I've got seven minutes. Where's this letter of yours, Roland? Let me see."

He picked up the letter and began to read it as he helped himself to another rasher of bacon. His agitation increased as he read.

"But I don't understand," he said impatiently. "What's all this about Mr Marston offering you a post in his business?"

"What's that, dear?" said Mrs Whately quickly. "Isn't Roland going into the bank after all?"

"Yes, of course he is going into the bank," her husband replied hastily. "It's all settled. Don't interrupt me, Roland. I can't understand what you've been doing!"

And he flung the back of his hand against his forehead, a favourite gesture when the pressure of the conversation grew intense.

"I don't know what it's all about, Roland," he continued. "I don't know anything about this man. Who he is, and what he is. And I don't know why you've been arranging all these things behind my back."

Roland expressed surprise that his father had not welcomed the offer of so promising a post. But Mr Whately was too flustered to consider the matter in this light. "It may be a better job," he said, "I don't know. But the bank has been settled and I can't think why you should want to alter things. At any rate, I can't stop to discuss it now," and a minute later the front door had banged behind a querulous, irritable little man, who considered no one had any right to disturb—especially at the breakfast-table—the placid course of his existence. As he left the room he flung the letter upon the table, and Mrs Whately snatched it up eagerly. Roland watched carefully the expression of her face as she read it. At first he noted there only a relieved happiness, but as she folded the letter and handed it back he saw that she was sad.

"Of course it's splendid, Roland," she said. "I'm delighted, but.... Oh, well, I do think you might have told us something about it before."

"I wanted to, mother, but one doesn't like to shout till one's out of the wood."

"With friends, no, but with one's parents—surely you might have confided in us."

There was no such implied disapproval in April's reception of the news. He had not seen her since the afternoon when he had kissed her, and he had wondered in what spirit she would receive him. Would there be awkward stammered explanations? Would she be coy and protest "that she had been silly, that she had not meant it, that it must never happen again?" He had little previous experience to guide him and he was still debating the point when he arrived at No. 73 Hammerton Rise.

What April Curtis did was to open the door for him, close it quickly behind him as soon as he was in the porch, take him happily by both hands and hold her face up to be kissed. There was not the least embarrassment in her action.

"Well?" she said, on a note of interrogation.

For answer he put his hand into his pocket, drew out Mr Marston's letter and gave it to her.

April pulled it out of the envelope, hurriedly unfolded it, and ran an engrossed eye over its contents.

"Oh, but how splendid, Roland; now it's all right. Now there's no need to worry about anything. Come at once and tell mother. Mother, mother!" she shouted, and catching Roland by the hand dragged him after her towards the drawing-room.

Mrs Curtis had, through the laborious passage of fifty-two uneventful years, so trained her face to assume on all occasions an expression of pleasant sentimental interest in the affairs of others that by now her features could not be arranged to accommodate any other emotion. She appeared therefore unastonished when her name was called loudly in the hall, when the drawing-room door was flung open and a flushed, excited April stood in the doorway, grasping by the hand an equally flushed but embarrassed Roland. Mrs Curtis laid her knitting in her lap; a kindly smile spread over her glazed countenance.

"Well, my dear, and what's all this about?" she said.

"Oh, it's so exciting, mother. Roland's not going into a bank after all."

"No, dear?"

"No, mother. A Mr Marston, you know the man whom Roland went to stay with last week, has offered him a post in his firm. It's a lovely job. He'll be travelling all over the world and he's going to get a salary; of how much is it—yes, a hundred and fifty pounds a year and all expenses paid. Isn't it splendid?"

Mrs Curtis purred with reciprocated pleasure: "Of course it is, and how pleased your parents must be. Come and sit down here; yes, shut the door, please. You know I always said to Mr Whately, 'Roland is going to do something big; I'm sure of it.' And now you see my prophecy has come true. I shall remind Mr Whately of that next time he comes round to see me, and I shall remind him, too, that I said exactly the same thing about Arthur. 'Mr Whately,' I said," and her voice trailed off into reminiscences.

But though Mrs Curtis was in many—and indeed in most—ways a troublesome old fool, she was not unobservant. She knew that a young girl does not rush into a drawing-room dragging a young man by the hand simply because that young man has obtained a lucrative post in a varnish factory. There must be some other cause for so vigorous an ebullition. And as Mrs Curtis's speculation was unvexed by the complexities of Austrian psychology, she assumed that Roland and April had fallen in love with each other. She was not surprised. She had indeed often wondered why they had not done so before. April was such a dear girl, and Roland could be trained into a highly sympathetic son-in-law. He listened to her conversation with respect and interest, whereas Ralph Richmond insisted on interrupting her. Roland would make April a good husband. Certainly she had been temporarily disquieted by Mr Whately's sudden decision to remove his son from school; but no doubt he had had this post in his mind's eye and had not wished to speak of it till everything had been fixed.

Mrs Curtis's reverie traversed into an agreeable future; she pictured the wedding at St Giles; they would have the full choir. There would be a reception afterwards at the Town Hall. April would look so pretty in orange blossom. Arthur would be the best man. He would stand beside the bridegroom, erect and handsome. "What fine children you have, Mrs Curtis!" That's what everyone would say to her. It would be the prettiest wedding there had ever been at St Giles.... She collected herself with a start. She must not be premature. Nothing was settled yet; they were not even engaged. And of course they could not be engaged yet. They were too absurdly young. Everyone would laugh at her. Still, there might be an understanding. An understanding was first cousin to an engagement; it bound both parties. And then April and Roland would be allowed to go about together. It would be so nice for them.

When Roland had gone, she fixed on her daughter a deep, questioning look, under which April began to grow uncomfortable.

"Well, mother?" she said.

"You like Roland very much, don't you, dear?"

"We're great friends."

"Only friends?"

April did not answer, and her mother repeated her question. "But you're more than friends, aren't you?" But April was still silent. Mrs Curtis leant forward and took April's hand, lifted for a moment out of her vain complacency by the recollection of herself as she had been a quarter of a century ago, like April, with life in front of her. Through placid waters she had come to a safe anchorage, and she wondered whether for April the cruise would be as fortunate, the hand at the helm as steady. Her husband had risked little, but Roland would scarcely be satisfied with safe travel beneath the cliffs. Would April be happier or less happy than she had been? Which was the better—blue skies, calm water, gently throbbing engines, or the pitch and toss and crash of heavy seas?

"Are you very fond of him, dear?" she whispered.

"Yes, mother."

"And he's fond of you?"

"I think so, mother."

"Has he told you so, dear?"

"Yes."

A tear gathered in the corner of her eye, stung her, welled, fell upon her cheek, and this welcome relief recalled her to what she considered the necessities of the moment.

"Of course I shall have to speak to the Whatelys about it."

A shocked, surprised expression came into April's face.

"Oh, but why, mother?"

"Because, my dear, they may have other plans for Roland."

"But ... oh, mother, dear, there's no talk of engagements or anything; we've just ... oh, why can't we go on as we are?"

Mrs Curtis was firm.

"No, my dear," she said, "it would be fair neither to you nor to them. It's not only you and Roland that have to be considered. There's your father and myself and Mr and Mrs Whately. We shall have to talk it over together."

And so when Roland returned that evening from an afternoon with Ralph he found his father and mother sitting in the drawing-room with Mrs Curtis.

"Ah, here's Roland," said Mrs Curtis. "Come along, Roland, we've just been talking about you."

Roland entered and sat on the chair nearest him. He looked from one to the other, and each in turn smiled at him reassuringly: their smile said, "Now don't be nervous. We mean you well. You've only got to agree to our conditions and we'll be ever so nice to you." In the same way, Roland reflected, the Spanish Inquisitors had recommended conversion to the faith with a smile upon their lips, while from the adjoining room sounds came that the impenitents would be wise to associate with furnaces and screws and pliant steel.

"Yes, Roland," said Mr Whately, "we've been talking about you and April."

"Damn!" said Roland to himself. It was like that ridiculous Dolly affair all over again. It was useless, of course, to be flustered. He was growing accustomed to this sort of scene. He supposed that April had got frightened and told her mother, or perhaps the maidservant had seen them kissing in the porch. In any case it was not very serious. They would probably forbid him to see April alone. It would be rather rotten; but the world was wide. In a few weeks' time he would be going abroad; he could free himself of these entanglements, and when he returned he would decide what he should do. He would be economically independent. In the meantime let them talk. He settled himself back in his chair and prepared to hear at least, with patience, whatever they might have to say to him. What they did have to say came to him as a surprise.

"I was talking to April about it this morning," said Mrs Curtis. "Of course I've noticed it for a long time. A mother can't help seeing these things. Several times I've said to my husband: 'Father, dear, haven't you noticed that Roland and April are becoming very interested in each other?' and he's agreed with me. Though I haven't liked to say anything. But then this morning it was so very plain, wasn't it?" She paused and smiled. And Roland, feeling that an answer was expected of him, said that he supposed it was.

"Yes, really quite clear, and so afterwards I had a talk with my little April and she told me all about it. And, of course, we're all of us very pleased that you should be fond of one another, but you must realise that at present you're much too young for there to be any talk of marriage."

"But..." Roland began.

"Yes, I know that you've got a good post in this varnish factory; but as I was saying to Mr Whately before you came, you're only on probation, and it's a job that means a lot of travelling and expense that you wouldn't be able to afford if you were a married man or were even contemplating matrimony."

"But..." Roland began again, and again Mrs Curtis stopped him.

"Yes, I know what you're thinking; you say that you are content to wait; that four years, five years, six years—it's nothing to you, that you want to be engaged now. I can quite understand it. We all can. We've all been young, but I'm quite certain that..."

Roland could not believe that it was real, that he was sitting in a real room, that a real woman was talking, a real scene was in the process of enaction. He listened in a stupefied amazement. What, after all, had happened? He had kissed April three times. She had asked no vows and he had given none. They were lovers he supposed, but they were boy and girl lovers. The romances of the nursery should not be taken seriously. By holding April's hand and kissing her had he decided the course of both their lives? What were they about, these three solemn people, with their talk of marriage and engagements?

"But you don't understand," he began.

"Oh, yes, we do," Mrs Curtis interrupted. "We old people know more than you think."

And she began to speak in her droning, mellifluous voice of the sanctity of love and of the good fortune that had led him so early to his affinity. And then all three of them began to speak together, and their words beat like hammers upon Roland's head, till he did not know where he was, nor what they were saying to him. "It can't be real," he told himself. "It's preposterous. People don't behave like this in real life." And when his mother came across and kissed him on the forehead and said, "We're all so happy, Roland," he employed every desperate device to recall himself to reality that he was accustomed to use when involved in a nightmare. He fixed his thoughts upon one issue, focused all his powers on that one point: "I will wake up. I will wake up."

And even when it was all over, and he was in his bedroom standing before the looking-glass to arrange his tie, he could not believe that it had really happened. It was impossible that grown-up people should be so foolish. He could understand that Mrs Curtis should be annoyed at his attentions to her daughter. He had been prepared for that. If she had said, "Roland, you're both of you too old for that. It was well enough when you were both children, but it won't do now; April is growing up," he could have appreciated her point of view. Perhaps they were too old for the love-making of childhood. But that she should take up the attitude that they were too young for the serious matrimonial entanglements of man and womanhood! It was beyond the expectation of any sane intelligence.

In a way he could not help feeling annoyed with April. If she had not told her mother nothing would have happened.

"Oh, but how silly," she said, when he told her about it next day. "I do wish I had been there. It must have been awfully funny!"

Roland had not considered it in that light and hastened to tell her so.

"I felt a most appalling fool. It was beastly. I can't think why you told your mother anything about it."

She looked up quickly, surprised by the note of impatience in his voice.

"But, Roland, dear, what else could I do? She asked me and I couldn't tell a lie. Could I?"

"I don't know," said Roland. And he began to walk backwards and forwards, up and down the room. "I suppose you couldn't help it, but.... Oh, well, what did you say to her?"

"Nothing much. She asked me.... Oh, but, Roland, do sit down," she pleaded, "I can't talk when you're walking up and down the room."

"All right," said Roland, sitting down. "Go on."

"Well, she asked me if I liked you and I said that we were great friends, and then she asked if we weren't more than friends."

"Oh, yes, yes, I know," said Roland, rising impatiently from his chair and walking across the room. "Of course you said we were, and that I had been making love to you, and that—oh, but what's the good of going on with it. I know what she said and what you said, and the whole thing was out in three minutes, and then your mother comes round to my mother and they talk and they talk, and that's how all the trouble in the world begins."

While he was actually speaking he was sustained by the white heat of his impatience, but the moment he had stopped he was bitterly ashamed of himself. What had he done? What had he said? And April's silence accentuated his shame. She neither turned angrily upon him nor burst into tears. She sat quietly, her hands clasped in front of her knees, looking at the floor.

After a while she rose and walked across to the window. Her back was turned to him. He felt that he must do something to shatter the poignant silence. He drew close to her and touched her hand with his, but she drew her hand away quietly, without haste or anger.

"April," he began, "I'm...."

But she stopped him. "Don't say anything. Please don't say anything."

"But I must, April. I've been a beast. I didn't mean it."

"It's quite all right. I've been very foolish. There's nothing more to be said."

Her voice was calm and level. She kept her back turned to him, distant and unapproachable. He did not know what to do nor what to say. He had been a beast to her. He knew it. And because he had wronged her, because she had made him feel ashamed of himself, he was angry with her.

"Oh, very well then," he said. "If you won't talk to me, I'm going home."

He turned and walked out of the room. In the porch he waited for a moment, thinking that she would call after him. But no sound came from the drawing-room, not even the rustle of clothes, that might have indicated the change of her position. "Oh, well," he said, "if she's going to sulk, let her sulk," and he walked out of the house.

For the rest of the day he endured the humiliating discomfort of contrition. He was honest with himself. He made no attempt to excuse his behaviour. There was no excuse for it. He had behaved like a cad. There was only one thing to do and that was to grovel as soon as possible. It would be an undignified proceeding, but he was quite ready to do it, if he could be certain that the performance would be accepted in the right spirit. It was not easy to grovel before a person who turned her back on you, looked out of the window and refused to listen to what you had to say.

When evening came he decided that he might do worse than make a reconnaissance of the enemy's country under the guidance of an armed escort—in other words, that if he paid a visit to the Curtises' with his father he would be able to see April without having the embarrassment of a private talk forced on him.

And so when Mr Whately returned from the office he found his son waiting to take him for a walk.

"What a pleasant surprise," he said. "I never expected to find you here. I thought you would be spending all your time with April now."

Roland laughed.

"Well, as a matter of fact," he said, "I thought we might go round and see the Curtises together."

"And you thought you wanted a chaperon?"

"Hardly that."

"But you felt shy of facing the old woman?"

"That's more like it."

"All right, then, we'll tackle her together."

Roland was certain, when they arrived, that the idea of employing his father as a shield was in the nature of an inspiration. April received him without a smile; she did not even shake hands with him. Fortunately, in the effusion of Mrs Curtis's welcome, this omission was not noticed.

"I'm so glad you have come, both of you. April told me, Roland, that you had been round to see her this morning, and I must say I began to feel afraid that I should never see you again. I thought you would only want to come round when you could have April all to yourself. It would have been such a disappointment to me if you had; I should have so missed our little evening talks. As I was saying to my husband only yesterday, 'I don't know what we should do without the Whatelys,' and he agreed with me. You know, Mr Whately, there are some people whom we quite like, but whom we shouldn't miss in the least if they went away and we never saw them again, and there are others who would leave a real gap. It's funny, isn't it? And it's so nice, now, to think that Roland and April—though we mustn't talk like that, must we, or they'll begin to think they're engaged. And we couldn't allow that, could we, Mr Whately?"

His body rattled with a deep chuckle. Out of the corner of his eye Roland flung a glance at April, to see what effect this wind of words was having on her, but her face was turned from him.

Mrs Curtis then proceeded to speak of Arthur and of the letter she had received from him by the evening post. "He says—now what is it that he says? Ah, yes, here it is; he says, 'As I am too old for the Junior games, I have been moved into the Senior League.' Now that's very satisfactory, isn't it, Mr Whately, that he should be in the Senior League? I always said he would be good at games, and April too, Mr Whately; she would have been very good at games if she had played them. When they used to play cricket in the nursery she used to hit at the ball so well, with her arms, you know. She would have been very good, but she hasn't had the time and they don't go in for games very much at St Stephen's. Now what do you think of that new frock of hers? I got it so cheap—you can't think how cheaply I got it. And then I got Miss Smithers to make it up for her, and April looks so pretty in it; don't you think so, Mr Whately?"

"Charming, of course, Mrs Curtis, absolutely charming!"

"I thought you'd like it. And I'm sure Roland does too, though he would be too shy to own to it. You know, Mr Whately, I felt like telling her when she put it on that Roland would have to be very careful or he would find a lot of rivals when he came back from Brussels."

It was more than April could bear. She had endured a great deal that day and this was the final ignominy.

"How can you, mother?" she said. "How can you?" and jumping to her feet, she ran out of the room, slamming the door behind her.

The sudden crash reverberated through the awkward silence; then came the soft caressing voice of Mrs Curtis: "I'm so sorry, Mr Whately; I don't know what April can be thinking of. But she's like that sometimes.

These young people are so difficult; one doesn't know where to find them. Yes, that's right, Roland, run and see if you can't console her."

For Roland had risen, moved deeply by the sight of April's misery, her pathetic weakness. It was not fair. First of all he had been beastly to her, then her mother had made a fool of her. He found her in the dining-room, huddled on a chair beside the fire. She turned at once to him for sympathy. She stretched out her arms, and he ran towards them, knelt before her and buried his face in her lap.

"We have been such beasts to you, April, all of us. I have felt so miserable about it all day. I didn't know what to do. I thought you would never forgive me. I don't deserve to be forgiven; but I love you; I do, really awfully!"

"That's all right," she said; "don't worry," and placing her hand beneath his chin she raised gently his face to hers.

It was a long kiss, one of those long passionless kisses of sympathy, pity and contrition that smooth out all difficulties, as a wave that passes over a stretch of sand leaving behind it a shining surface. For a long while they sat in each other's arms, saying nothing, his fingers playing with her hair, her lips from moment to moment meeting his. When at last they reverted to the subject of their morning's quarrel there was little possibility of dissension.

It was with a gay smile that she asked him why he had been so angry with her. "Why shouldn't our parents know, Roland? They would have had to some day."

"Oh, yes, of course, but— —"

"And surely, Roland dear," she continued, "it's better for us that they should know. I should have hated having to do things in secret. It would have been exciting, of course; I know that; but it wouldn't have been fair to them, would it? They are so fond of us; they ought to have a share in our happiness."

"That's just what I felt," Roland objected. "I had felt that our love had ceased to be our own, that they had taken too big a share of it. It didn't seem to be our love affair any longer."

"Oh, you silly darling!" and she laughed happily, relieved of her fear that there might be some deeper cause for Roland's behaviour to her. "Why should you worry about that? What does it matter if other people do know about it? Why, what's an engagement but a letting of a lot of other people into our secret; and when we're married, why, that's a telling of everyone in the whole world that we're in love with one another. What does it matter if others know?"

"I suppose it doesn't," Roland dubiously admitted.

"Of course it doesn't. The only thing that does matter," she said, twisting a lock of his hair round her little finger and smiling at him through half-closed eyes, "is that we've made up our silly quarrel and are friends again," and bending forward she kissed him quietly and happily.

He was naturally relieved that the sympathy between them had been re-established; but he realised how little he had made her appreciate his misgivings. Indeed, he would have found it hard to explain them to himself. Their love was no longer fresh and spontaneous. Its growth, as that of a wild flower that is taken from a hedge and planted in a conservatory, would be no longer natural. Other hands would tend it. In April's mind the course of love was marked by certain fixed boundaries—the avowal, the engagement, the marriage service. She did not conceive of love as existing outside these limits. She had never been in love before; and naturally she regarded love as a state of mind into which one was suddenly and miraculously surprised, and in which one continued until the end of one's life. There was no reason why she should think differently. Her training had taught her that love could not exist outside marriage—marriage that ordained one woman for one man.

But it was different for Roland, who had learnt from the vivid and fleeting romances of his boyhood that love comes and goes, irresponsible as the wind that at one moment is shaking among the branches, scattering the leaves, tossing them in the air, only to subside a moment later into calm.

These misgivings passed quickly enough, however, in the delightful novelty of the situation. It was great fun being in love; to wake in the early morning with the knowledge that as soon as breakfast was over you would run down the road and be welcomed by a charming girl, whom you would counsel to shut the door behind you quickly so that you could kiss her before anyone knew you were in the house, who would then tilt up her face prettily to yours. It was charming to sit with her in the drawing-room and hold her hand and rest your cheek against hers, to answer such questions as, "When did you first begin to love me?"

Often they would go for walks together in the autumn sunshine; occasionally they would take a bus and ride out to Kew or Hampstead, and sit on the green grass and hold hands and talk of the future. These talks were a delicious excitant to Roland's vanity. His ambitions were strengthened by her faith in him. He saw himself rich and famous. "We'll have a wonderful house, with stables and an orchard, and we'll have a private cricket ground and we'll get a pro. down from Lord's to look after it. And we'll have fine parties in the summer—cricket and tennis during the day, and dances in the evening!"

"And a funny little cottage," she would murmur, "somewhere down the river, for when we want to be all by ourselves."

It was exciting, too, when other people, grown-up people, made significant remarks.

One afternoon he was at a tea-party and a lady asked him if he would come round to lunch with them the next day. "We've got a nephew of ours stopping with us. An awfully jolly boy. I'm sure you and he would get on well together." Roland, however, had to excuse himself on the grounds of a previous engagement.

"I'm awfully sorry," he said, "but I've promised to go on the river."

"With April Curtis? Ah, I thought so."

And the smile that accompanied the question made Roland feel very grown up and important.

These weeks of preparation for the foreign tour Roland considered however, in spite of their charm, as an interlude, a pause in the serious affairs of life. It was thus that he had always regarded his holidays. He had divided with a hard line his life at school and his life at home. The two were unrelated. April and Ralph, his parents and the Curtises belonged to a world that must remain for him always episodic. It was a pleasant world in which from time to time he might care to sojourn. But what happened to him there was of no great importance.

As he leant over the taffrail of the steamer and felt the deck throb under him he knew that his real life had begun again. What significance had these encumbrances of his home life if he could cast them off so easily? Already they were slipping from him. The waves beat against the side of the ship, splashing the spray across the deck, and the sting of the water on his face filled him with a buoyant confidence. The thud of the engines beat through his body to a tune of triumph.

The grey line that was England faded and was lost.

CHAPTER XI
THE ROMANCE OF VARNISH

Aseparation of six months makes in the middle years of a man's life little break in a relationship. Human life was compared over two thousand years ago by a Greek philosopher to the stream that is never the same from one moment to another. And though, indeed, nothing is permanent, though everything is in flux, the stream during the later stages of its passage flows quietly through soft meadows to the sea. A man of forty-five who has been married for several years may leave his family to go abroad and returning at the end of the year find his wife, his home, his friends, to all appearances, exactly as he left them.

Roland returned from Belgium a different person. He was no longer a schoolboy; he was a business man. He had been introduced to big financiers; he had listened to the discussion of important deals; he had witnessed the signatures of contracts. In the evenings he had sat with Marston and gone carefully over the accounts of the day's transactions.

"There's not much profit here," Marston would say, "hardly any, in fact, when we've taken over-head charges, office expenses and all that into consideration. But we're not out for profits just now. We're building up connections. If we can make these foreign deals pay their way we're all right. We shall crowd the other fellows out of the market, we shall make ourselves indispensable, and then we can shove our prices as high as we blooming well like."

To Roland it was a game, with the thrills, the dangers, the recompenses of a game. He did not look on business as part of the social fabric. He did not regard wealth as a thing important in itself. A credit balance was like a score at cricket. You were setting your brains against an opponent's. You made as many pounds as you could against his bowling. He did not allow first principles to attach disquieting corollaries. He did not ask himself whether it was just for a big firm to undersell their smaller rivals and drive them out of the market by the simple expedient of taking money out of one pocket and putting it into another. Business was a game: if one was big enough to take risks one took them.

Within a month Gerald was writing home to his father with genuine enthusiasm.

"He really is first class, father. I thought he would be pretty useful, but I never expected him to be a patch on what he is. He's really keen on the job and he's got the hang of it already. He ought to do jolly well when he comes out here alone. The big men like him; old Rosenheim told me the other day that it was a pleasure to see him about the place. 'Such a relief,' he said, 'after the dried-up hard-chinned provincials that pester me from morning to night.' I believe it's the best thing we ever did, getting Roland into the business."

Roland, realising that his work was appreciated, grew confident and hopeful of the future. They were happy days.

It is not easy to explain the friendship of two men. And Roland would have been unable to say why exactly he valued the companionship and esteem of Gerald Marston more highly than that of the many boys, such as Ralph Richmond, whom he had known longer and, on the whole, more intimately. Gerald never said anything brilliant; he was not particularly amusing; he was often irritable and moody. But from the moment when he had seen him for the first time in Brewster's study Roland had recognised in him a potential friend. Later, when they had met at the Oval, he had felt that they understood each other, that they spoke the same language, that there was between them no need for the usual preliminaries of friendship. And during their weeks in France and Belgium this relationship or intuition was fortified by the sharing of common interests and common adventures.

The majority of these adventures were, it must be confessed, of doubtful morality, for it was only natural that Roland and Gerald should in their spare time amuse themselves after the fashion of most young men who find themselves alone in a foreign city.

In the evenings, after they had balanced their accounts, they used to walk through the warm lighted streets, surrounded by the stir of a world waking to a night of pleasure, select a brightly coloured café, sit back on the red plush couch that ran the length of the room, and order iced champagne. The band would play soft, sentimental music that, mixing with the wine in their heads, would render them eager, daring and responsive, and when two girls walked slowly down the centre of the room, swaying from the hips, and casting to left and right sidelong, alluring glances, naturally they smiled back, and indicated two vacant seats on either side of them. Then there would be talk and laughter and more champagne, and afterwards.... But what happened afterwards was of small importance. Gerald had had too much experience to derive much excitement from bought kisses. And for Roland, these romances were the focus of little more than a certain lukewarm kindliness and curiosity. They were not degrading, because they were not regarded so. They were equally unromantic, because neither was particularly interested in the other. Indeed, Roland was a little dismayed to find how slight, on the whole, was the pleasure, even the physical pleasure, that he received from his companion's transports; these experiences, far from having the devastating effect that they are popularly supposed to have on a young man's character, would have had in Roland's life no more significance than an act of solitary indulgence, had they not been another bond between himself and Gerald. And this they most certainly were.

It was amusing to meet in the morning afterwards and exchange confidences. And as everything is transmuted by the imagination, Roland in a little while came to look on those evenings—the wine, the music, the rustle of skirts, the low laughter—not as they had been actually, but as he would have wished to have them. They became for him a gracious revel. And in London his thoughts would wander often from his ink-stained desk, from the screech of the telephone, from the eternal tapping of the typewriter, to those brightly coloured cafés, with their atmosphere of warm comfort, the soft sensuous music, the cool sparkling champagne, the low whisper at his elbow. When he went out to lunch with Marston he would frequently contrast the glitter of a Brussels restaurant with the tawdry furniture and over-heated atmosphere of a City eating-house.

"A bit different this, isn't it?" he would say. "Do you remember that evening when we went down the Rue de la Madeleine and found a café in that little side street?"

"That was where we met the jolly little girl in the blue dress, wasn't it?"

"Yes. And do you remember what she said about the old Padre?"

And they would laugh together over the indelicacies that had slipped so charmingly in broken English from those red lips.

But Gerald was the one figure that remained distinct for Roland. The girls, for the most part, resembled each other so closely that he could only in rare instances recall their features or what they had worn or what they had said. He remembered far more vividly his walks with Gerald through the lighted streets, their confidences and hesitations. Should they go into this café or into that: and then when they had selected their café how Gerald would open the wine list and carefully run his finger down the page, while the waiter would hover over him: "Yes, yes, sir, a very good wine that, sir, a very good wine indeed!" And then when the wine was ordered how they would look round at the girls who sat in couples at the marble-topped tables, sipping a citron or a bock. "What do you think of that couple over there?" "Not bad, but let's wait a bit; something better may turn up soon"; and a little later: "Oh, look, that girl over there, the one with the green dress, just beneath the picture; try and catch her eye, she looks ripping!" They had been more exciting, those moments of expectation, than the subsequent embraces.

Gerald was always the dominant figure.

It was the expression of Gerald's face that Roland remembered most clearly on that disappointing evening when they had taken two chorus girls to dinner at a private room and Roland's selected had refused champagne and preferred fried sole to pheasant—an abstinence so alarming that, in spite of Roland's protests, Gerald had suddenly decided that they would have to catch a train to Paris that evening instead of being able to wait till the morning.

And it was Gerald whom Roland particularly associated with that ignominious occasion on which he had thought at last to have discovered real romance.

They had dropped into a restaurant in the afternoon for a cup of chocolate, and had seen sitting by herself a girl who could hardly have been twenty years of age. She wore a wide-brimmed hat, under which Roland could just see, as she bent her head over her ice, the tip of her nose, the smooth curve of a cheek, the strain on the muscles of her neck. She raised the spoon delicately to her mouth, her lips closed on it and held it there. Her eyelids appeared to droop in a sort of sensual contentment. Roland watched her, fascinated: watched her till she drew the spoon slowly from her mouth. She lingered pensively, and between the even rows of her white teeth the red tip of her tongue played for a moment on the spoon. At that moment she raised her eyes, observed that Roland was staring at her, smiled, and dropped her eyes again.

"Did you see that?" whispered Roland excitedly. "She smiled at me, and she's ripping! I must go and speak to her!"

"Don't be a fool," said Gerald; "a smile may not mean anything. Besides, she's obviously not a tart and she may be known here. If she is she won't want to be seen talking to a stranger. You sit still, like a good boy, and see if she smiles at you again."

Against his will Roland consented. But he had his reward a few minutes later when she turned her chair to catch the waitress's attention, and her eyes, meeting his, smiled at them again—a challenging, alluring smile that seemed to say, "Well, are you brave enough?" He was dismayed, however, to notice that she had turned in order to ask for her bill. He saw her run her eye down the slip of paper, take some money from her purse and begin to button on her gloves, long gauntlet gloves that fastened above the elbow.

"She's going! what shall I do?" he asked.

For answer Marston took a piece of paper from his pocket and wrote on it: "Meet me at the Café des Colombes to-night at eight-thirty."

"Now, walk up to the counter and pretend to choose a cake; if she wants to see any more of you she will drop her handkerchief, or purse, or at any rate give you an opportunity of speaking to her; if she does, slip this note into her hand. If she doesn't, you can buy me an éclair, and thank your lucky stars that you've been preserved from making a most abandoned fool of yourself."

Roland was in such a hurry to get to the counter that he tripped against a table and only saved himself from falling by gripping violently the shoulder of an elderly bourgeois. By the time he had completed his apologies his charmer had very nearly reached the door.

"It's all up," he told himself; "she thinks me a clumsy fool, that it's not worth her while to worry about, I ought to have gone straight up to her at once"; and he followed with dejected eyes her progress towards the door.

She was carrying in one hand an umbrella and in the other a little velvet bag. As she raised her hand to open the door, the bag slipped from her fingers and fell upon the floor. There were three persons nearer to the bag than Roland, but before even a hand had been stretched out to it he had precipitated himself forward, had picked it up and was handing it to the lady. She smiled at him with gracious gratitude. So far all had gone splendidly. Then he began to fumble. The note was in the other hand, and in the flurry of the moment he did not know how to manœuvre the bag and the note into the same hand. First of all, he tried to change the bag from the right hand to the left. But his forefinger and thumb were so closely engaged with the note that the remaining three fingers failed to grasp the handle of the bag. He made a furious dive and caught the bag in his right hand just before it reached the floor. Panic seized him. He lost all sense of the proprieties. He handed the bag straight to her, and then realising, before she had had time to take it from him, that somehow or other the note also had to come into her possession, he offered it to her between the forefinger and thumb of his left hand with less secrecy than he would have displayed in giving a tip to a waiter. The sudden change of the lady's expression from inviting kindliness to a surprised affronted indignation threw him into so acute a fever of embarrassment that once again he endeavoured to move the bag from the right hand to the left. Again he fumbled, but with a different result.

He piloted the bag successfully into the lady's hands, but allowed the note to slip from between his fingers. It fell face upwards on the floor.

Several ways of escape were open to him. He might have affected unconcern, and either picked up the piece of paper or left it where it lay. He might have kicked the note away and walked forward to open the door. He might have placed his foot on the note till the attention of the room was once again directed to its separate interests. None of these things, however, did he do. He did what was natural for him in such an unexpected situation. He did nothing. He stood quite still and gazed at the note as it lay there startlingly white against the black tiles of the floor. The eyes of everyone in the room appeared to be directed towards it. The features of the startled lady assumed an expression of horrified amazement. Two waitresses leant over the counter in undisguised excitement; another stopped dead with a tray in her hand to survey the incriminating document. The fat gentleman against whom Roland had collided began to make some unpleasantly loud remarks to his companion. An old woman leant forward and asked the room in general what was happening. From a far corner came the horrible suppression of a giggle.

The lady herself, who was, as a matter of fact, perfectly respectable, though she liked to be thought otherwise, and had dropped her bag accidentally, was the first to recover her composure. She fixed on Roland a glance of which as a combination of hatred and contempt he had never seen the equal, turned quickly and walked out of the restaurant. The sudden bang of the door behind her broke the tension. The various spectators of this entertaining interlude returned to their ices and their chocolate, the waitresses resumed their duties, the patron of the establishment fussed up the centre of the room, and Gerald, who had watched the scene with intense if slightly nervous amusement, left his table, picked up the note, and taking Roland by the arm, led him out of the public notice, and listened to his friend's solemn vow that never again, under any circumstances, would he be induced to open negotiations with any woman, be she never so lovely, who did not by her dress, her manner and the places she frequented proclaim unquestionably her profession.

It was hardly surprising that as a result of these adventures a more developed, more independent Roland returned at the end of his six months' tour, a Roland, moreover, with a different attitude to himself, his future, his surroundings, who was prepared to despise the chrysalis from which he had emerged. His school-days appeared trivial.

"What a deal of fuss we made about things that didn't really matter at all," he said to Gerald as they leant over the taffrail and watched the dim line that was England grow distinct, its grey slowly whitening as they drew near. "What a fuss about one's place in form, one's position in the house; whether one ragged or whether one didn't rag. I can see all those masters, with their solemn faces, thinking I had perjured my immortal soul because I had walked out with a girl. They really thought it mattered."

How puny it became in comparison with this magnificent gamble of finance! What were marks in an exam. to set against a turnover of several thousands? Duty, privilege, responsibility; what had they been but the brightly coloured bricks with which children play in the nursery; and as for the fret and fever concerning their arrangement, where could be found an equivalent for the serious absorption of a child?

In the same way he thought of his home and the environment of his boyhood. What a grey world it had been! How monotonous, how arid! He remembered sitting as a child at the bars of his nursery window watching the stream of business men hurrying to their offices in the morning, their newspapers tucked under their arms. They had seemed to him like marionettes. The front door had opened. Husband and wife had exchanged a brusque embrace; the male marionette had trotted down the steps, had paused at the gate to wave his hand, and as he had turned into the street the front door had closed behind him. Always the same thing every day. And then in the evening the same stream of tired listless men hurrying home, their bulky morning paper exchanged for the slim evening newssheet. They would trot up the white stone steps, the front door would swing open, again in the porch the marionettes would kiss. It had amused him as a child, this dumb show, but as a boy he had come to hate it—and to fear it also. For he knew that this was the life that awaited him if he failed to turn to account his superior opportunities. The fear of degenerating into a suburban business man had been always the strongest goad to his ambition. But now he could look that fear confidently in the face. He had won through out of that world of routine and friction and small economies into one of enterprise and daring and romance.

And April: he had not thought very much about her during his six months' absence; she belonged to the world he had outgrown, a landmark on his road of adventure. And it was disconcerting to find on his return that she did not regard their relationship in this light. Roland had grown accustomed to the fleeting relationships of school that at the start of a new term could be resumed or dropped at will. He had not realised that it would be different now; that six months in Belgium were not the equivalent of a seven weeks' summer holiday; that he would be returning to an unaltered society in which he would be expected to fulfil the obligations incurred by him before his departure. It was the reversal of the Rip Van Winkle legend.

Roland had altered and was returning to a world that was precisely as he had left it.

Nothing had changed.

On the first evening he went round to visit April, and there was Mrs Curtis as she had always been, sitting before the fire, her hands crossed over her bony bosom. She welcomed him as though he had been spending a week-end in Kent.

"I'm so glad to see you, Roland, and have you had a nice time? It must be pleasant for you to think of how soon the cricket season will be starting. I was saying to our little April only yesterday: 'How Roland will be looking forward to it.' What club are you thinking of joining?"

"The Marstons said something to me about my joining their local club."

"But how jolly that would be! You'll like that, won't you?"

Her voice rose and fell as it had risen and fallen as long as Roland's memory had knowledge of her. The same clock ticked over the same mantelpiece; above the table was the same picture of a cow grazing beside a stream; the curtains, once red, had not faded to a deeper brown; the carpet was no more threadbare; the same books lined the shelves that rose on either side of the fire-place; in the bracket beside the window was the calf-bound set of *William Morris* that had been presented to April as a prize; on the rosewood table lay yesterday's copy of *The Times*. Mrs Curtis and her setting were eternal in the scheme of things.

April, too, was as he had left her. Indeed, her life in his absence had been a pause. She had no personal existence outside Roland. She had waited for his return, thinking happily of the future. She had gone to school every morning at a quarter to nine and had returned every evening at half-past five. During the Christmas holidays she had read *Nicholas Nickleby* and *Vanity Fair*. She was now half-way through *Little Dorrit*. At the end of the Michaelmas term she had gained a promotion into a higher form and in her new form she had acquitted herself creditably, finishing half-way up the class. At home she had performed cheerfully the various duties that had been allotted to her. But she had regarded those six months as an interlude in her real life: that was Roland's now. Happiness could only come to her through him; and, being sure of happiness, she was not fretful nor impatient during the delay. She did not expect nor indeed ask of life violent transports either of ecstasy or sorrow. Her ideas of romance were domestic enough. To love and to be loved faithfully, to have children, to keep a home happy, a home to which her friends would be glad to come—this seemed to her as much as any woman had the right to need. She felt that she would be able to make Roland happy. The prospect was full of a quiet but deep contentment.

Roland had no opportunity of speaking to her on that first evening; Mrs Curtis, as usual, monopolised the conversation. But he sat near to April. From time to time their eyes met and she smiled at him. And the next morning when he came round to see her she ran eagerly to meet him.

"It's lovely to have you back again," she said; "you can't think how I've been looking forward to it!"

Roland was embarrassed by her eagerness. He did not know what to say and stood beside her, smiling stupidly.

She pouted.

"Aren't you going to kiss me?" she said. And a moment later: "I shouldn't have thought, after six months, you'd have needed asking!"

Roland met her reproach with a stammered apology.

"I felt shy. I thought you might have got tired of me, all that long time."

"Oh, but Roland, how horrid of you!" And she moved away from him. But he took her in his arms and made love prettily to her and consoled her.

"I daresay," she said, "I daresay. But you didn't write to me so very often."

"I wanted to, but I thought your mother wouldn't like it."

"Oh, but, Roland, that's no excuse; she expected you to. There's an understanding." Then with a quiet smile: "Do you remember the row we had about that understanding?"

"I was a beast."

"No, you weren't, I was a silly."

"I was miserable about it."

"So was I. I didn't know what to do with myself. I thought you'ld never speak to me again, that you'd gone off in a huff, like the heroes in the story books."

"But the heroes always come back in the story books."

"I know, and that's just why I thought that very likely you wouldn't in real life. I was so unhappy I cried myself to sleep."

"We were sillies, weren't we?"

"But it was worth it," said April.

"Worth it?"

"Don't you remember how nice you were to me when we made it up?"

They laughed and kissed, and the minutes passed pleasantly. But their love-making fell short of Roland's ideal of love. It was jolly; it was comfortable; but it was little more. He was not thrilled when the back of his hand brushed accidentally against hers; their kisses were hardly a lyric ecstasy. Even when he held her in his arms he was conscious of himself, outside their embrace, watching it, saying to himself: "Those two are having a good time together," and being outside it he was envious, jealous of a happiness he did not share. It was someone else who was holding April's hand, someone else's head that bent to her slim shoulder. It was an exciting experience. But then had it not been exciting to walk across Hampstead Heath on a Sunday evening and observe the feverish ardours of the prostrate lovers.

He despised himself; he reminded himself that he was extraordinarily lucky to have a girl such as April in love with him; he was unworthy of her. Was not Ralph eating out his heart with envy? And yet he was dissatisfied. The Curtises' house had become a prison for him; a soft, warm prison, with cushions and shaded lights and gentle voices, but it was a prison none the less. He was still able to leave it at will, but the time was coming when that freedom would be denied him. In a year or two their understanding would be an engagement; the engagement would drift to marriage. For the rest of his life he would be enclosed in that warm, clammy atmosphere. There was a conspiracy at work against him. His father had already begun to speak of his marriage as an accomplished fact. His mother was chiefly glad he was doing well in business because success there would make an early marriage possible. On all sides inducements were being offered him to marry—marriage with its corollary to settle down. Marry and settle down, when he was still under twenty!—before he had begun to live!

CHAPTER XII
MARSTON & MARSTON

During the weeks that immediately followed his return, Roland found that he was, on the whole, happiest when he was at the office. He had less there to worry him. His work was new and interesting. Mr Marston had decided that before Roland went on his tour alone he should acquire a general knowledge of the organisation of the business. And so Roland spent a couple of weeks in each department, acquainting himself with the routine.

"And a pretty good slack it will be," Gerald had said. "It's the governor's pet plan. He made me do it. But you won't learn anything that's going to be of the least use to you. All you've got to do in this show is to be polite and impress opulent foreigners. You don't need to know the ingredients of varnish nor how we arrange our advertising accounts. And you can bet that the fellows themselves won't be in any hurry to teach you. The less we know about things the better they're pleased. They like to run their own show. If I were you I should have as lazy a time as possible."

Under ordinary circumstances Roland would have followed this advice. He had learnt at Fernhurst to do as much work as was strictly necessary, but no more. He had prepared his lessons carefully for his house tutor and the games' master, the two persons, that is to say, who had it in their power to make his existence there either comfortable or the reverse. He had also worked hard for the few masters, such as Carus Evans, who disliked him. That was part of his armour. When Carus Evans had said to him for the third day running, "Now, I think we'll have you, Whately," and he had translated the passage without a slip, he felt that he was one up on Carus Evans. But for the others, the majority with whom he was only brought into casual contact, and who were pleasantly indifferent to those who caused them no trouble, he did only as much work as was needful to keep him from the detention-room. Roland had rarely been inconvenienced by uncomfortable scruples about duty.

At any other time he would have spent the days of apprenticeship in placid idleness—discussion of cricket matches; visits to the window and subsequent speculation on the prospects of fine weather over the week-end; glances at his watch to see how soon he could slip from the cool of the counting house into the hot sunshine that was beating upon the streets; pleasant absorption in a novel. But Roland was worried by the family situation; he was finding life dull; he was prepared to abandon himself eagerly to any fresh enthusiasm. For want of anything better to do, without premeditation, with no thought of the power that this knowledge might one day bring him, he decided to understand the business of Marston & Marston.

On the first morning he was handed over to the care of Mr Stevens, the head of the trade department. Mr Stevens was a faithful servant of the firm, and, as is the way with faithful servants, considered himself to be more important than his employers.

"They may sit up in that board-room of theirs," he would say, "and they may pass their resolutions, and they may decide on this and they may decide on that, but where'ld they be without their figures, I'd like to know. And who gives them their figures?"

He would chuckle and scratch his bald head, and issue a fierce series of orders to the packers. He bore no malice against his directors; he was not jealous; he knew that there were two classes, the governing and the governed, and that it had been his fate to be born among the governed.

"There always have been two classes and there always will be two classes. We can't all be bosses." It was a law of nature. And he considered his performances more creditable than those of his masters.

"These directors," he would say, "they were born into the business. They've stayed where they was put; they haven't gone up and they haven't gone down. But I—I started as a packer and I'm now head of the trade department; and look you here, Jones," he would suddenly bellow out, "if you hammer nails into a box at that rate you'll not only not be head of a trade department, you'll blooming soon cease to be a packer!"

It was natural that Mr Stevens should, from his previous experience of Gerald and certain other young gentlemen, regard Roland as an agreeable trifler on the fringe of important matters.

"Well, well, sir, so you've come along to see how we do things down here. I expect we shall be able to show you a thing or two. Now, if you was to go and sit over in that corner you'd be out of the way and you'd be able to see the business going on."

"I daresay, Mr Stevens, but that won't help me very far, will it?"

"I wouldn't say that, sir; nothing like seeing how the machinery works."

"But I might as well go and ask an engine-driver how a train worked and then be told to sit in a corner of the platform at a railway station and watch the trains go by. I should see how they worked but I shouldn't know much about them."

Mr Stevens chuckled and scratched the bald patch on his head appreciatively.

"You see, Mr Stevens," Roland continued, "I don't know anything about this show at all and I know that you're the only person in the place who can help me."

It was a lucky shot. Roland was not then the psychologist that he was to become in the days of his power. He worked by intuition. What he had intended for a graceful compliment was a direct appeal to Mr Stevens' vanity, at the point where it was most susceptible to such an assault. It was a grief at times to Mr Stevens that the authorities should regard him as little more than a useful servant, who carried out efficiently the orders that they gave him. Mr Stevens was not ambitious; the firm had treated him fairly, had recognised his talents early and had promoted him. He had no quarrel with the firm, but he knew—what no one else in the building, with the possible exception of Perkins, the general manager, did know—that for a long time he had ceased to carry out to the letter the instructions that had been given him, and that Mr Marston had only a general knowledge of a department that he himself knew intimately. He had arranged numerous small improvements of which Mr Marston was ignorant, and had exploited highly profitable exchanges of material with other dealers. Mr Marston may have perhaps noticed in the general accounts a gradual fall in packing expenses, but if he had he had attributed it, without much thought, to the increased facilities for obtaining wood and cardboard. He did not know that as the result of most delicate manœuvring and an intricate system of exchange conducted by Mr Stevens his firm was being supplied with cardboard at the actual cost price.

Mr Stevens did not tell him. He enjoyed his little secret. Every year he would consult the figures, scratch his bald head and chuckle. What a lot he had saved the firm! He looked forward to the day when he should tell Mr Marston. How surprised they would all be! They had never suspected that funny old Stevens was such a good business man. In the evening hours of reverie and after lunch on Sunday he would endow the scene with that dramatic intensity that he had looked for but had not yet found in life.

There were other moments, however, when he longed for appreciation. He wished that someone would realise his importance without having to have it explained to him. So that when Roland said to him, "You're the only person in the place who can help me," he was startled into the indulgence of his one weakness.

"Well, well, sir," he said, and his face flushed with pleasure, "I daresay if you put it like that"; and taking Roland by the arm he led him away into his study and began to explain his accounts, his invoices, his receipts and his method of checking them. And because he had found an appreciative audience he proceeded to reveal one by one his little secrets. "Mr Marston doesn't know I do this, and don't tell him, I'm keeping it as a surprise; but you can see that by letting the wood merchants have that extra percentage there, I can get tin-foil cheap enough to be able to pack our stuff at two per cent. less than it would cost ordinarily. Think what I must have saved the firm!"

There could be no question of his value; but what Roland did not then appreciate — what, for that matter, Mr Stevens himself did not appreciate — was the value of this work in relation to the general business of the firm. Mr Stevens was a specialist. He understood his own department but he understood nothing else. He did not realise that on the delicate balance of that two per cent, it had been possible to undersell a dangerous rival.

The same conditions, Roland discovered, existed in several other departments. Each head worked independently of the other heads. Mr Marston, sitting at his desk, co-ordinated their work. A one-man business: that was Mr Marston's programme. One brain must control, otherwise there would be chaos. One department would find itself working against another department. He believed in departments because they stood for the delegation of routine work, but they must be subordinate departments. There were moments, however, when Roland wondered whether Mr Marston's hold on the business had not relaxed with the years. A great deal was going on of which he was ignorant. He had started the machinery and the machinery still ran smoothly, but was the guiding hand ready to deal with stoppages? Roland wondered. How much did Mr Marston really know? Had he kept up with modern ideas, or was he still living with the ideas that were current in his youth? But more than this even, Roland wondered how much Perkins knew.

He did not like Perkins. "A good man," Mr Marston had called him, "as good a general manager as you're likely to find anywhere. Not a social beauty; silent, and all that, but a good strong man. You can trust him."

Roland did not agree with this estimate. First impressions are very often right; he was inclined to trust his intuition before his reason, and his first impression of Perkins was of an embittered, jealous man. "He hates me," Roland thought, "because I'm stepping straight into this business through influence, with every prospect of becoming a director before I've finished; while he's sweated all his life, and worked from nothing to a position that for all his ability will never carry him to the board-room." He was a man to watch. The people who have been mishandled by fortune show no mercy when they get the chance of revenge.

Perkins was scrupulously polite, but Roland felt how much he resented his intrusion, and Gerald was inclined to endorse this opinion.

"Oh, yes, a sour-faced ass," he said; "father thinks a lot of him, though. It's as well to keep on the right side of him. He can make things rather awkward if you don't. He keeps an eye on most of the accounts, and he watches the travellers' expenses pretty closely. If he gets annoyed with you he might start questioning your extras."

They laughed, remembering how they had entered under the heading "special expenses" the charges for a lurid evening at a certain discreet establishment in the Rue des Colombes.

On the whole, Roland was happy at the office, but the evenings were distressing: the bus ride back; the walk up the hot stuffy street towards his home; the subsequent walk with his father; the same walk every day along the hard, flag-stoned roads, during which they met the same dispirited men hurrying home from work. London was horrible in June, with its metallic heat, its dust, and the dull leaves of the plane-trees scattering their mournful shadows. How sombre, too, were the long evenings after the wretched two-course dinner, in the small suburban drawing-room—ill lit, ill ventilated, meanly furnished. It was not surprising that he should accept eagerly the Marstons' frequent invitations to spend the week-end with them in the country; it was another world, a cleaner, fresher world, where you were met at the station, where you drove through a long, winding drive to an old Georgian house, where you dressed for dinner, where you drank crusted port as you cracked your walnuts. Yet it was not this material well-being that he so highly valued as the setting it provided for a gracious interchange of courtesy, for the leisured preliminaries of friendship, for ornament and decoration.

Was anything in his life better than that moment on a Friday evening when from the corner seat of a railway carriage he watched the smoke and chimneys of London fall behind him, when through the window he saw, instead of streets and shops and houses, green fields and hedges and small scattered villages, and knew that for forty-eight hours he could forget the fretted uneasiness of his home.

He was invited during August to spend a whole week at Hogstead. Several others would be there, and there would be cricket every day.

"We can't do without you," Mr Marston had said, "and what's more, we don't intend to."

"Of course, we don't," said Muriel; "you've got to come!"

Naturally Roland did not need much pressing.

CHAPTER XIII
LILITH OF OLD

Roland made during this week the acquaintance of several members of the family who had hitherto been only names to him. There was Gerald's uncle Arnold, a long mean-faced man, and his wife, Beatrice. Afterwards, when he looked back and considered how large a part she had played, if indirectly, in his life, and for that matter in the lives of all of them, he could not help thinking that his first sight of her had been prophetic, certainly dramatic. He had just arrived, had been met by Muriel and Mr Marston and his brother in the hall, and Muriel had insisted on taking him away at once to see her rabbits. She had come to regard him as her special friend. Gerald's other friends were too stiff and grown up; Roland was nearer to her own age and he did not patronise her.

"Come along," she said, "you've got to see my rabbits before dinner-time."

"Will they have grown up by to-morrow?" he asked.

"Well, they won't be any younger, will they? They are such dears," and she had taken his hand, pulling him after her. They ran down the curving path that sloped from the house to the cricket field. "I keep them in that little shed behind the pavilion," she said. They were certainly delightful, little brown and white balls of fur, with stupid, blinking eyes. Roland and Muriel took them out of the cage and carried them on to the terrace that ran round the field, and sat there playing with them, offering them grass and dandelions.

A grass path ran between great banks of rhododendrons from the terrace towards the garden, and at the end a pergola stretched a red riot of roses parallel to the field. Suddenly at the end of the path, at the point where it met the pergola, Roland saw, framed in an arch of roses, a tall, graceful woman walking slowly on Gerald's arm, her head bent quietly towards him. At that distance Roland could not distinguish her features, but the small oval face set in the mass of light yellow hair was delicate and the firm outlines of her body suggested that she had only recently left her girlhood behind her.

"Who's that?" asked Roland.

"That! Oh, that's Aunt Beatrice."

"But who's Aunt Beatrice?"

"Uncle Arnold's wife."

"What!"

Roland could hardly believe it: so young a woman married to that shrivelled, prosaic solicitor.

"Oh, yes," said Muriel, "they've been married nearly three years now; and they've got such a darling little girl: Rosemary; you'll see her to-morrow. She's got the loveliest hair. It crinkles when you run your fingers through it."

"But—oh, well, I suppose it's rather cheek, but he's years older."

"Uncle Arnold?" replied Muriel cheerfully. "Oh, yes, I think he must be nearly fifty." Then after a pause, light-heartedly as though the possession of a family skeleton was something of an honour, "I don't think they like each other much."

"How do you know?" Roland asked.

"They are always quarrelling. I never saw such a couple for it. If there's a discussion he's only got to take one side for her to take the other."

"Well, I don't see very well how she could be in love with him, he's such a...." Roland paused, realising that it would be hardly good manners to disparage Muriel's uncle. But she did not intend him to leave the sentence unfinished.

"Yes," she said, "such a.... Go on!"

"But I didn't mean that."

"Yes, you did."

"No, I didn't; really I didn't. I'm sure your uncle's awfully nice, but he's so much older, and you can't be in love with someone so much older than yourself."

"I see; you're forgiven"; then after a pause and with a mischievous smile: "Have you ever been in love, Roland?"

"Yes."

"Oh, how lovely!" and she turned quickly and sat facing him, her knees drawn up, her hands clasped in front of them. "Now tell me all about it. I've always wanted to have a talk with someone who's really been in love, and I never have."

"What about Gerald?"

She pouted. "Gerald! Oh, well, but he laughs at me, and besides——But come on and tell me all about it."

She made a pretty picture as she sat there, her face alight with the eagerness of curious girlhood, and Roland felt to the full the fascination of such a confessional. "It was a long time ago," he said, "and it's all over now."

"Never mind that," Muriel persisted. "What was her name?"

"Betty."

"And was she pretty?"

"Of course; I shouldn't have been in love with her if she hadn't been."

Muriel tossed back her head and laughed. "Oh, but how absurd, Roland! Some of the ugliest women I've ever seen have managed to get husbands."

"And some pretty hideous-looking men get pretty wives."

"But I suppose the pretty wives think their ugly husbands are all right."

"And equally I suppose the handsome husbands think their plain wives beautiful."

They laughed together, but Muriel raised a warning finger. "We are getting off the point," she said. "I want to know more about your Betty. Was she dark?"

"Darkish—yes."

"And her eyes; were they dark too?"

"I think so; they were bright."

"What, aren't you sure? I don't think much of you as a lover."

"But I can never remember the colour of people's eyes," he pleaded. "I can't remember the colour of my mother's or my aunt's, or——"

"Quick, shut your eyes; what's the colour of my eyes?"

"Blue," Roland hazarded.

"Wrong. They're green. Cat's eyes. You ought to be ashamed of yourself. I shall write and tell your Betty about it."

"But that's all over long ago, I told you."

"How did it end?"

"It never began," laughed Roland: "she never cared for me a bit."

Muriel pouted. "How unromantic," she said; then added with the quick, mischievous smile, "and how silly of her!"

As he dressed for dinner that evening Roland wondered what perverse impulse had made him speak to Muriel of Betty rather than of Dolly; of either of them rather than of April; of an unsuccessful love affair that was over rather than of a successful one that was in progress. Muriel would far rather have heard of April than of Betty. How she would have pestered him with questions! Where had they met? When had he first known he was in love with her? What had he said to her? How had she answered him? It would have been great fun to confide in her. He had been foolish not to tell her. She was such a jolly girl. She had looked charming as she had sat back holding her knees, with her clear skin and slim boyish figure, and her brightly tinted lips that were always a little parted before her teeth, beautifully even teeth they were, except just at the corner of her mouth where one white tooth slightly overlapped its neighbour. She was the sort of girl that he would like to have had for a sister. He had always regretted that he had not had one, and between Muriel and himself there could have been genuine, open comradeship. She would have been a delightful companion. They would have had such fun going about together to parties, dances and the Oval. She would have received so charmingly his confidence.

And yet, on the whole, he did not know why, he was rather glad that he had not told her about April.

That night Roland sat next Beatrice at dinner, and was thus afforded an opportunity of confirming or rejecting his first impression of her. She was only twenty years old, but she looked younger, not so much on account of her slim figure and small, delicate, oval face as of her general pose and the girlish untidiness that made you think that she had not taken very long over her toilet. Her light yellow hair was drawn back carelessly from the smooth skin of her neck and forehead. It looked as though it had been crushed all the afternoon under a tightly fitting hat, and that when Beatrice had returned from her walk, probably a little late, she had flung the hat on the bed, and deciding that she could not be bothered to take down her hair and put it up again had been content to draw her comb through it once or twice with hurried, impatient fingers. This negligence, which might have been charming as the setting for mobile, vivacious features, was out of keeping with the tranquillity of her face, her quiet gestures and lack of action. She had not learnt how to dress and carry herself, and this was an omission you would hardly expect in a woman who had been married for three years.

And yet she was beautiful, or perhaps not so much beautiful as different. She suggested tragedy, mystery, romance. What, Roland asked himself, lay behind the wavering lustre of her eyes? And, looking at the meagre, uninspired features of her husband, he wondered how she could have ever brought herself to marry him. He was a very good fellow, no doubt, of whom one might grow fond—but love—to be held in his arms, to be kissed by those dry lips! He shuddered, revolted by this dismal mating of spring and autumn.

She did not talk very much, though occasionally, when her husband made a particularly definite statement, she would raise her head and say rather contemptuously: "Oh, Arnold!" to which he would reply with heavy worded argument: "My dear girl, what you don't understand is...." It was uncomfortable, and Roland, looking round the table, wondered whether the family was aware of it. They did not appear to be. At one end of the table Mr Marston was discussing, in his jovial, full-blooded manner, the prospects of the cricket week, and, at the other, Mrs Marston was informing a member of the Harrow XI. that their opponents of the morrow had recruited a couple of blues from a neighbouring village. Gerald and Muriel were both laughing and chatting, and the other members of the party seemed equally not to notice the close atmosphere of impending conflict. Perhaps they had grown accustomed to it.

Roland listened carefully to all that Arnold Marston said, both during dinner and afterwards when the ladies had gone upstairs and the port had been passed for the second time round the table. He was hard, dogmatic and, at the same time, petulant in his talk. He quickly assumed that everyone who did not agree with him was ignorant and a fool. As he talked his fingers performed small gestures of annoyance; they plucked at the table-cloth, fingered the water-bowl, heaped the salt into small pyramids upon his plate. They were discussing the pull shot, then something of an innovation, and Roland maintained that it was absurd for school coaches not to allow boys to hit across long hops. "Why, do you know that at Fernhurst you are expected to apologise to the bowler if you make a pull shot."

"And quite right, too," said Mr Arnold.

"But, why?" Roland answered him. "The pull's perfectly safe; it's a four every time and you can't get more than a single if you play back to it with a straight bat."

"I daresay, I daresay, but cricket's cricket, and you have got to play it with a straight bat. You've got to play according to rules."

"But there's no rule that says you mayn't hit a long hop with a crooked bat."

Mr Arnold fidgeted angrily.

"My dear boy, it's no good arguing. I've been playing cricket and watching cricket for forty years, and the good batsmen always played a straight ball with a straight bat."

"There are a good many who don't."

"That means nothing. A big man's a rule to himself. The pull's a dangerous stroke; it's all right in village cricket perhaps, but no one who doesn't play with a straight bat would get into a county side."

"But isn't it the object of the game to make runs?"

"Not altogether—even if you do get four runs from it instead of one, which I am prepared to doubt. We wear our clothes to keep our bodies warm, but you wouldn't be pleased if your tailor made your coat button up to the throat, and said: 'It covers more of you, sir; you'll be warmer that way, and the object of clothes is to keep you warm.'"

There was a general laugh at Roland's expense, and before it had subsided Mr Marston had introduced another subject. Roland was annoyed; he had a distaste for anything that savoured of cleverness. He regarded it as an unfair weapon in an argument. An argument should be a weighing of facts. Each side should produce its facts, and an impartial witness should give judgment. It was not fair to obscure the issue with an untrue, if amusing, simile. And once the laugh is against you it is no good continuing an argument. Arnold Marston had learnt this on his election platform. He had once been asked what his party proposed to do for the unemployed; it was an awkward question, that gave many opportunities for adverse heckling. But he had obscured the issue with a laugh: "When my party gets in there will be no unemployment." And the meeting had gone home with the opinion that he was a jolly fellow—not too serious—the sort of man that anyone could understand. It was a good trick on the platform, but it was very annoying at the dinner-table, at least so the discomfited found. And Roland felt even more aggrieved as they were leaving the room and the silly ass in the Harrow XI. slapped him on the back and informed him that, "The old man got in a good one on you there." He could understand Beatrice hating him.

He did not have another opportunity of speaking to her that evening, but as he sat in the big drawing-room among the members of the house party his attention drifted continually from the agreeable, superficial conversation that had been up to now so sympathetic to him. These trivial discussions of cricket, their friends, their careers, and, in a desultory manner, of life itself, had been invaded by a stern, critical silence. His eyes kept turning towards

Beatrice as she sat in a deep arm-chair, her hands folded quietly in her lap; they followed her when she walked to the window and stood there, her arm raised above her head, looking into the garden. He would have liked to go across the room and speak to her; but what would he have been able to say? He could not tell what thoughts were passing beneath the unruffled surface: was she fretting impatiently at the tedious cricket shop? Was she criticising them all?—she, who had seen deeper and farther and come nearer to tragedy than any of them—or was she what she appeared—a young woman moved by the poetry of a garden stilled by moonshine? When she turned away he thought that he detected a movement of her shoulders, a gesture prompted by some wandering thought or gust of feeling, that would have been significant to one who knew her, but for him was meaningless. And that night he lay awake for nearly an hour, a long time for one who thought little and to whom sleep came easily, remembering her words and actions, the intonation of her voice, and that movement by the window. As he began to lose control over thoughts she became transfigured, the counterpart of those princesses, shut away in high-walled castles, of whom he had dreamed in childhood; her husband became an ogre, leering and vindictive, who laughed at him from the turrets of impregnable battlements.

Breakfast at Hogstead was a haphazard business. It began at eight and ended at ten. No one presided over it. There were cold things on the sideboard to which you helped yourself. As soon as you came down you rang the bell and a maid appeared to ask you whether you would prefer tea or coffee and whether you would take porridge. You then sat down where you liked at the long wide table.

When Roland came down the next morning at about a quarter to nine he found the big rush on; from half-past eight to half-past nine there were usually six or seven people at the table. Before that time there was only Mrs Marston and anyone who had been energetic enough to take a dip in a very cold pond that was protected from sunshine by the northern terrace of the cricket field. By a quarter to ten there was usually only a long table, covered with dirty plates, to keep company with Mr Marston, who, strangely enough, was a late riser. There were eight people in all having breakfast when Roland arrived, or, to be more exact, there were seven, for Gerald had finished his some time before, but as he had had a bathe he preferred to remain at the table and inform everyone of his courage as they came down.

"I can't think why everyone doesn't bathe in the morning," he was saying; "makes one feel splendidly fit. I'm absolutely glowing all over."

"So you've told us before," said Muriel.

"I've told you, but I haven't told Roland. Roland, why didn't you come and have a bathe this morning, you old slacker? Do you no end of good."

"Puts one's eye out," said Roland, repeating the old Fernhurst theory that cricket and swimming are incompatible.

"Rot, my dear chap; nothing like a bathe, nothing like it. I bet you I shall skittle them out this afternoon, and I don't see why I shouldn't make a few runs either."

Roland had by this time satisfied the maid's curiosity as to his beverage and had helped himself to a plate of tongue and ham. He turned round with the plate in his hand and looked to see where he should sit. There was a vacant place beside Gerald to which he would have been expected to direct himself; there was also a vacant place beside Beatrice: he chose the latter, and hardly realised till he had drawn back the chair that Gerald was at the opposite end of the table.

Several thoughts passed with incredible swiftness through his brain. Had anyone noticed what he had done? Would they think it curious? More important still, would Beatrice resent it? From this last anxiety he was soon freed, for Beatrice, without apparently having observed his presence, rose from the table and went into the garden. He was left with an empty chair on either side of him and no one for him to talk to; Gerald and Muriel were beyond the reach of anything less than a shout.

He finished his breakfast hurriedly in an enforced silence and walked out into the garden in the secret hope of finding Beatrice. In this he soon succeeded. She was playing croquet with her daughter on the lawn. Roland stood watching them for a moment and then walked slowly across the lawn. Beatrice glanced up at him and then went on with her game. She did not even smile at him. It would have been too much perhaps to have expected her to ask him to join them, but she might surely have made some sign of comradely recognition. After all, he had the night before taken her down to dinner; he had endeavoured to be as nice as he could to her, and it annoyed him and, at the same time, attracted him to feel that he had made absolutely no impression on her.

Roland was not one of those who analyse their emotions. When he was attracted by some new interest he did not put himself in the confessional, and he did not now ask himself why or how Beatrice had appealed to him.

As a matter of fact, she did not attract him physically. Her beauty added to the glamour that enriched her loneliness, but did not touch him otherwise. It was interest he felt for her, a compelling interest for someone outside the circle of his own experience, who was content to disparage what he admired and had filled her own life with other enthusiasms. She was remote, inscrutable. She lived and ate and talked and moved among them, but she had no part there. And because he was so interested in her he was desperately anxious that she should feel some interest in him. She was a mystery for him, but he was not content she should remain a mystery; he wanted to understand her, to become friends, so that in her troubles she should turn to him for sympathy and guidance. How wonderful that would be, that this aloof and beautiful woman should share with him an intimacy that she denied her husband. He would watch her as he had watched her the previous evening moving among her friends, indifferent and apart from them, and they would sit, as they had sat, hardly noticing her, talking of their own affairs, perhaps casting towards her a glance of casual speculation: "What is she really?" they would say, and then put her from their mind and return to their bridge and their billiards and their cricket shop. But he would know, and as she turned from the window he would appreciate the significance of that little movement, that hesitation almost of the shoulders, and she would turn her eyes to him, those sad, disdainful, dove-coloured eyes of hers, that invited nothing and offered nothing, but would become for him flooded with sympathy and gentle friendship; there would be no need for words—just that meeting of the eyes across a crowded drawing-room.

Immersed in reverie, he walked up and down the long grass path that ran from the cricket field to the rose garden, and when his name was shouted suddenly, shrilly and from very close, he approximated to that condition of dismay that the vernacular describes as "jumping out of one's skin." He turned, to see Muriel standing two yards behind him, her hands upon her hips, shaking with laughter.

"I have been watching you for ten minutes," she said as soon as she had recovered her breath, "and it's the funniest sight I've seen; you've been walking up and down the path with your head in the air, and your hands clenched together behind your back, and your lips were moving. I'm certain you were talking to yourself. I couldn't think what you were doing. I sat behind that bush there and watched you going up and down and up and down, your hands clenched and your head flung back and your lips moving, and then at last I guessed——"

"Well, what was it?"

"You were composing poetry. Now, don't laugh, I'm serious, and I want to know who you were composing it for."

"Well, who do you think it was?"

"That girl, of course."

"What girl?"

"Why, the girl you told me about yesterday!"

"Oh, that——"

"Yes; oh, that! But you were now, weren't you?"

"No, I wasn't. You can't see me wasting my time on poetry. Besides, I couldn't do it."

"Then, what were you doing?"

"Thinking."

"Who about?"

"You, of course."

"Oh, no," she said, shaking her head, the light hair scattering in the sunlight. "Oh, no, no, no! If you had been thinking about me, it might have occurred to you that I had no one in this large party to amuse me and that I might very likely be lonely. And if you had thought of that, and had gone on thinking that, with your head flung back——"

"Yes, I know all about that head."

"Well, if you had been thinking of me all that time, and hadn't considered it worth your while to come and see what I was doing, I should be very cross with you. But as I know you weren't I don't mind. But come along now; what was it all about?" And, sitting down on the garden seat, she curled herself into a corner and prepared herself for catechism. "Now, come on," she said, "who was it?"

"Well, if you want to know, it was your Aunt Beatrice."

Muriel pouted.

"Her! What do you want to think about her for?"

"I don't know. She's rather interesting, don't you think?"

"No, I don't," and Muriel spoke sharply in a tone that Roland had never before encountered.

"But——" he began.

"Oh, never mind," she said, "if you've been thinking about Aunt Beatrice for the last ten minutes you won't want to talk about her now. Come and have a game of tennis."

And she jumped up from her seat and walked up towards the house. Roland felt, as he prepared to follow her, that it was an abrupt way to end a conversation that she had forced on him.

And that night, as he undressed, Roland had to own to himself that altogether it had not been a satisfactory day. There had been the incident at the breakfast-table, the rebuff on the croquet lawn, the coldness that had arisen between himself and Muriel, and then, although he had done fairly well in the cricket match, he had not achieved the goal which, he had to confess, had been his great incentive to prowess—namely, the approval of Beatrice.

He had made twenty-seven in the first innings—a good twenty-seven, all things considered. He had had two yorkers in his first over. He had played a large part in the gradual wearing down of the bowling, that had paved the way for some heavy hitting by the tail. He had made several very pretty shots. There had been that late cut off the fast bowler—a beauty; he had come down on it perfectly, and it had gone past second slip out of reach of the third man for three; and then there had been that four off the slow bowler who had tied up Gerald so completely; he had played him quite confidently. Mr Marston had, indeed, complimented him on the way he had placed the short-pitched balls in front of short-square for singles. It had been a pretty useful innings, but though he had kept turning his eyes in the direction of the pavilion, and especially to the shaded side of it, where the ladies reclined in deck-chairs, he had failed to discover any manifestation of excitement, pleasure or even interest on the part of Beatrice in his achievements. True, he had once seen her hands meet in a desultory clap, but that clap had rewarded what was, after all, a comparatively simple hit, a half-volley outside the off stump that he had hit past cover to the boundary, and as that solitary clap came a full thirty seconds after the rest of the pavilion had begun clapping, and ceased a good thirty seconds before anyone else clapping in the pavilion ceased, he was obliged to feel that the applause was more the acquittal of a social duty than any recognition of his own prowess, and when he was finally given leg before to a ball, that would certainly have passed a foot above the stumps, she did not smile at him with congratulations nor did she attempt to console him, though he gave her every opportunity of doing so had she wished by walking round three sides of a rectangle, and reaching the dressing-room by means of the shaded lawn on the left of the pavilion. No. His cricket had not interested her in the least, and it was exasperating to see her face kindle with enthusiasm when the wicket keeper and the slow bowler put on fifty runs for the last wicket through a series of the most outrageous flukes that have ever disgraced a cricket field.

Not a single ball was hit along the ground and only rarely did it follow the direction in which the bat was swung. Length balls on the off stump flew over the head of mid-on, of point, and second slip, to fall time after time providentially out of reach. The fielding side grew exasperated; slow bowlers tried to bowl fast and fast bowlers had a shot with lobs; full pitches even were attempted, and these, too, were smitten violently over the heads of the instanding fieldsmen and out of reach of the deeps. It was a spectacle that would at ordinary times have flung Roland into convulsions of delight, but on this occasion it annoyed him beyond measure. He felt as must a music-hall artist whose high-class performance has been received with only mild approval when he watches the same audience lose itself in caterwauls of hilarious appreciation at the debauched antics of a vulgar comedian with a false nose and trousers turned the wrong way round who sings a song about his "ma-in-law and the boarding-house." For there was Beatrice, who had hardly taken the trouble to watch his innings, laughing and clapping the preposterous exhibition of this last wicket pair. It was a real relief to him when the slow bowler, in a desperate effort to hook an off ball to the square by boundary, trod on his middle stump and nearly collapsed amid the debris of the wicket.

Altogether it had been an unsatisfactory day and it was typical of the whole week. He had looked forward to it eagerly, he had meant to enjoy himself so much—the quiet mornings in the garden, the inspection of the wicket, the change into flannels, the varying fortune of cricket, the long enchantment of a warm, heavy afternoon, and afterwards the good dinner, the comradeship, the kindly interplay of talk, till finally sleep came to a mind at harmony with itself and full of agreeable echoes. How good these things had seemed to him in imagination. But, actually, there was something missing. The weather was fine, the cricket good, the company agreeable, but the harmony was broken. He was disquieted. He did not wake in the morning with that deep untroubled sense of enjoyment; he had, instead, a belief that something was going to happen; he was always looking to the next thing instead of abiding contentedly in the moment.

And this mental turmoil could only be attributed to the presence of Beatrice. She disturbed him and excited him. His eyes followed her about the room. Whenever he was away from her he wondered what she was doing and wished she would come back; but in her presence he was unhappy and self-conscious. He hardly joined in the general conversation of the table for shyness of what she would think of him. On the few occasions when he sat next to her he could think of nothing to say to her, nothing, that is to say, that was individual, that might not have been, and as a matter of fact probably had been, said to her by every other young man in the room.

He would hazard some remark about the weather—it was rather hot: did she think there was any danger of a thunderstorm?

"I hope not," she would answer; "it would spoil everything, wouldn't it?" She assumed the voice of a mother that is endeavouring to reassure a small child. Cricket was like a plaything in the nursery. "That is what she takes me for," he said to himself—"an overgrown schoolboy"; and he prayed for an opportunity of saying something brilliant and evocative that would startle her into an interest for him. If only he could lead the conversation away from heavy trivialities to shadowy conjectures, wistful regrets; if only they could talk of life and its disenchantments, its exquisite gestures; of sorrow, happiness and resignation. But how were they to talk of it? If she thought about him at all, which was doubtful, or in any way differentiated him from the other young men of the party, she would probably consider that he was flattered by her gracious inquiries about his batting average. How was she to know what he was feeling; and how was he to introduce so portentous a subject? He recognised with a smile what a sensation he would cause were he to lean across to her and say: "What do you, Mrs Arnold, consider to be the ultimate significance of life?" His question would be sure to coincide with one of those sudden silences that occur unexpectedly in the middle of a meal, and his words would fall into that pool of quivering silence, scattering ripples of horror and dismay. Mr Marston would stare at him, Muriel would giggle and say she had known all the time he was a poet, and the other members of the party would gaze at him in astonished pity. "Poor fellow!" their glances would say; "quite balmy!" And Beatrice? she would dismiss the situation with an agreeable pleasantry that would put everyone save Roland at his ease. He did not in the least see how he was to win her confidence.

His looks had not impressed her, as, indeed, why should they? His features were neither strikingly handsome nor strikingly ugly; they were ordinary. He was not clever, at least his cleverness did not transpire in conversational brilliance and repartee; and she was not interested in cricket. He envied the ease with which Gerald talked to her, the way they laughed and ragged each other. They were such good friends. It had been in Gerald's company that he had first seen her. Was Gerald in love with her, he wondered. Gerald had never confided to him any recent love affair, and perhaps this was the reason. It was not unlikely. She was young, she was lonely, she was beautiful. He asked Muriel whether she thought there was any cause for his anxiety.

"What!" she said. "Gerald and Aunt Beatrice in love with each other!"

"Yes; why not. She's not in love with her husband, and I don't see why at all——" He stopped, for Muriel was fixing him with a fierce and penetrative glare.

"No," she said, "there's not the least danger of Gerald falling in love with Aunt Beatrice, but if you aren't very careful, someone else will be very soon!"

He laughed uncomfortably.

"Oh, don't be silly!"

"So you know who I mean, don't you?"

"You mean me, I suppose."

"Of course."

He tried to dismiss the subject with a laugh.

"And that would never do, would it?"

It was not successful. Muriel looked more annoyed than he had ever seen her before. It was absurd of her. She must know that he was only ragging. They had always been so open with one another, so charmingly indiscreet.

"No, it wouldn't," she said.

He waited, thinking she was going to add some qualification to this plain denial. Her lips indeed began to frame a syllable, when in response to some swift resolution she shook her head. "Oh, well," she said, "it doesn't matter."

There was no use denying it: it had not been the week he had expected.

CHAPTER XIV
THE TWO CURRENTS

Roland returned home dissatisfied with himself and anxious to vent the dissatisfaction on someone else. He was in a mood when the least thing would be likely to set him into a flaring temper, and at dinner his father provided the necessary excitant. They were considering the advisability of having the dining-room repapered and Mr Whately was doubting whether such an expensive improvement would be possible for their restricted means.

"I don't know whether we can manage that just now," he said. "We have had one or two little extras this last year or so; there was that new stair carpet and then the curtains on the second landing. I really think that we ought to be a little careful just now. Of course later on, when Roland and April are married——" And he paused to beam graciously upon his son before completing the sentence. "As I was saying, when Roland and April——" But he never completed the sentence. It remained for ever an anacoluthon. It was that beam that did it. It exasperated Roland beyond words. Its graciousness became idiocy.

"I wish you wouldn't talk like that, father," he said. "We've heard that joke too often."

There was an uncomfortable silence. Mr Whately was for a moment too surprised to speak. He had made that little pleasantry so often that it had become part of his conversational repertory. He could not understand Roland's outburst; at first he was hurt; then he felt that he had been insulted, and, like all weak men, he was prone to stand upon his dignity.

"That's not the way to talk to your father, Roland."

"I'm sorry, father, but oh, I don't know, I...." Roland hesitated, and the matter should then have been allowed to drop. Mrs Whately had indeed prepared to interfere with an irrelevant comment on a friend's theory of house decoration, but Mr Whately, having once started on an assault, was loath to abandon it. "No, Roland, that's not at all the way to speak to me, and I don't know what you've got to be impatient with me about. You know quite well that you're going to marry April in time."

"I know nothing of the sort."

"Don't be absurd; of course you do; it was arranged a long time ago."

"No, it wasn't; nothing's been arranged. We're not engaged, and I won't have all this talk about 'when Roland and April are married.' Do you hear? I will not have it!"

It was a surprising outburst. Roland was usually so even-tempered, and the moment afterwards he was bitterly ashamed of himself.

"I'm sorry," he said. "I didn't know what I was saying."

For a moment his father did not answer him. Then: "It's all right, Roland," he said; "we understand."

But Roland saw quite clearly he was not forgiven, that his behaviour had increased the estrangement that had existed between his father and himself ever since, without asking parental advice, he had abandoned the idea of the bank. They did not talk much after dinner, and Mr Whately went to bed early, leaving Roland and his mother alone. It was easier now that he had gone.

"I feel such a beast," Roland said. "I don't know what made me do it. I was worried and tired. I didn't enjoy myself as much as I had hoped to down at Hogstead."

"I know, dear, I know. We all feel like that sometimes, but I don't see why that particular thing should have upset you. After all, it's a very old joke of father's; you've heard it so often before."

"I know, mother, I know. I don't know what it was."

He could not make clear to her, if she was unable to appreciate through her intuition, his distaste for this harping on his marriage, this inevitable event to which he had to come, the fate that he could in no way avoid.

"Really, dear," his mother went on, "I couldn't understand it. You haven't had any row with April, have you?"

"Oh, no; nothing like that, nothing."

"Then really, dear— —"

"I know, mother, I know."

It was no good trying to explain to her. Could anyone ever communicate their grief, or their happiness for that matter, to another? Was it not the fate of every human soul to be shut away from sympathy behind the wall he, himself, throws up for his defence?

"And, dear, while we're on the question," his mother was saying, "both father and I have been thinking that—well, dear, you've been spending rather a lot of money lately, and we thought that, though you have such a certain post, you really ought to take the opportunity of putting by a little money for setting up your house later on. Don't you think so, dear?"

"I suppose so, mother."

"You see you've got practically no expenses now. I know you pay us something every week, and it's very good of you to, but you could quite easily save fifty pounds a year."

"Yes, I suppose so."

"And don't you think you ought to?"

"I'll try, mother, I'll try."

She rose from her chair, walked across to him, and, bending down, kissed his forehead.

"We do feel for you, dear," she said, "really we do."

"I know you do, mother."

For a long while after she had left him Roland remained in the drawing-room; he was burdened by a confused reaction against the influences that were shaping his future for him. He supposed he was in love with April, that one day he would marry her; but was there any need for this insistence upon domesticity? Could he not be free a little longer? His eyes travelled miserably round the small, insignificant drawing-room. The window curtains had long since yielded their fresh colour to the sunshine and hung dingily in the gaslight. The wall-paper was shabby and tawdry, with its festooned roses. The carpet near the door was threadbare; the coverings to the stiff-backed chairs were dull and crinkly. This was what marriage meant to men and women in his position. He contrasted the narrow room with the comfort and repose of Hogstead. What chance did people stand whose lives were circumscribed by endless financial difficulties, who could not afford to surround themselves with deep arm-chairs and heavy carpets and warm-coloured wall-papers? It was cruel that now, at the very moment when he had begun to escape from the drab environment of his childhood, these fetters should be attached to him. It was cruel. And rising from his chair he walked backwards and forwards, up and down the room. The days of his freedom were already numbered. They would be soon ended, the days of irresponsible, unreflecting action. It was maddening, this semblance of liberty where there was no liberty. He recalled a simile in a novel he had once read, though the name of the book and of the author had escaped

140 | The Lonely Unicorn

his memory, in which human beings were described as fishes swimming in clear water, with the net of the fisherman about them. He was like that. He was swimming in clear water, but at any moment the fisherman might lift the net and he would be gasping and quivering on the bank.

Next day, in pitiful reaction, he presented to Mr Marston a request to be allowed to commence his foreign tour immediately instead of, as had been previously arranged, in the beginning of the autumn.

"But, my dear fellow," Mr Marston expostulated, "you surely don't want to go in the very middle of the cricket season, when you're in such splendid form? Think what games you'll be missing. There's the Whittington match in August. We simply can't do without you. And then there's that game against Hogstead in September, in which you did so splendidly last year. It's no good, my dear fellow, we simply can't spare you."

But Roland was stubborn.

"I'm very sorry, sir," he said, "but I do feel that I ought to be going out there soon, and July and August will be slack months—just the time to see people and form alliances. In the autumn they would be too busy to worry about me."

Mr Marston shrugged his shoulders. It was annoying, but still the business came first, he supposed.

"All right, my dear fellow. I daresay you are right. And I am glad to see you are so keen on your work. I only wish Gerald was."

"Oh, but I think he is really, sir," said Roland, who, for one horrible moment, had a feeling that he was playing a mean trick on Gerald. At school he had resented the way that little Mark-Grubber Shrimpton had gone up to Crusoe at the end of the hour to ask his questions. He had found a nasty name for such behaviour then, and was there so much difference between Shrimpton's thirst for knowledge and his own desire to travel when he might have been playing cricket? But Mr Marston speedily reassured him.

"Oh, yes; Gerald—he's keen enough of course, and, after all, he's rather different. He's known all along there was no necessity for him to over-exert himself, and I daresay he's heard so much shop talked that he's got pretty sick of the whole thing. You have come fresh to it."

"Then I may go, sir?"

"Yes, yes, if you want to. I'll ask Mr Perkins to make an arrangement. I expect we'll be able to get rid of you next week."

And so it was arranged.

The Lonely Unicorn | 141

Two days before his departure, as he was bounding downstairs on his way to lunch, Roland was suddenly confronted at the turn of the staircase below the second landing by a tall, graceful figure, in a wide-brimmed hat and light crinkly hair. He gave a surprised gasp. "I am so sorry," he began; then saw that it was Beatrice. "Oh, how do you do, Mrs Arnold?" It was rather dark and for a moment she did not recognise him.

"Oh, but of course—why, it's Mr Whately! And how fortunate! I was wondering how I should ever get to the top of these enormous stairs. I can't think why you don't have a lift. I've come to see Gerald. Do you think you could run and tell him I'm here? I suppose I should have gone and asked one of your clerks, but they do so embarrass me. Oh, thank you so much. It is kind."

Within a minute Roland had returned with the news that Gerald had already gone out to lunch, that his secretary did not know where he had gone, but that he had left a message stating that he was not to be expected back before three.

A look of disappointment crossed her face.

"Oh, but how annoying!" she said. "And I had wanted him to take me out to lunch. We haven't seen each other for such a long time. I suppose it's my own fault. I ought to have let him know. All the same, thank you so much, Mr Whately."

She had half turned to go, when Roland, with one of those sudden inspirations, of which a moment's thought would have rendered him incapable, suggested that she should come out and lunch with him instead. "It would be so delightful for me if you would."

As she turned towards him, her features expressing an obvious surprise, he wondered how on earth he had had the courage to ask her. He had never seen her look more beautiful than she did, standing there in the half light of the staircase, her pale blue dress silhouetted against the dull brown of the woodwork, and one arm flung out along the banister. For a moment he thought that she was going to refuse, then the look of surprise passed into a gracious smile.

"But how kind of you, Mr Whately: I should love to."

He took her to a smart but quiet restaurant that was mostly used by city men wishing to lunch unobtrusively with their secretaries, and they were lucky enough to find a corner table. At first he found conversation a little difficult; the waiter was so slow bringing the dishes. There were uncomfortable pauses in their talk. But by the time they had finished their fish, and drunk a little wine, Roland's nervousness had passed. It was a delight to look at her, a delight to listen to the soft intonations of her voice; and here in the quiet intimacy of the restaurant he was able to appreciate even more acutely than at Hogstead the mystery and romance that surrounded her. The pathos of her life was actual to him; they were discussing a new novel that had been much praised, but of which she had complained a falsity to life.

"But then you are so different from the rest of us," he had said.

"Ah, don't say that," she replied quickly. "I'm so anxious to be the same as all of you, to live your life and share your interests. It's so lonely being different."

She made him talk of himself, of his hopes and his ambitions. And he told her that in two days' time he would be going abroad.

"In the middle of August! Before the cricket season's over! What horrid luck!"

"Oh, no, I wanted to go," said Roland. "I was getting tired of things. I wanted a change."

She looked at him with curiosity, a new interest for him in her deep dove-coloured eyes.

"You, too!" she said.

"I don't know what it is," Roland continued. "I feel restless; I feel I must break loose. It's all the same, one day after another, and what does it lead to?"

She leant forward, her elbows on the table, her face resting upon the backs of her hands.

"Ah, don't I know that feeling," she said; "one waits, one says, 'Something is sure to happen soon.' But it doesn't, and one goes on waiting. And one tries to run away, but one can't escape from oneself." Their eyes met and there seemed to be no further need for words between them. Roland's thoughts travelled into spaces of vague and wistful speculation. A profound melancholy consumed him, a melancholy that was at the same time pleasant—a sugared sadness.

"What are you thinking of, Roland?" The use of his Christian name caused no surprise to him; it was natural that she should address him so. He answered her, his eyes looking into hers.

"I was thinking of how we spend our whole lives looking forward to things and looking back to things and that in itself the thing is nothing."

She smiled at him. "So you've found that out too?" she said. Then she laughed quickly. "But you mustn't get mournful when you are with me. You've all your life before you and you're going to be frightfully successful and frightfully happy. I shall so enjoy watching you. And now I must really be rushing off. You've given me a most delightful time"; and she began to gather up her gloves and the silk purse that hung by a gold chain from her wrist.

Roland could do little work that afternoon; his thoughts wandered from the ledger at his side and from the files of the financial news. And that evening he was more acutely aware than usual of the uncoloured dreariness of his home. For him Beatrice was the composite vision of that other world from which the course of his life was endeavouring to lead him. She represented, for him, romance, adventure, the flower and ecstasy of life.

But two days later he felt once again, as he leant against the taffrail to watch the English coast fade into a dim haze, that he was letting drop from his shoulders the accumulated responsibilities of the past six months. Did it matter then so much what happened to him over there behind that low-lying bank of cloud if he could at any moment step out of his captivity, relinquish his anxieties and enter a world that knew nothing of April or of his parents, that accepted him on his own valuation as a young man with agreeable manners and a comfortable independence? Who that held the keys of his dungeon could be called a prisoner?

PART III
THE FIRST ENCOUNTERS

CHAPTER XV
SUCCESS

He felt less certain of his freedom when he watched, three months later, the white coast of England take visible shape on the horizon. He should have been feeling very happy. He was returning to his friends, his home, his girl. And he was returning with credit. He had not made, it is true, large profits for the firm, but that had not been expected of him. He had done what he had been told to do. He had established important connections, made friends with two large business men, and, incidentally, brought several thousand pounds' worth of business to the firm of Marston & Marston. He had done better than had been expected. When he had written home and told Mr Marston that M. Rocheville was prepared to sign a contract for varnish on behalf of the Belgian Government, Mr Marston had dropped the letter on his desk and had sat back in his chair amazed at this good fortune; and when, a fortnight later, the news arrived of a possible combination with the German firm of Haupsehr & Frohmann, Mr Marston had jumped from his seat and walked backwards and forwards, up and down the office. And for two days he disconcerted his secretary by muttering in the middle of his dictation: "Marvellous boy! marvellous boy!"

And he had been marvellous both in his fortune and in his audacity. He had met M. Rocheville under circumstances of ridiculous improbability. He was dining at a small restaurant in Antwerp; he had just ordered his meal and had commenced his study of the wine list when he became conscious of a commotion at the table on his left. There was a mingling of voices, reproachful, importunate, and one in particular feebly explanatory. Roland listened, and gathered from the torrent of words that the owner of the feeble voice had lost his purse and was trying to explain that he had friends in the town and would return and settle the account on the next day. But the proprietor, from a long experience of insolvent artists, actors, courtesans and other dwellers on the fringe of respectability, demanded a more substantial guarantee than the card which the subject of the misfortune was offering him.

"No, no," he was saying, "it is not enough; you will leave me your watch and that ring upon your second finger and you may go. Otherwise— —" And he shrugged his shoulders. To this the prosperous little gentleman, whom an empty bucket beneath the table proved to have dined expensively, would not agree. It was a personal affront, an insult to his name, and he brandished his card in the face of the proprietor; it availed little, and the intervention of the police was imminent when Roland heard the name "Rocheville" flung suddenly like a spear among the waiters.

On the waiters it had no effect; they winked, nodded, smiled to one another. They had heard that tale before. Many indignant customers had flourished the trade-mark of their reputation. Had not a poet produced once from his pocket the review of his latest book as a proof of his nobility? To the waiters the word "Rocheville" meant nothing; to Roland it meant much. The most important man in the Army Ordnance Department was named Rocheville. He might not be the same man, of course, but it was worth the experiment; certainly it was worth the loss of fifty francs that he would charge to the firm as a "special expense."

He rose from his seat and walked across to M. Rocheville.

"I beg your pardon, sir," he said. "I trust you will forgive me if I am committing an impertinence, but from what I overheard I gathered that you had lost your purse. If that is so, please allow me to lend you whatever you may need to settle your account."

"But, sir—no, really I couldn't; it would be an unthinkable liberty."

But Roland insisted. And having appeased the proprietor, who retired in a profusion of bows, he turned again to meet M. Rocheville's thanks.

"But it was nothing, sir, really it was nothing, and I could not endure the sight of a gentleman being submitted to such an inconvenience."

Monsieur Rocheville executed an elaborate bow.

"It is too kind of you, and if you will give me your address I will see that a cheque is sent to you to-morrow."

"But I'm afraid that I go to Brussels first thing to-morrow, and I am not certain at which hotel I shall be stopping. But it does not matter."

"But it does, of course it does," M. Rocheville expostulated. "How shall we manage it?"

For a moment he paused, his hand raised to his forehead, essentially, Roland thought, the gesture of a bureaucrat.

"Yes, yes, I have it," said M. Rocheville: "you will come back with me to some friends of mine that live here and we will arrange it."

"Well, then," said Roland, "if that is so, will you not do me the honour first of sitting at my table while I finish my meal and sharing a bottle of wine with me?"

M. Rocheville had already drunk a full bottle of champagne, but he had lived on perquisites for so long that he could not resist the temptation of accepting any offer that put him under no pecuniary obligation. And, besides, this was a confoundedly pleasant young man, who had saved him from an undignified situation, and in whose company he would no doubt pass agreeably a couple of hours.

"I should be delighted," he said; "and do you know my name?"

"I'm afraid not," said Roland.

With a slightly diffident flourish M. Rocheville handed his card to his young companion. It was for this moment that Roland had arranged his dramatic sequence. He examined the card carefully, then looked up with a surprised, half-modest, half-excited expression on his face.

"You aren't—you aren't *the* Monsieur Rocheville?"

A slow smile spread itself over the ample features of the bureaucrat. It was a long time since his vanity had been so delicately tickled, and after the insults he had received from the waiter this recognition of his value was very pleasant.

"Yes," he said, "I suppose I am."

"The Monsieur Rocheville who manages the Ordnance administration?" Roland persisted.

It was a sweetly sugared pill. To think that this young foreigner should know all about him. He, himself, was perhaps more important than he had been led to think—a prophet in his own country; but abroad, in England, they estimated truly the value of his services. He was inclined to agree with them; too much praise was given to the Generals and Commanders of Army Corps. He always experienced a slight impatience when he heard eulogies of the exploits of Malplaquet and Marshal Ney and Turin. They had done the spectacular work. The light of popular approval had to be focused somewhere: but that in itself proved nothing. Mankind was an ass. Was not authority delegated? Was not the private soldier less valuable than the colonel? Was not the colonel less valuable than the general? In the same way might not the general be less valuable than the organisation which provided him with food, with cannons, with rifles; with ammunition, and, as far as that went, with his army too. The farther one was from the firing line the more important one became. The organisation, was it not himself? A sound line of argument. And he sat back contentedly in the chair that Roland offered him and lifted the glass that Roland had filled for him.

He raised it to the light, then gently, very gently advanced his lips to it. He rolled the rich, heavy Volnay on his tongue. It was good. A little shudder ran through his body. The wine had warmed him. He sat back in his chair and smiled. It was good to be appreciated. And Roland in this respect accommodated him to the full. By the time Roland had finished his dinner the old man was in a state of maudlin self-pity and self-complacency. "I am not understood"; that was the burden of his complaint.

And then, very carefully, very gently, Roland introduced his own subject—the sale of varnish. Monsieur Rocheville lamented the inferiority of the Belgian species. It would not polish and it was so dear. But what would you! The Belgians were interested only in husbandry and food and wantonness. Monsieur Rocheville's eyes glistened as he brought out the word, and in another minute Roland would have been forced to attend to a recital of the Rocheville enterprises in the lists of gallantry; this, however, he evaded. If varnish in Belgium was so dear, why did he not send for it elsewhere—to Germany, or France, or Italy? He had heard there was very good varnish to be obtained in Italy. And when M. Rocheville advanced the theory that one should encourage national industries, Roland persuaded him that there was nothing that could better encourage the Belgian varnish industry than a removal of the Government's patronage.

"If they think they are certain of your custom they won't work. Why should they? Commerce is competition. You stimulate competition and you'll find your industry is a hundred per cent. more healthy in five years' time than it will be if you let it go on on the old lines: buying dear and buying bad." M. Rocheville agreed. How true it all was and how clearly this young man understood it—a delightful young man, on the whole the most delightful young man he had ever met. It was a pity that he insisted on talking about varnish all the time. There were so many much more interesting things that they could have found to discuss together. Still, it was all very warm and nice and comfortable.

Looking back the next day, and trying to reconstruct the sequence of their conversation, M. Rocheville found it impossible to recall the exact moment at which Roland had stated his interest in Marston & Marston's varnish and made his proposal that the Belgian Government would do well in the future to deal with his firm direct. As far as he could remember, there had been no such exact statement in so many words. They had discussed varnish from every point of view—from the international standpoint, from the financier's standpoint; they had even touched on the vexed question of retail business, and also the refractory behaviour of trade unions. They had discussed varnish indeed so thoroughly that it was impossible to recall what had, and what had not, been said. One thing alone M. Rocheville could recall with painful distinctness—that there had come a point in the conversation when he had realised that this engaging young man was offering to sell him a very large quantity of varnish—good varnish—better than the Belgian firms could supply and at the same price. There was no question of buyer or seller, no bargaining, no haggling. It was altogether different from his usual harsh business interviews, that were so distressing to a man of taste. In the same way that this young man had rendered him assistance in that trying altercation with the proprietor, so did he now in this matter of varnish lay his undoubted talents and experience at his disposal. It was a charming, friendly action, and the young man was so business-like. He had produced from his pocket a printed contract in which he had made certain alterations "between friends," he had called it, the cancellation of two or three small clauses; he had spread the document on the table for him to sign. He had then given M. Rocheville a similar agreement signed by his firm, and he had then ordered another glass of Benedictine, and the conversation turned from varnish into more intimate channels. He could not remember about what he had talked, but he felt that, at such an hour, their comments on whatever topic they had chosen to discuss must have been profound. In describing the occasion to a friend he waved a hand vaguely: "For two hours, he and I, we talked of life."

Then they had visited a M. Villeneuve to settle the matter of the loan. Roland had demurred, but M. Rocheville had insisted. And this part of the evening, owing to the sudden change of air, he could recall more clearly. Monsieur Villeneuve was in bed when they arrived and did not extend to him a very cordial welcome. But the loan was at last successfully negotiated, and Roland then discovered that in five hours' time he would have to catch a train and that it would be agreeable to spend those five hours in sleep. But M. Rocheville was very loath to part with him. For a long while he stood in the porch and, as far as Roland could discern any clear intention behind his confused utterances, appeared to be suggesting that Roland should still further trespass on the hospitality of M. Villeneuve.

"Then, perhaps, if you cannot do that," M. Rocheville persisted, "you will come and spend a week-end with me before you return. You have my card. I have a nice house in Brussels, very quiet and comfortable. I am not married."

But Roland had reminded him that he was very busy, and that he did not know if he would have time, but that he would certainly try to arrange a lunch at their next visit.

"And in the meantime I will see that you get that varnish."

"Ah! that varnish," said M. Rocheville. And observing that he was now standing alone in the porch, with no one to whom he might address his profound reflections upon the mortality of man, he walked slowly towards the gate, a little puzzled by Roland's conduct and by his own.

"A delightful young man," he said, then paused as though he must qualify this estimate, but his Latin cynicism saved him. "Well, well," he said, "an agreeable interlude."

That was Roland's first triumph, and the other, if less adroitly stage-managed, was more audacious, and owed its success to skill as much as to good fortune.

Haupsehr & Frohmann directed one of the largest polish factories in the south of Germany; they supplied, indeed, practically the whole of the Rhineland with their goods, and Roland had considered that a meeting between them might prove profitable. He found, however, that it was impossible to obtain an interview with either Herr Haupsehr or Herr Frohmann. "They will not look at English goods." That was what everyone told him, and a carefully worded request for an interview that he addressed to the head of the firm was answered by return of post with a bald statement that Herren Haupsehr and Frohmann did not consider a personal interview would further the interests of either Mr Roland Whately, representative of Marston & Marston, or of themselves. And Roland was thus driven to the reluctant conclusion that his advisers were correct. If he were to effect an introduction it would have to be done by guile.

He awaited his opportunity, and the opportunity came to him in the passport office. He had gone to fulfil some trifling by-law concerning the registration of aliens. For a long time he had sat in a draughty corridor, and then for a long time he had stood beside a desk while a busy bureaucrat attended to someone else's business, and when at last he had succeeded in making his application a bell rang in the next room, and without an apology his interlocutor rose from his chair and hurried to the next room.

"How terrified they are of their chiefs," Roland thought. He had by now become accustomed to the trepidation of officials. How typical was that desk of the words that were written and the sentences framed at it; precise, firm, tabulated and impersonal: the plain brass inkstand, with red and black inkpots; the two pens, the blotter, the calendar, the letter files, the box for memoranda; and the mind of that fussy little official was exactly like his desk, and, leaning over, Roland tried to see to whom the letter on the blotter was addressed.

As he did so, his eye fell on a slip of pasteboard that had been put behind the inkstand. It was a calling card, the calling card of a Herr Brumenhein, and on the top, in handwriting, was inscribed the words: "To introduce bearer." The name Brumenhein was familiar to Roland, though in what connection he could not recall. At any rate, the fact that he recollected the name at all proved that it was the appendage of an important person, and as it was always useful to possess the means of being introduced under the auspices of a celebrity, Roland picked up the card and placed it in his pocket-book.

When he returned to the hotel he made inquiries about the unknown patron, and learned that Herr Brumenhein was a very distinguished Prussian minister, and one who was honoured by the confidence of the Crown Prince. "He will be a great man one day," said the hotel proprietor.

"As great as Griegenbach?"

"Who knows?—perhaps, and it is said the Crown Prince is not too fond of Griegenbach."

And then Roland's informant proceeded to enlarge on the exaggerated opinion Griegenbach had held of his own value since his successful Balkan diplomacy. "He thinks he is indispensable and he makes a great mistake. No one is indispensable. The post of minister is more important than the man who fills it."

Roland, of course, agreed; he always agreed with people. It was thus that he had earned the reputation of being good company, and at this moment, even if he had held contrary opinions as to the relations of the moment and the man, he would have been unable to develop them in an argument. He was too busy wondering how best he could turn this discovery to his advantage. And it was not long before the thought was suggested to him that this card might very easily procure him the desired interview with Herr Haupsehr. It was a risky game of course, but then what wasn't risky in high finance? It was quite possible that Herren Haupsehr and Brumenhein were the oldest of friends, that awkward questions would be asked and his deceit discovered. But, even if it was, he could, at the worst, only be kicked downstairs, and that was an indignity he could survive. It would destroy for ever the possibility of any negotiations between himself and the German firm, but that, also, was no serious drawback, for, as things were, there seemed little enough prospect of opening an account. He could not see how he would be in any the worse position were he to fail, whereas if he brought it off.... It was a dazzling thought.

And so at eleven o'clock next morning Roland presented himself at the entrance of Herr Haupsehr's office. He asked no questions; he made no respectful inquiry as to whether at that moment Herr Haupsehr was, or was not, engaged. He assumed that whatever occupied that gentleman's attention would be instantly removed on the announcement that a friend of Herr Brumenhein's was in the building. Roland said nothing. He flourished his card in the face of the young lady who stood behind the door marked "Inquiries."

"You wish to see Herr Haupsehr?"

Roland bowed, and the young lady disappeared. She returned within a minute.

"If you will please to follow me, sir."

He was conducted through the counting-house and into the main corridor, up a flight of stairs, along another corridor, till they reached a door marked "Private," before which the young lady stopped. Roland made an interrogatory gesture of the hand towards it.

"If you please, sir," she said.

Roland did not knock at the door. He turned the handle and entered the room with the gracious condescension of a general who is forced to visit a company office. It was a large room, with a warm fire and easy-chairs and an old oak desk. But Herr Haupsehr was not sitting at his desk: he had advanced into the centre of the room, where he stood rubbing his hands one against the other. Some men reach a high position through truculence, others through subservience, and Herr Haupsehr belonged to the second class. He was a little man with a bald head and with heavy pouches underneath his eyes. He fidgeted nervously, and it was hard to recognise in this obsequious figure the dictator of that letter of stern refusal.

"Yes," he said, "you are a friend of Herr Brumenhein?" In the eyes of Herr Haupsehr had appeared annoyance and a slight distrust at the sight of so young a visitor, but the sound of the magic name recalled him to servility.

"Yes," he repeated, "yes; and what is it that I may have the honour to do for a friend of Herr Brumenhein?"

Roland made no immediate reply. He drew off his gloves slowly, finger by finger, and placed them in the pockets of his great-coat, which garment he then proceeded to remove and lay across the back of one of the comfortable, deep arm-chairs. He then took out his pocket-book, abstracted from it a card and handed it to Herr Haupsehr. So far he had not spoken a word. Herr Haupsehr examined the card carefully, raising it towards the light, for he was shortsighted, and found the unusual English lettering trying to his eyes. He read out the words slowly: "Mr Roland Whately, Marston & Marston, Ltd." He stretched his head backwards, so that his gaze was directed towards the ceiling. "Mr Roland Whately, Marston & Marston, Ltd...." the name was familiar, but how and in what connection? There were so many names. He shook his head. He could not remember, but it did not matter. Roland had watched him anxiously; he had mistrusted that gaze towards the ceiling, and it was a big relief when Herr Haupsehr stretched out his hand and indicated one of the large arm-chairs—"And what is it that I can do for you?"

Roland then began to outline the scheme that had suggested itself to him. The scheme was to the advantage of the German as well as to himself. Haupsehr & Frohmann were the biggest dealers in polish in South Germany. That was granted. But there were rivals, very dangerous rivals, the more dangerous because they were specialists, each of them, in one particular line of polish, and a specialist was always better, if more expensive, than a general dealer. Now what Roland suggested was that Haupsehr should devote his attention solely to metal polish, should become specialists in a large sense, and that he should rely for the varnish solely on Marston & Marston.

"Don't worry about varnish," Roland said: "we'll let you have it a lot cheaper than these rivals of yours can produce it at. There won't be much actual profit in it for you, not directly, but it will allow you to put all your capital into the metal polish and, by smashing your rivals, it'll leave you with a clear market."

The German considered the plan. It was a good one, he could see its advantages. He would be trading, of course, with a nation for which he had no great affection, but, even so, Herr Brumenhein apparently thought well of it.

The Lonely Unicorn | 153

"Oh, yes, he thought it a capital idea," said Roland. "He's most anxious to see trade alliance between Great Britain and Germany. He's so afraid there may be ill-feeling. I told him that that was, of course, absurd, but still — —"

"Yes, yes," said Herr Haupsehr, "I see, of course; but there are difficulties, grave difficulties."

Roland could see that he was beginning to waver, that he was anxious to postpone his decision, and that would, of course, be fatal. Roland had learnt early that when a man says to you: "Look here, I can't decide now, but I'll write and let you know in a day or two," he has already decided against you. And so Roland played Herr Brumenhein for all he was worth. Having discovered that Herr Haupsehr had never met the great man, Roland felt himself at liberty to tell his story as amply as possible.

"But you should meet him," he said; "a most charming companion. He comes over and stays with us nearly every summer."

"Really! Every summer?"

"Oh, yes, nearly always. And he's the coming man, of course. Not a doubt of it. Griegenbach's day is done."

Herr Haupsehr affected surprise. He respected every minister till he was out of office.

"Oh, yes, not a doubt of it. He thinks he's more important than his job—a big mistake. A minister's post is more important than the man who fills it."

With that Herr Haupsehr agreed. Himself had revered authority all his life. This young man showed considerable sagacity. The job was bigger, always bigger, than the man.

"Yes, he's the coming man," Roland went on; "we can see it more clearly over in England perhaps than you can over here. If I were a German I would back Herr Brumenhein with every bit of influence I possessed."

And, indeed, so admirably did he present the future greatness of Herr Brumenhein that Herr Haupsehr got the impression that he had only to agree to these varnish proposals to be offered an important post in the ministry. It was not stated in so many words, but that was the suggestion. And, in the end, preliminary arrangements were drawn up and a contract signed. Herr Haupsehr showed Roland to the door with intense civility.

"And I was wondering," he said, "do you think it would be altogether wise if I were to write personally to Herr Brumenhein and tell him that I have met you and agreed to your plan? Would it be wise?" And he stood nervously fidgeting from one foot to the other—the eternal sycophant.

Roland scratched his chin thoughtfully. Then, after a moment's deliberation:

"No," he said. "On the whole, no. I don't think it would be wise. Herr Brumenhein is very busy. I think it would be better to wait till he visits us again in England and I shall tell him— —"

"You will tell him all about me and my willingness, yes?"

"Of course, of course."

"You are too kind, sir; too kind."

"Aufwiedersehn."

"Aufwiedersehn."

Hands were shaken, the door closed, and Roland was in the passage, the contract safe in his breast pocket.

With two such feats accomplished Roland should certainly have been returning home with a light heart. He would be praised and made much of. For at least a fortnight conversation would centre round his exploits. His return was that of a general entering his city after a successful battle—a Roman triumph. But for all that he was dispirited. On his journey out he had experienced the exhilaration of freedom, and on his return he was obsessed by the gloom of impending captivity. To what, after all, was he coming back?—worries, responsibilities, the continual clash of temperaments. How fine had been the independent life of vagabondage that he had just left, where he could do what he liked, go where he liked, be bound to no one. There had been a time when the sights and noises of London had been inexpressibly dear to him. His heart had beaten fast with rapture on his return from Fernhurst, when he had watched the green fields vanish beneath that sable shroud of roofs and chimney-stacks. But now there was no magic for him in the great city through which he was being so swiftly driven. Autumn had passed to winter; the plane-trees were bare; dusk was falling; the lamplighter had begun his rounds. For many it was a moment of hushed wonderment, of peace and benediction, but Roland stirred irritably in the corner of his cab, and there was no pleasure for him in the effusive welcome his mother accorded him. He did his best to respond to it, but it was a failure, and she noticed it.

"What's the matter, darling? Wasn't it a success? Didn't you do well over there?"

And behind her evident anxiety Roland detected, or fancied that he could detect, the suggestion of a hope that he had not done so well as he had expected.

"She would like to have comforted me," he thought. "Her husband has been a failure; he has had to depend upon her and so she has kept his love. She would like me to be the same." And this attitude, although he could understand it, exasperated him. He was aware that through his new friends he had become alienated from her, that she must be lonely now. But what would you? Life went that way.

They had tea together, and though Roland spoke amusingly and with animation about his experiences abroad, their talk was not intimate as it had been. There was nothing said behind and apart from their actual words, and Mrs Whately imagined that he was impatient to see April.

As soon as they had finished tea she suggested that he should go round to her.

"I'm sure you must be longing to see her."

And when he had gone, she sat for a little while in front of the unwashed tea-things thinking how hard it was that a mother should have to yield her son to another woman.

She need not have. Roland, at the moment when she was thinking of him with melancholy regret, was far from being "dissolved in pleasure and soft repose." He was sitting, as he had so often sat before, on the chair beside the window-seat, in which April was forlornly curled, while Mrs Curtis expressed, to complete his depression, her opinion on the economic situation in Europe. Soon she abandoned these matters of high finance and reverted to simple matters of to-day—namely, her son and her daughter. It was "dear April" and "dear Arthur"; and Roland was reminded vividly of a bawdy house in Brussels and the old woman who had sat beside the fire, exhibiting her wares. That was what Mrs Curtis was at heart. He could see her two thousand years earlier administering in some previous existence to the lusts of Roman soldiery: "Yes, a dear girl, Flavia; and Julia, she's nice; and if you like them plump Portia's a dear, sweet girl—so loving. Dacius Cassius said to me only yesterday...." Yes, that was what she was, and beneath her sentimentality how cold, how hard, how merciless, like that woman in Brussels who had taken eighty per cent. of the girls' money. He was continuing to draw comparisons with a vindictive pleasure when he observed that she was collecting her knitting preparatory to a move.

"But I know you two'll want to be together. I won't be a troublesome chaperon," she was saying; "I'll get out of your way. I expect you've lots to say to each other."

And before Roland quite knew what was happening he was alone with April. He turned towards her, and as her eyes met his she blushed a little and smiled, a shy, wavering smile that said: "I am here; take me if you want me, I am yours" — a smile that would have been to anyone else indescribably beautiful, but that to Roland, at that moment, appeared childish and absurd. He did not know what to say. He was in no mood for protestations and endearments. He could not act a lie. There was an embarrassing pause. April turned her face away from him. He said nothing, he did nothing. And then very distinctly, very slowly, like a child repeating a lesson:

"Did you have a good crossing?" The tension was broken; he began to talk quickly, eagerly, inconsequently — anything to prevent another such moment. And then Mrs Curtis came back and the conversation was monopolised, till Roland reminded her that it was seven o'clock and that he would have to be getting back.

"I haven't seen my father yet."

"Of course, of course. We mustn't keep him, must we, April?"

Roland took his leave, but April did not, as was usual, follow him to the door. She remained huddled in the window-seat, and did not even turn her head in his direction. She was angry with him, and no doubt with good cause, he reflected; but Mrs Curtis had gone so suddenly; he had been taken off his guard. Heavens! but what a home-coming!

He felt happier though next morning when he walked into the office of Marston & Marston. Everyone was pleased to see him back: the girls in the counting-house smiled at him. He was informed by the lift-boy that his cricket had been sadly missed during the later half of the season, and Mr Stevens literally leapt from his desk to shake him by the hand. It was ripping to see Gerald again, to come into his room and hear that quietly drawled: "Well, old son," and resume, as he had left it, their old friendship.

"The governor's awfully pleased with you," said Gerald, "never seen the old boy so excited over anything before. He's been talking about nothing else. He keeps on saying: 'The fellow who can make fifty runs in half-an-hour can run a business.' But I'm damned if I know how you did it. I've gone over there with carefully prepared introductions and had a chat with a few johnnies, but you seem to have gone pirating about, holding up Government officials and boosting into financiers' offices. How's it done?"

Roland laughed.

"That's my secret."

"You are welcome to it," said Gerald; "and tell me, did you have any real adventures?"

"One or two."

"Where? Good ones?"

"Not bad. Brussels, the usual place."

Gerald shook his head. "You should give it up, old son, it isn't worth it."

Roland laughed. "I like your talking! Why, I never knew such a fellow as you for women."

"For women, yes, but not professionals."

"That's much worse."

But Gerald shook his head. "No, it isn't, my son. No man ever got any good yet out of going with professionals."

But before Roland had had time to elucidate this riddle Mr Marston had entered the room. He took Roland's hand in his and shook it heartily.

"This is splendid, my dear fellow, splendid! They told me you'd come back and I knew where I should find you. It's good to have you back, and you've done splendidly—far better, I don't mind telling you, than any of us expected. We all looked on this as a sort of trial. But, my word, you've brought it off."

"I've been telling him, father, that you've been going round London saying that the man who can make fifty runs in half-an-hour is sure to be able to run a business."

"And it's true," said Mr Marston, "it's true. If a man's got the pluck to face a ticklish situation at cricket, he can do anything. Business is only bluff, like cricket, making the bowler think you're set when you're really expecting every ball will be your last. If I've said it to Gerald once I've said it fifty times. 'My boy,' I've said, 'if you don't do another stroke of work in your life you'll be worth a salary of five hundred pounds a year for having brought young Whately to us.' Now come along and let's go over those accounts."

They spent over an hour together, and at the end of it Mr Marston rose from his desk perfectly satisfied.

"As far as I can see you haven't made a slip. It's first class absolutely. Now, you run along to Perkins and settle up your personal accounts with him, and then we'll go out and have lunch somewhere together, the three of us, and you can spend the afternoon at home. I daresay your girl's been missing you."

"I haven't got a girl, sir."

"What! a young fellow like you not got a girl! We shall have to see about that. Why, at your age I seem to remember...." And the old man winked his eye and chuckled gaily.

Perkins received Roland with considerable politeness, mingled for the first time with respect, also, Roland suspected, with a more deep dislike.

"Well, so you're back, are you? And they all tell me you've been doing great things—interviewing Government officials."

"I've had a bit of luck."

"Useful luck?"

"I suppose so."

"And now you want me to have a look at the accounts?"

"That's it."

"Right; bring them along."

Roland laid out his personal accounts, his hotel bills, his railway fares, his entertaining expenses.

"And, as far as I can see," he said, "there's a balance of about thirteen pounds in your favour."

"We'll have a look and see," said Mr Perkins, and he began to scrutinise the accounts carefully, adding up every bill, and checking the amount of the German balance-sheet. Roland had taken a great deal of trouble over these accounts. He would not have minded making a few slips in the figures he had placed before Mr Marston, but he was desperately anxious to present no weak spot to Perkins.

"Yes, yes," said Perkins, "these seem to be all right, and there's a balance, as you say, of thirteen pounds, five and threepence."

"Right," said Roland, and began to count out the money.

"Yes, but as far as I can see, there aren't any—well, how shall I put it?—any special expense accounts here. I usually let one or two of them through all right."

"No, I've stated what all my charges are for."

"Well, then, aren't there one or two little things? Usually you young gentlemen like to have a few extras put down." And his face, that was turned to Roland's, assumed a cunning, knowing smile, an unpleasant smile, the smile of a man in a subservient position who enjoys the privilege of being able to confer a favour on his superior, and at the same time despises his superior for asking it. Roland had known that it was in exactly this way that Perkins would offer to slip through a special expense account. He knew that by accepting this offer he would place himself eternally in Perkins's debt. That, as in Gerald's case, there would be between them an acknowledged confederacy. This he would never have. He had, as a matter of fact, incurred very few of the special expenses to which Perkins referred. He had worked hard; he had been alone. Solitary indulgence is never very exciting; one wants companionship, as in everything, and so he had confined his excesses to a couple of visits to a discreet establishment in Brussels, of which he had decided to defray the cost himself.

He was able, therefore, to meet Perkins's leer with a look of puzzled interrogation.

"I don't quite understand, Mr Perkins. I think you've all my accounts there, and I owe you thirteen pounds, five shillings and threepence; perhaps you'll give me a receipt."

In the look that they exchanged as Mr Perkins respectfully handed Roland the receipt, each recognised the beginning of a long antagonism.

"Thanks very much, Mr Perkins."

Roland walked out of the room jauntily. He had had the best of the first skirmish.

This victory put him on excellent terms with himself, and, later, a bottle of excellent Burgundy at lunch wooed him to so kindly a sympathy for his fellow-beings that any leader of advanced political opinions would have found him an easy victim to any theory of world-brotherhood. As, however, no harbinger of the new world accosted him on his way from the City to Charing Cross Station, Roland was free to focus his entire sympathy upon the forlorn figure of April. He thought of her suddenly just outside Terry's

Theatre, and the remembrance of his behaviour to her on the night before caused him to collide violently with an elderly gentleman who was walking in the opposite direction. But he did not stop to apologise; his sentimentality held a mirror to his guilt. What a selfish beast he had been. How miserable he must have made her. She must have so looked forward to his return. He had hardly written to her while he had been away. Poor little April, so sweet, so gentle. A wave of tenderness for her consumed him. They had shared so much together; he had confided in her his hopes and his ambitions. He worked himself into a temper of self-abasement. He must go to her at once and beg forgiveness.

He found her sitting in the arm-chair before the fire. She raised her eyes in mild amazement, surprised that he should visit her at such a time. She did not know how she should comport herself. Her dignity told her that she should rise and receive him coldly, but her instinct counselled her to remain seated and hear what he had to say. She obeyed her instinct. Roland flung his hat and stick on the cushioned window-seat and precipitated himself at her feet. She tried to push him away, but his voice murmuring the word "darling" overmastered her, and she let him put his arms round her and draw her head upon his shoulder.

"I feel such a beast, April, such a beast. All the day I have been cursing myself and wondering what on earth possessed me. I don't know what it was. But all the time I've been away I've been so looking forward to seeing you again. When I was all alone and unhappy I said to myself: 'Never mind, April's waiting,' and I thought how wonderful to see you again, and then— —Oh, I don't know, but when I came here last night and found your mother here—I don't know! All the time I was dying to speak to you, and she would go on talking, and I got more and more annoyed. And then, I don't know how it happened, but I found myself getting angry with you because of your mother."

"But you mustn't, Roland, really you mustn't. You shouldn't speak of mother like that; you know how good she's been to us."

"Oh, yes, I know it, of course I do. But can't you see what it was like last night for me coming back to you, and wanting you, and then to hear only your mother; and by the time she left us alone I had got so bad tempered that— —"

"Yes, you weren't very nice, were you?"

And he had begun to pour out a further torrent of explanation when he saw that a sly, mischievous smile was playing round the corners of her mouth and that she was no longer angry.

"Then you'll forgive me?" he said.

"But I don't know about that."

"Oh, but you have, haven't you? I know you have."

She began to remonstrate, to say that she had not forgiven him, that he had been most unkind to her, but she made no resistance when his hand slipped slowly round her neck and turned her face to his. And as he raised it, she pouted ever so slightly her lips towards those that sank to meet them. As their mouths met she passed one hand behind his head and pressed it down to her. It was a long embrace, and when she drew back from it, the lustre of her eyes had grown dimmed and misty.

"You've never kissed me like that before," she said.

"Perhaps I've never really loved you before."

"Oh, but I should hate to think that."

"But why?"

"Oh, I don't know. I'm silly, but if you only love me now, then before— oh, it doesn't matter, you love me now, don't you?"

And he answered her in the only possible way.

One hour they had together, an hour of rich enchantment. The blinds were drawn, the lamp unlighted; she sat on the floor with the firelight playing over her, leant back against him while he told her of Bruges and its waterways, the proud boulevards of Brussels, the great cathedral at Köln, the noble sweep of the Rhine and the hills on either side of it. She followed little of what he said to her; it was enough for her, after three long months, to be soothed by his presence, to hear his voice, to hold his hand in hers, and to feel from time to time his breath grow warm upon her neck and cheek as he bent to kiss her. It was the tenderest hour their love had brought to them.

But for Roland it was followed by a reaction. He felt, in a confused manner, that he had been playing a part, that he had said what was but half true. He had certainly been exasperated by Mrs Curtis's conversation, but it was her talk, the supreme futility of her talk, that had exasperated him. It had annoyed him in itself and not as being a barrier between himself and April. He had told a lie.

And it was not for the first time, he reminded himself. Half lies had been an essential part of their love-making. At every crisis of their relationship he had tampered with the truth. He had told her he had only made love to Dolly because she had rejected him that evening at the ball. He had told her that it was her belief in him that had inspired his success at Hogstead. He had mistaken the fraction for the whole. Were they never to meet on terms of common honesty? What was their love worth if it had to live on lies?

He returned home to find the drawing-room fire almost out.

"Will these servants never do their work?" he grumbled.

That evening the soup plates happened to be cold and the joint overdone.

"It gets worse every day," he said. "I don't know what that girl thinks she's paid for. She never does anything right."

And when he went upstairs to turn on a bath he discovered that all the hot water had been used in washing up the plates. He returned to the drawing-room in a fury of impatience.

"I do wish, mother," he said, "that you'd explain to Lizzie that there's no need for her to wash herself as well as the plates in that sink of hers."

"And I wish you wouldn't grumble the whole time, Roland," his mother retorted. "Lizzie's got a great deal to do. She has to do the cooking as well as the housework. I think that, on the whole, she manages very well."

"I am glad you think so," said Roland, and walked out of the room.

Next morning he found on his plate a letter from Mrs Marston, inviting him down for the week-end.

"It seems such a long time since that cricket week," she wrote, "and we all want to congratulate you on your splendid work. So do come."

He handed the letter across to his mother.

She raised her eyebrows interrogatively.

"Well, dear?"

"Of course I shall go."

She did not answer him, and he read in her silence a disapproval.

"You don't want me to," he said.

"I don't mind, dear. It's for you to decide."

"But you'd rather I didn't?"

"Well, dear, I was only thinking that as you've been away from us for three months, and...."

"Yes, mother, and what?"

"Well, dear, to go away, the very first week-end."

"But you'll be seeing lots of me all the week."

"I wasn't thinking of us, though of course we like to have you here. It was April; don't you think it might rather hurt her feelings?"

"Oh, bother April!"

"But, dear...."

"I know, mother, but it's April this and April that; it's nothing but April."

His mother raised to him a surprised, grieved face, but she made no answer, and Roland, standing beside the table, experienced the sensation of an anxious actor who has finished his speech in the middle of the stage and does not know how to reach the wings.

"You see, mother," he began, but she raised a hand to stop him.

"No, dear, don't explain: I understand."

He cursed himself, as he walked to the bus, for his ill-temper. What a beast he was—first to April, then to his mother; the two people for whom he cared most in the world. What was wrong? Why was he behaving like this? It had not been always so. At school he had had a reputation for good-naturedness—"a social lubricant," someone had called him—and at Hogstead he was still the same, cheerful, good-humoured, willing to do anything for anyone else. He became his old self in the company of Gerald and his father and the light-hearted, irresponsible Muriel. It was only at Hammerton that he was irritable and quick to take offence. His ill-humour fell away from him, however, the moment he reached the office.

"Well, old son," said Gerald, "and did you get a letter from the mater this morning?"

"Yes."

"And you're coming?"

"Well, I don't know yet."

"Oh, but of course you are. They'll all be fearfully annoyed if you don't, especially Muriel——"

"Muriel! Why, what did she say?"

"Nothing particular as far as I remember, but she seemed frightfully keen. She says you're the only one of my friends she's any use for. She finds them too stuck up—middle-aged at twenty she calls them. So you'll have to come."

"I suppose I shall."

"Of course you will. Sit down and write a note this minute, so that there's no chance of your thinking better."

When Roland returned home that night his mother made no reference to the scene at the breakfast table. They spoke at dinner of indifferent things, politics and personalities; but there was a brooding atmosphere of disquiet. Not until nearly bedtime did Ronald announce his intention of going down to Hogstead. His mother's reply expressed neither reproach nor disappointment.

"Yes, dear," she said; "well, I hope you'll enjoy yourself."

And just because her voice was even and unchallenging, Roland felt that he had to give some explanation.

"You see, mother, Mr Marston is, after all, my boss, and these visits— well, they're rather a royal command. They'd be a bit annoyed if I didn't go."

"Of course, dear, of course. We only want you to do what you think best."

But he knew that she was disappointed. She was right, too. He supposed he ought really to have stayed at home and gone for a walk with April. He felt guilty in his attitude towards April, guilty and, in a way, resentful, resentful against these repeated demands on his time and energy, against this assumption of an unflagging passion, an eternal intoxication. And yet he did feel guilty. Was he treating her as a boy ought to treat his girl? How rarely, for example, had he ever taken her anywhere. Ah, well, that at least he could remedy.

Next day, during his lunch hour, he went round to the box office of the Adelphi and bought three stalls for Thursday night. He returned home with the happy air of one that carries a delightful surprise in his pocket.

"Mother," he said, "what are you doing on Thursday night?"

"Nothing, dear, as far as I know."

"Well, would you like to come out somewhere with me?"

"You know I always like to go out anywhere with you."

"And April?"

"Of course, dear."

"Well, then, what do you say to a dinner in Soho and the Adelphi afterwards?"

"But, dear—oh, you don't mean it?"

"Yes, I do, mother. I wanted to celebrate my return, so I got the three seats. I've booked the table, and there we are."

Her face flushed with pleasure.

"Oh, but you shouldn't have, really you shouldn't, and you don't want me."

"Of course we do, mother, and anyhow we could hardly go alone."

"And have you told April?"

"No, I'm just off to tell her."

He bent down, kissed her, then straightened himself and ran out of the room. She heard his footsteps clatter on the stairs, then move about in the bedroom above her, and then once more clatter on the stairs. She sighed, her eyes dimming a little, but glad, inexpressibly glad, that he should still need her in his happiness.

Roland found April alone.

"I've got a surprise for you," he said.

"What is it?"

"What do you think?"

"A box of chocolates."

"Do you want a box of chocolates?"

"I should like one."

"Right! Then I'll go and get you one." And he turned towards the door, but she ran after him and caught him by the sleeve of his coat.

"Don't be silly," she said; "come back!"

"But you said you wanted a box of chocolates."

"But I want to know what your surprise is first?"

"Well, then, have a look in my pockets and see if you can find it."

She put both her hands in his coat pockets, and quickly, before she knew what he was doing, his arms were round her, and he had drawn her close to him. Her hands were prisoners in his pockets and she was powerless. Slowly he put his face to hers and kissed her.

"That's not fair," she said.

"It's very nice."

"I daresay, but I want to know what your surprise is?"

For answer he placed the envelope in her hand; she looked puzzled, but when she had opened it she gave a little cry of delight.

"Oh, Roland, how dear of you!"

"Then you'll come?"

"Of course. Oh, Roland, dear! It's years since I went to a theatre. I shall love it."

He was delighted with the success of his plan. He felt happy and confident. How pretty, how charming April was; how much he was in love with her. He took her on his knee and insisted on rearranging her hair.

"But you're only making it worse," she complained.

"Oh, no, I'm not; I'm getting on splendidly. You just wait and see," and he continued to stroke her hair, dividing it so that he could kiss her neck.

"It's in an awful state," she said, "and someone is sure to come before I can tidy it."

"Don't you worry," he said, drawing his fingers along the curved roll of hair. And then suddenly it all came down; the long tresses fell in a cascade about them, covering them in a fine brown net.

"Oh, you beast, you beast!" she said, struggling to get up.

But he held her close.

"Oh, no; it's ripping like that. You look lovely."

"Do I?"

"And, look, I can kiss you through your hair," and he drew a thin curl across her mouth and laid his upon it, moving his lips slightly up and down till he had drawn the hair into their mouths and their lips could meet.

"But you did it on purpose, I'm sure you did. It couldn't have happened like that of its own, all of a sudden."

"Well, what if it didn't! You look simply ripping."

She laughed happily, hiding her face upon his shoulder.

"It's very wrong of you, though."

"What! wrong to make you look pretty!"

And she could not refrain from kissing him.

"What would mother say?"

"She's out."

"But if she came in?"

"She won't."

"Well, at any rate, I shall have to go and put it up."

"No, please don't."

"But suppose someone comes in?"

"They won't. And besides, if they did, they ought to think themselves jolly lucky; you look simply lovely!"

"Do I?" The words came in a soft whisper from lips almost touching his.

"As always." The hand that lay in his pressed tightly. "You'll stay like that, won't you?"

"If you're good."

"Darling!"

He did not tell her about the dinner. He suggested that he should call for her at six, and she was too excited at the time to take into account so material a consideration as food. But her eyes sparkled with pleasure when he took her into the little Soho restaurant where he had booked a table. She had never been in such a place before and her delight in the unfamiliar room and food was joy to Roland. For her it was a place of mystery and enchantment. She asked him hurried, excited questions: What sort of people came here? Did he think the lady in the corner was an actress? Who had painted the brightly coloured fresco? He persuaded her to take half-a-glass of wine; she sipped at it in a fascinating, nervous manner, with little pecks, as though she thought it were going to burn her, and between each sip she would smile at Roland over the rim of the wine-glass. As she sat she flung to left and right quick, eager glances at the waiter, the hangings, the occupants of the other tables. Her excitement charmed Roland. It was like seeing a child play with a new toy. In a way, too, it was an excitant to his vanity, a tribute to his manhood, to his superior knowledge of the world. And in the theatre, when the light was turned out, he sat close to her and held her hand tightly at the moments of dramatic tension; and when she marvelled at the beauty of the heroine he whispered in her ear: "Nothing like as pretty as you are!" And Mrs Whately, sitting on the other side of Roland, glanced at them from time to time with a kind indulgence, remembering her youth, and her early love-making. It was a memorably happy evening. When Roland walked back with April and kissed her good-night in the doorway she said nothing, but her hand clenched tightly on the lapel of his coat. And when he returned home he saw in his mother's eye an expression of love and gratitude that had not been there for a long while.

He walked upstairs in a mood of deep contentment. After he had undressed he stood for a moment at the open window, looking out over the roofs and chimney-stacks of London. Behind a few window-panes glowed the faint light of a candle or a lamp, but the majority of the houses were obscured in darkness. Hammerton was asleep. But the confused murmur of traffic and the faint red glow in the sky reminded him that the true London, the London that he loved, was only now waking to a night of pleasure. Ah, well, to-morrow he would be at Hogstead. He flung back his arms with the proud relief of one who has fulfilled his obligations and is at liberty to take his own enjoyment.

CHAPTER XVI
LILITH AND MURIEL

Roland was in the true holiday mood as he stepped into the afternoon train to Hogstead. He had before him the prospect of sixty hours of real happiness. He would be made much of, he would be congratulated, he would be able, on occasions, to lead the conversation. It was no small feat that he had accomplished. He had won the appreciation of a family that was satisfied with itself and was inclined to regard its own achievements as the summit of human ability and ambition. It had been simple in comparison to make an impression on April—a dinner in a Soho restaurant. Muriel and Beatrice would have accepted such an evening as a matter of course, an affair of everyday occurrence. His heart beat quickly as he thought of Beatrice. Would she be there, he wondered. Would she have heard of his success? What effect would it have made on her? She might regard it as much or little. One never knew. Muriel, though, had been impressed; that he knew for certain. It would be great fun receiving her congratulations. He thought of her as he had left her four months ago, a tousle-headed Muriel, a little girl who had charmed him with her chatter and had been so unexpectedly petulant when he had questioned her about her aunt. He had not realised that at seventeen four months make a big difference with a girl. No one had told him that she had put her hair up and that her skirts would only reveal the instep of her ankle. He had left her a girl and she had become a woman.

She was the first person he saw on his arrival. A footman had just taken his bag and was helping him off with his coat when the drawing-room door opened, there was a rustle of skirts, and Muriel came impulsively to greet him.

He drew back in surprise at the sight of her tall, graceful figure, with the long, tightly fitting skirt and hair no longer tossing mischievously about her shoulders, but gathered behind her neck in a long, wide curve.

"What's the matter, Roland?" she asked.

"But, Muriel," he said.

"Well?"

"You are so changed."

She broke into a peal, a silvery peal, of laughter.

"So you have noticed it? We wondered whether you would. Mother thought you would, but I said you wouldn't. And Gerald had a bet with father about it and he's won, so he'll have to take us all to a theatre. Come and tell them about it."

Roland followed her in amazement. The change in her was so unexpected. He had always looked on her as a little girl whom he had teased and played with, and now, suddenly, in a night, she had grown up into a daughter of that other world of which he had caught fleeting, enticing glimpses at restaurants and theatres. He watched her as she laughed and talked, unable to realise that this was the little girl with whom he had played last summer. And yet to him she was unaltered. She offered him the same frank comradeship. She took him for a walk after tea and spoke with real enthusiasm of his success.

"I can't say how glad I am, Roland. I was so awfully anxious for you to come off. I was so afraid something might go wrong. I think it's wonderful of you."

Her words thrilled him. It was something to win the admiration of a girl like Muriel. April was naturally impressed by his achievements. Of course it would be wonderful to her that he should visit great cities and dabble in high finance. It was like a fairy story that had come true. But Muriel had spent all her life in that world. She had travelled; her parents were rich. She was accustomed to the jargon of finance. It would have been a feat for him, a newcomer to that world, to have proved himself able to move comfortably there, but to have impressed her with his achievements ... and when she began to ask him how he had manœuvred those big interviews his flattered vanity could not allow him to hold his secret.

"But I've told no one," he said, "not even my people."

"That's all the more reason why you should tell me."

"Will you promise to keep it a secret?"

"On my honour."

And so he told her of his fortune and adroitness, how he had met Monsieur Rocheville in the restaurant and how he had tricked Herr Haupsehr with the magic name of Brumenhein. She laughed heartily and asked him questions. What would happen if the two ever met?

"The Lord knows," said Roland. "But in the meantime we shall have sold many gallons of varnish, and perhaps we shall have become indispensable to the old fellow."

They made no mention during their walk of Beatrice. For some unexplained reason Roland had felt shy of asking Muriel whether she was to be one of the party. He had been content to wait and, on their return, he experienced, as he pushed open the drawing-room door, a sudden surprising anxiety. Would Beatrice be there? He assumed composure, but he could not prevent his eyes travelling quickly round the room in search of her. When he saw that she was not there he felt a sudden emptiness, a genuine disappointment. She would not be coming, then. And now that she was not there half his excitement, his enthusiasm, was gone. He sat beside Mrs Marston and discussed, without interest, the costliness of Brussels lace, and wondered how soon he could conveniently go and change for dinner. The minutes dragged by.

And then at last, in that half-hour when the room was slowly emptying, the door opened and he saw Beatrice, her slim figure silhouetted against the dull red wall-paper of the hall. His heart almost stopped beating. Would she notice him, he wondered. Had she forgotten their lunch together? Had the growing intimacy between them been dispelled by a four months' absence? He watched her walk slowly into the room, her hair, as ever, disordered about her neck and temples, and on her features that look of difference, of being apart, of belonging to another world, that appearance of complete detachment. Then suddenly she saw Roland, and smiled and walked quickly forward, her hand stretched out to him.

"I've been hearing so much about you," she said. "They tell me you've been doing wonderful things. Come and sit with me over here and tell me all about it."

And once again the love of vanity prompted him to confess his secret.

"But you won't tell anyone, will you?" he implored.

She smiled. "If I can keep my own secrets, surely I can keep yours," she said. Then, after a pause, "And they tell me Gerald won his bet."

He blushed hotly. "Yes."

"I knew he would," she said, and she leant forward, as she had at the restaurant, her hands pillowing her chin, her eyes fixed on his.

Roland laughed nervously. "But I don't see why," he began.

She shook her head. "That's the mistake all you men make. You think a woman sees nothing unless she's not watching you the whole time. But she does."

It flattered him to be included under the general heading of "you men." And at that moment Muriel came into the room. She was wearing a low evening dress, wonderfully charming in her new-found womanhood. Roland's eyes followed her in admiration.

"Isn't she pretty?" he said. "That pale blue dress; it's just right. It goes well with her complexion. Pale colours always do."

Beatrice did not answer for a moment; then she gave a little sigh. "Yes, very pretty. I envy her."

Roland turned quickly to her a look of surprised interrogation.

"But you! Why, you look younger than any of us."

She shrugged her shoulders. "Perhaps; but what's the use of it to me? Ah, don't say anything, please. You mustn't waste your time on me. Go on and talk to Muriel."

Dinner that evening was a jovial meal. Muriel having announced with due solemnity that Gerald had won his bet, she proceeded to decide at what theatre Mr Marston should fulfil his obligation.

"And don't you think," said Muriel, "that Roland ought to come with us? If it weren't for him we shouldn't be going at all."

"I suppose he ought, the young rascal, though I can't think why he should have spotted it. Muriel was an untidy little scamp when he went away, and she's an untidy little scamp now he's come back."

"Oh, father!"

"Yes, you are. You can't tell what's on purpose with you and what isn't; you're all over the place."

It was perfectly untrue, of course, but they laughed all the same.

"That's a poor excuse, father," said Gerald. "I knew he'd spot it. It's through spotting things like that that he manages to wangle interviews with all these pots."

"Perhaps it is, perhaps it is; I'm bothered if I know how he does it." And Roland and Muriel exchanged a swift glance of confederacy: a feeling that was increased when the last post arrived and Mr Marston interrupted the general conversation with a piece of news his letter had brought him.

"My dear, here's a funny thing. I never saw it in the papers, though I suppose it must have been in them. But that fellow Brumenhein is dead."

"Brumenhein!"

"Yes, you know—the fellow whom the Kaiser thought such a lot of. People said he might very likely supplant Griegenbach."

"I didn't dare look at you," Roland said to Muriel afterwards. "I couldn't have kept a straight face if I had."

"And what a bit of luck."

"It may save me a lot of unpleasantness later on."

"You're a wonderful boy."

They were saying good-night to each other on the landing, and Muriel, who slept on the second floor, was standing on the stairs, leaning over the banisters. Her words made Roland feel very brave and confident.

"And to think that you didn't expect me to notice that you had put your hair up!"

He meant it as a joking repartee to her compliment, but the moment after he had said it he felt frightened. They looked at each other and said nothing. There was a moment of chill, intense embarrassment, then Muriel gave a nervous laugh and, turning quickly, ran up to her bedroom.

PART IV
ONE WAY OR ANOTHER

CHAPTER XVII
THREE YEARS

The next three years of Roland's life were an amplification of those three days, and nothing would be gained by a detailed description of them. The narrative would be cut across frequently by visits to Europe, dropped threads would have to be gathered up, relationships reopened. The action was delayed, interrupted and, at times, held up altogether. The trips abroad were always altering Roland's perspective, and the sense of distance made him reconsider his attitude. Four months after the events described in the last chapter he had reached a state of acute reaction against his home, his parents and, in a way, against April, because of her connection with that world from which he was endeavouring to escape. Very little was needed to drive him into declared revolt, but at that moment he was sent abroad and, once abroad, everything became different. He began to accuse himself of selfishness and ingratitude. His parents had denied themselves comfort and pleasure to send him to an expensive school; they had given him everything. Like the pelican, they had gone hungry so that he should be full. Since he could remember, the life of that family had centred round him. Every question had been considered on the bearing it would have on his career. Was this the manner of repayment? And it was the same with April. He forgot her mother and her home; he remembered only her beauty and her love for him, her fixed, unwavering love, and the dreams that they had shared. He always returned home in a temper of sentimentality, full of good resolutions, promising himself that he would be gentle and sympathetic to his parents, that he would never swerve from his love for April. The first days were invariably soft and sweet: but in a short time the old conflict reasserted itself; the bright world of Hogstead stood in dazzling contrast to the unromantic Hammerton. He became irritated, as before, by the trifling inconveniences of a house that lacked a parlourmaid; unpunctual, unappetising meals; and, more especially, by the endless friction imposed on him by the company of men and women who had been harassed all their lives by the fret and worry of small houses and small incomes. Trivial, ignoble troubles, that was the misfortune of everyone fated to live in Hammerton. And April was a part of it. He was very fond of her; indeed, he still thought he was in love with her, but love for Roland was dependent on many other things, was bound up with his other enthusiasms and reactions. He enjoyed her company and her caresses. In her presence he was capable of genuine tenderness; but it was so easy. April responded so simply to any kindness shown to her. There was no uncertainty about her. He missed the swift anger of the chase.

More and more frequently he found himself receiving and accepting invitations to spend the week-end at Hogstead; and always when he announced his intention of going there he was aware of silent criticism on the part of his parents. He felt guilty and ashamed of himself for feeling guilty. It became a genuine struggle for him to pronounce the words at breakfast. It was like confessing a secret, and he hated it. Had he not a right to choose his friends? Then would come a reaction of acute self-accusation and he would improvise a treat, a theatre or a picnic. His emotions would fling it like a sop to his conscience: "There, does that content you? Now may I go and live my own life?" Afterwards, of course, he was again bitterly ashamed of himself.

But always on the ebb-flow of his contrition came fear—the instinct of self-preservation, to save, at all costs, his individuality from the fate that threatened it. Whenever things seemed likely to reach a head, a European trip would intervene, and the whole business would have to begin again. An action that would ordinarily have completed its rhythm within three or four months was lengthened into three years; in the end inevitably the curve of the parabola was reached. The time was drawing near when Roland would have to make his decision one way or another.

He was by now earning a salary of four hundred pounds a year, and marriage—marriage as his parents understood it—was well within his means. Up till now, whenever any suggestion about the date of his marriage had been advanced, he referred to the uncertain nature of his work.

"I never know where I'm going to be from one week to another. Marriage is out of the question for a chap with a job like that."

Their engagement was still unannounced. He had retained that loophole, though at the time it was not so that he had regarded it.

Ralph had asked him once whether he was engaged. And the question had put him on his guard. He didn't like engagements. Love was a secret between two people. Why make it public? He must strike before the enemy struck. In other words, he must come to an agreement with April before her mother opened negotiations. That evening he had brought up the subject.

He was sitting in the window-seat, while she was on a stool beside him, her head resting against his knees and his hand stroking slowly her neck and hair and cheek.

"You know, darling," he said, "I've been thinking about our engagement."

"Yes, dear."

"Well, are you awfully keen on an engagement?"

"But how do you mean? We shall have to be engaged some time, shan't we?"

"Oh, of course, yes. But there's no need for a long engagement, is there? What I mean is that we could easily get engaged now if we wanted to. But it would be a long business, and oh, I don't know! Once we're engaged our affairs cease to be our own. People will be asking us 'When's the happy day?' and all that sort of thing. Our love won't be our own any longer."

"It's just as you like, dear."

It was so nice to sit there against his knee, with his fingers against her face. Why should they worry about things? It would be nice to be engaged, of course, and to have a pretty ring, but it didn't matter. "It's just as you like," she had said, and they had left it at that over two years ago and there had been no reason to rediscuss it. But he knew that now the whole matter would have to be brought up. It had been decided that he was to remain in London for a couple of years in charge of the Continental branch; he would have to go abroad occasionally, but there would be no more long trips. He was in a position to marry if he wanted to. His family would expect him to, those of his friends who had heard of the "understanding" would expect him to, Mrs Curtis would expect him to, and he owed it to April that he should marry her. For years now he had kept her waiting. There was not the slightest doubt as to what was his duty.

Nothing, however, could alter the fact that there was nothing in the world that he wanted less than this marriage. It would mean an end to all those pleasant week-ends at Hogstead. It was one thing to invite a young bachelor who was no trouble to look after and who was amusing company; it was quite another thing to entertain a married couple. He would no longer be able to throw into his business that undivided energy of his. He would not be free; he would have to play for safety. As his friendship with the Marstons began to wane, he would become increasingly every year an employee and not an associate. He would belong to the ruled class. And it would be the end, too, of his pleasant little dinner-parties with Gerald. He would have to be very careful with his money. They would be fairly comfortable in a small house for the first year or so, but from the birth of their first child their life would become complicated with endless financial worries and would begin to resemble that of his own father and mother, till, finally, he would lose interest in himself and begin to live in his children. What a world! The failure of the parent became forgotten in the high promise of the child, and that child grew up only to meet and be broken by the conspiracy of the world's wisdom and, in its turn, to focus its thwarted ambitions on its children, and then its children's children. That was the eternal cycle of disillusion; whatever happened he must break that wheel.

But the battle appeared hopeless. The forces were so strong that were marshalled against him. What chance did he stand against that mingled appeal of sentiment and habit? All that spring he felt himself standing upon a rapidly crumbling wall. Whenever he went down to Hogstead he kept saying to himself: "Yes, I'm safe now, secure within time and space. But it's coming. Nothing can stop it. Night follows day, winter summer; one can't fight against the future, one can't anticipate it. One has to wait; it chooses its own time and its own place." At the office he was fretful and absent-minded.

"What's the matter with you?" Gerald asked him once.

"Nothing."

"Oh, but there must be, you've been awfully queer the last week or so."

Roland did not answer, and there was an awkward silence.

"I say, old man, I don't quite like asking you, but you're not in debt or anything, are you? Because if you are, I mean——"

"Oh, no, really. I'm not even 'overdrawn.'"

In Gerald's experience of the world there were two ills to which mankind was heir—money and woman. The subdivisions of these ills were many, but he recognised no other main source. If Roland was not in debt, then there was a woman somewhere, and later in the day he brought the matter up again.

"I say, old son, you've not been making an ass of yourself with some woman, have you? No one's got hold of you, have they?"

"Lord, no!" laughed Roland. "I only wish they had!"

But Gerald raised a warning finger.

"Touch wood, my son. Don't insult Providence. You can take my word for it that sooner or later some woman will get hold of you and then it's the devil, the very devil. Did I ever tell you about the girl at Broadstairs?" And there ensued the description of a seaside amour, followed by some shrewd generalities on the ways of a man with—but to conclude the quotation would be hardly pertinent. At any rate, Gerald told his story and pointed his moral.

"You may take my word for it, adultery is a whacking risk. It's awfully jolly while it lasts, and you think yourself no end of a dog when you offer the husband a cigar, but sooner or later the wife clings round the bed-post and says: 'Darling, I have deceived you!' And then you're in it, up to the ruddy neck!"

Roland laughed, as he always did, at Gerald's stories, but it hurt him to think that his friend should have noticed a change in him. If he was altered already by a few weeks of Hammerton, what would he be like in five years' time after the responsibilities of marriage had had their way with him? And marriage was not for five years, but for fifty.

He never spoke to Gerald of April now. There had been a time in the early days of their friendship when he had confided in him, under an oath of secrecy, that he hoped to marry her as soon as his position permitted. And Gerald had agreed with him that it was a fine thing to marry young, "and it's the right thing for you," he added; "some fellows are meant for marriage and others aren't. I think you're one of the ones that are." A cryptic statement that Roland had, at the time, called in question, but Gerald only laughed. "I may be wrong," he had said, "one never knows, but I don't think I am." Often afterwards he had asked Roland about April and whether they were still in love with each other as much as ever, and Roland, his vanity flattered by the inquiry, had assured him of their constancy. But of late, when Gerald had made some light reference to "the fair April," Roland had changed the conversation, or, if a question were asked, had answered it obliquely, or managed to evade it, so that Gerald had realised that the subject was no longer agreeable to him, and, being blessed with an absence of curiosity, had dropped it from his repertoire of pleasantries. But he did not connect April with his friend's despondency.

CHAPTER XVIII
THREE DAYS

The summer was nearly over, however, before the crisis came. It was on a Friday evening in the beginning of September, and Roland was sitting with his mother, as was usual with them, for a short talk after his father had gone to bed. He could tell that something was worrying her. Her conversation had been disjointed and many of her remarks irrelevant. And suddenly his instinct warned him that she was going to speak to him about April. He went suddenly still. If someone had thrown a stone at him at that moment he would have been unable to move out of the way of it. He could recollect distinctly, to the end of his life, everything that had passed through his mind during that minute of terrifying silence that lay between his realisation of what was coming and the first sound of that opening sentence.

"Roland, dear, I hope you won't mind my mentioning it, but your father and I have been talking together about you and April."

He could remember everything: the shout of a newsboy in the street—"Murder in Tufnell Park!" the slight rustle of the curtain against the window-sill; the click of his mother's knitting-needles. And, till that moment, he had never noticed that the pattern of the carpet was irregular, that on the left side there were seven roses and five poppies and on the right six roses and six poppies. They had had that carpet for twenty years and he had never noticed it before. His eyes were riveted on this curious deformity, while through the window came the shriek of the newsboy—"Murder in Tufnell Park!" Then his mother's voice broke the tension. The moment had come; he gathered his strength to him. As he had walked five years earlier, with unflinching head, up the hill to Carus Evans, so now he answered his mother with an even voice:

"Yes, mother?"

"Well, dear, we've been thinking that you really ought to be settling something definite about yourself and April."

"But we didn't want to be engaged, mother."

"I wasn't thinking of that, dear. I know about that. It's a modern idea, I suppose, though I think myself that it would have been better some time ago, but it's not an engagement so much we're thinking of as of your marriage."

It was more sudden than Roland had expected.

"Oh, but—oh, surely Mrs Curtis would never agree. She'd say we were much too young."

"Well, that's what we thought, but I went round and saw her the other day, and she quite agreed with us that it was really no good waiting any longer. You are making a lot of money, and it's quite likely that Mr Marston will raise your salary when he hears you're going to be married; and after all, why should you wait? As I said to your father: 'They've known each other for a long time, and if they don't know their minds now they never will.'"

Roland did not know what to say. He was unarmed by a sympathy and kindness against which he could not fight.

"It's awfully decent of you." Those were the only words that occurred to him, and he knew, even as he uttered them, that they were not only completely inadequate, but pitifully inexpressive of his state of mind.

"We only want to do what will make you happy, and it is happier to marry young, really it is!"

He made a last struggle.

"But, mother, don't you think that for April's sake—she's so young. Isn't it rather hard on her to be loaded with responsibilities so early?"

"It's nice of you to think that, Roland. It shows you really care for her; but I think that in the end, when she's an old woman like I am, she'll be glad she married young."

And then, because Roland looked still doubtful, she offered him the benefit of what wisdom the narrow experiences of her life had brought her. She had never unlocked her heart before; it hurt her to do it now and her eyes welled with tears. But she felt that, at this great crisis of his life, she must be prepared to lay before her son everything that might help him in it. It might be of assistance to him to know how these things touched a woman, and so she told him how she too had once thought it cruel that responsibilities should have been laid on her so soon.

"I was only nineteen when I married your father, and things were very difficult at first. It was a small house, we had no servant, and I had to get up early in the morning and light the fires and get the breakfast things ready, and all the morning I had to scrub and brush and wash up. I had no friends.

And then, after tea, I used to lie down for an hour and rest, I was so tired, and I wanted to look fresh and pretty for your father when he came home. And there were times when I thought it was unfair; that I should have been allowed to be free and happy and unworried like other girls of my age. I used to see some of my school friends very occasionally and they used to tell me of their balls and parties, and I was so envious. And then very often your father was irritable and bad-tempered when he came back, and he found fault with my cooking, and I used to go away and cry all by myself and wonder why I was doing it, working so hard and for nothing. And then I began to think he didn't love me any more; there was another girl: she was fresher; she didn't have to do any housework. There was nothing in it; it never came to anything. Your father was always faithful; he's always been very good to me, but I could see from the way his face lighted up when she came into the room that he was attracted by her, and I can't tell you how it hurt me. I used to think that he preferred that other girl, that he thought her prettier than I was. It wasn't easy those first three years. When you've been married three years you're almost certain to regret it and think you could have done better with someone else, but after ten years you'll know very well that you couldn't, because, Roland, love doesn't last; not what you mean by love; but something takes its place, and that something is more important. When two people have been through as much together as your father and I have, there's—I don't know how to put it—but, you can't do without each other. And it makes a big difference the being married early. That's why I should like you and April to marry as soon as ever you can. You'd never regret it."

The tears began to trickle slowly down her cheeks; she tried to go on, but failed.

Roland did not know what to do or say. He had never loved his mother so much as he did then, but he could not express that love for her with words. He knelt forward and put his arms round her and drew her damp cheek to his.

"Mother," he whispered. "Mother, darling!"

For a long time they remained thus in a silent embrace. Then she drew back, straightened herself, and began to dab at her eyes with a handkerchief.

"It'll be all right, mother," he said.

She did not answer, but smiled a soft, glad smile, and taking his hand pressed it gently between hers.

"As long as you're happy, Roland," she said.

And so the crisis had come and had been settled. In those few minutes the direction of fifty years had been chosen finally. It was hard, but what would you? Life went that way. At any rate he would have those first few scented months; that at least was his. For a year he and April would be indescribably happy in the new-found intimacy of marriage, and afterwards—but of what could one be certain? For all he knew life might choose to readjust itself. One could not have anything both ways; indeed, one paid for everything. The Athenian parent had been far-seeing when he knelt before the altar in prayer that the compensating evil for his son's success might be light. One should do what lay to hand. As he curled himself in his bed he thought of April, and his heart beat quickly at the knowledge that her grace and tenderness would soon be his.

He shut away all thought of the dark years that must follow the passing of that first enchantment and fixed his mind on the sure pleasures that awaited him. How wonderful, after all, marriage could be. To return home at the end of the day and find your wife waiting for you. You would be tired and she would take you in her arms and run cool fingers through your hair, and you would talk together for a while, and she would tell you what she had done during the day, and you would tell her of whom you had met and of the business you had transacted, and you would bring your successes and lay them at her feet and you would say: "I made so much money to-day." And your words would lock that money away in her little hand—"All yours," they would seem to say. Then you would go upstairs and change for dinner, and when you came down you would find her standing before the fire, one long, bare arm lying along the mantelpiece, and you would come to her and very slowly pass your hand along it, and, bending your head, you would kiss the smooth skin of her neck. And could anything be more delightful than the quiet dinner together? Then would come the slow contentment of that hour or so before bedtime, while the warmth of the fire subsided slowly and you sat talking in low tones. And, afterwards, when you were alone in the warm darkness to love each other. Marriage must be a very fine adventure.

The next day brought with it its own problems, and on this Saturday morning in early autumn the white mist that lay over the roofs of Hammerton was a sufficient object of speculation. Did it veil the blue sky that adds so much to the charm of cricket, or a grey, sodden expanse of windy, low-flying clouds. It was the last Saturday of the cricket season. Roland was, naturally, bound for Hogstead, and there is no day in the whole year on which the cricketer watches the sky with more anxiety. In May he is impatient for his first innings, but as he walks up and down the pavilion in his spiked boots and hears the rain patter on the corrugated iron roof he can comfort himself with the knowledge that sooner or later the sun will shine, if not this week, then the next, and that in a long season he is bound to have many opportunities of employing that late cut he has been practising so assiduously at the nets. In the middle of the season he is a hardened warrior; he takes the bad with the good; he has outgrown his first eagerness; he has become, in fact, a philosopher. Last week he made seventy-two against the Stoics and was missed in the slips before he had scored. Such fortune is bound to be followed by a few disappointments. But at the end of the season a wet day is a dire misfortune. As he sits in the pavilion and watches the rain sweep across the pitch he remembers that only that morning he observed the erection of goal posts on the village green, that the winter is long and slow to pass, that for eight months he will not hold a bat in his hands, that this, his last forlorn opportunity of making a century, is even now fast slipping from him.

The depression of such a day is an abiding memory through the grey months of January and December, and, though Roland had had a fairly successful season, he was naturally anxious to end it well. He was prepared to distrust that mist. He had seen many mists break into heavy sunshine. He had also seen many mists dissolve into heavy rain. He knew no peace of mind till the sky began to lighten just before the train reached Hogstead, and he did not feel secure till he had changed into flannels and was walking down to the field on Gerald's arm, their shadows flung hard and black upon the grass in front of them.

It was a delightful morning; the grass was fresh with the dew which a slight breeze was drying; there was hardly a worn spot on the green surface, against which the white creases and yellow stumps stood in vivid contrast. An occasional cloud cut the sunlight, sending its shadow in long ripples of smoke across the field.

"And to think," said Gerald, "that this is our last game this season."

But for Roland this certainty marred the enjoyment of the blue sky and the bright sunshine. "This is the last time," he repeated to himself. For eight months the green field, so gay now with the white figures moving in the sunlight, would be desolate. Leaves would be blown on to it from the trees; rain would fall on them. The windows of the pavilion would be barred, the white screens stacked in the shelter of a wall.

After his innings he sat beside Muriel in the deck-chair on the shaded, northern terrace. But he felt too sad to talk to her and she complained of his silence.

"I don't think much of you as a companion," she said. "I've timed you. You haven't said a word for ten minutes."

He laughed, apologised and endeavoured to revert to the simple badinage that had amused them when Muriel was a little girl in short frocks, with her hair blowing about her neck, but it was not particularly successful, and it was a relief when Gerald placed his chair on the other side of Muriel and commenced a running commentary on the game. Roland wanted to be alone with his thoughts. Occasionally a stray phrase or sentence of their conversation percolated through his reverie.

"What a glorious afternoon it's going to be," he heard Muriel say. "It seems quite absurd that this should be your last game. One can't believe that the summer's over. On a day like this it looks as though it would last for ever!"

The words beat themselves into his brain. It was over and it was absurd to dream. The autumn sunshine that had lured her into disbelief of the approach of winter had made him forget that this day at Hogstead was his last. By next year he would be married; the delightful interlude would be finished. He would have passed from the life of Hogstead, at any rate in his present position. If he returned it would be different. The continuity would have been broken.

Out of the corner of his eye he caught a glimpse of Muriel's profile; how pretty she was; quite a woman now; and he turned his chair a little so that he could observe her without moving his head. Yes, she was really pretty in her delicate porcelain fashion; she was not beautiful. But, then, beauty was too austere. Charm was preferable. And she had that charm that depends almost entirely on its setting, on a dress that is in keeping with small dainty features. The least little thing wrong and she would have been quite ordinary.

What would happen to her? She would marry, of course; she would find no lack of suitors. Already, perhaps, there was one whom she had begun slightly to favour. What would he be like? To what sort of a man would she be attracted? Whoever he was he would be a lucky fellow; and Roland paused to wonder whether, if things had been different, if he had been free when he had met her first, she could have come to care for him. She had always liked him. He remembered many little occasions on which she had said things that he might have construed into a meaning favourable to himself. There had been that evening on the stairs when they had felt suddenly frightened of each other, and since then, more than once, he had fancied that they had stumbled in their anxiety to make impersonal conversation.

How happy they would have been together. They would have lived together at Hogstead all their lives, a part of the Marston family. Hammerton would have ceased to exist for him. They would have built themselves a cottage on the edge of the estate; their children would have passed their infancy among green fields, within sound of cricket balls.

At the far end of the field, on the southern terrace, Beatrice was sitting alone, watching Rosemary play a few yards away from her. She must have been there during the greater part of the morning, but Roland had not noticed her till she waved a hand to attract his attention. He rose at once and walked across to her. He felt that a talk with her would do him good.

They had seen a good deal of each other intermittently during the past three years, and each talk with her had been for Roland a step farther into the heart of a mystery. Gradually they had come to talk in shorthand, to read each other's thoughts without need of the accepted medium of words, so that when in reply to a complimentary remark about the fascination of her hat she made a quiet shrug of her shoulders, he knew that it was prompted by the wound of her wasted beauty. And on that late summer morning, with its solemn warning of decay, Roland felt brave enough to put to her the question that he had long wished to ask.

"Why did you marry him?" he said.

His question necessitated no break in the rhythm of her reverie. She answered him without pausing.

"I didn't know my own mind," she said. "I was very young. I wasn't in love with anyone else. My mother was keen on it. I gave way."

Beatrice spoke the truth. Her mother had honestly believed the match to be to her daughter's advantage. Her own life had been made difficult through lack of money. She had always been worried by it, and she had naturally come to regard money as more important than the brief fluttering of emotion that had been the prelude to the long, bitter struggle. It had seemed to her a wonderful thing that her daughter should marry this rich man. Herself had only been unhappy because she had been poor; her daughter would be always rich.

"How did you meet him?" Roland asked.

"I was his secretary. Romantic, isn't it? The poor girl marries the rich employer. Quite like the story books." And her hands fluttered at her sides.

Roland sought for some word of sympathy, but he was too appalled by the cruel waste of this young woman's beauty, of her enormous potentialities flung away on an ageing, withered man, who could not appreciate them. Her next sentence held for him the force of a prophetic utterance.

"When you marry, Roland," she said, "choose your own wife. Don't let your parents dictate to you. It's your affair."

As their eyes met it seemed to him that they were victims of the same conspiracy.

"One can't believe that the summer is over on a day like this. It looks as though it would last for ever!" The words ran like a refrain among his thoughts all the afternoon. He had a long outing. Hogstead had imported for the final match talent that was considerable but was not local. The doctor had persuaded a friend to bring his son, a member of the Rugby XI. It was discovered that an old blue was spending his honeymoon in a farmhouse a few miles away and a deputation had been dispatched to him; while, at the last moment, the greengrocer had arranged a compromise on a "to account rendered" bill with a professional at the county ground. Hogstead was far too strong for Mr Marston's side and all the afternoon Roland chased terrific off drives towards the terraces. The more tired he became the deeper grew his depression. The sun sank slowly towards the long, low-lying bank of cloud that stretched behind the roofs of the village; the day was waning, his last day. Came that hour of luminous calm, that last hour of sunlight when the shadows lengthen and a chilling air drives old players to the pavilion for their sweaters. Above the trees Roland could see the roof of the house; the trees swayed before its windows; the sunlight had caught and had turned the brass weathercock to gold. Never again, under the same conditions, would he see Hogstead as he in the past had so often seen it, standing above the trees, resplendent in the last glitter of sunset. It was only five years ago that he had come here for the first time, and yet into those five years had been crowded a greater measure of happiness than he could hope to find in the fifty years that were left him.

At the end of the day Mr Marston's eleven had half-an-hour's batting, during which Roland made one or two big hits. But it was an anticlimax, and his innings brought him little satisfaction. It was over now. He walked back to the pavilion, and with dismal efficiency collected his boots and bat and pads and packed them into his bag. What would he be like when he came to do that next? What would have happened to him between then and now? He came out of the pavilion to find Muriel standing on the step, waiting, presumably, for her brother. The need for sympathy, for feminine sympathy, overwhelmed him, and he asked her whether she would come for a walk with him—only a short stroll, just for a minute or two. She looked at him in surprise.

"But it's so late, Roland," she said; "we'll have to go and change for dinner in a minute."

The Lonely Unicorn | 187

"I know, I know, but just for a minute—do."

He was not ready yet for the general talk and laughter of the drawing-room; he wanted a few minutes of preparation.

"Do come," he said.

She nodded, and they turned and walked together towards the end of the cricket ground. She did not know why he should want her to come with him at such an unusual time, but she could see that he was unhappy, that he needed sympathy, and so, after a second's hesitation, she passed, for the first time in her life, her arm through his. He looked at her quickly, a look of surprise and gratitude, and pressed her arm with his. He said nothing, now that she was with him. He did not feel any need of words; it was her presence he wanted, and all that her presence meant to him. But she, being ignorant of what was in his mind, was embarrassed by his silence.

"That was a jolly knock of yours," she said at last.

"Oh! not bad, but in a second innings!"

"Rather like that one of yours five years ago."

"What! Do you remember that?"

"Of course; it was a great occasion."

"For me."

"And for us."

The past and the emotions of the past returned to him with a startling vividness. He could recall every moment of that day.

"I was so anxious to come off," he said. "You know I was to have gone into a bank and Gerald brought me down in the hope that your pater would take to me. I was frightfully nervous."

"So was I."

"But you'd never seen me."

"No, but Gerald had talked to me about you, and I thought it such rotten luck that a fellow like you should have to go into a bank. There'd been a row, hadn't there?"

They had reached the hedge that marked the boundary for the Marston estate; there was a gate in it, and they walked towards it. They stood for a moment, her arm still in his, looking at the quiet village that lay before them. Then Roland dropped her arm and leant against the gate.

"Yes, there'd been a row," he said, "and everything was going wrong, and I saw myself for the rest of my life a clerk adding up figures in a bank."

He paused, realising the analogy between that day and this. Then, as now, destiny had seemed to be closing in on him, robbing him of freedom and the chance to make of his life anything but a grey subservience. He had evaded destiny then, but it had caught him now. And he leant on the gate, hardly seeing the labourers trudging up the village street, talking in the porch of the public-house; their women returning home with their purchases for Sunday's dinner.

Again Muriel was oppressed by his silence.

"I remember Gerald telling us about it," she said, "and I was excited to see what you'd be like."

"And what did you think of me when you saw me?"

"Oh, I was a little girl then"; she laughed nervously, for his eyes were fixed on her face and she felt that she was blushing.

"Yes, but what did you think?" he repeated; "tell me."

Her fingers plucked nervously at her skirt; she felt frightened, and it was absurd to be frightened with Roland, one of her oldest friends.

"Oh, it's silly! I was only a little girl then. What does it matter what I thought? As a matter of fact," and she flung out the end of her confession carelessly, as though it meant nothing, "as a matter of fact, I thought you were the most wonderful boy I'd ever seen." And she tried to laugh a natural, offhand laugh that would make an end of this absurd situation, but the laugh caught in her throat, and she went suddenly still, her eyes fixed on Roland's. They looked at each other and read fear in the other's eyes, but in Roland's eyes fear was mingled with a desperate entreaty, a need, an overmastering need, of her. His tongue seemed too big for his mouth, and when at last he spoke, his voice was dry.

"And what do you think of me now?"

She could say nothing. She stood still, held by the grey eyes that never wavered.

"What do you think of me now?" he repeated.

She made a movement to break the tension, a swift gesture with her hand that was intended for a dismissal, but he was standing so close that her hand brushed against him; she gave a little gasp as his hand closed over it and held it.

"You won't tell me," he said. "But shall I tell you what I thought of you then? Shall I tell you? I thought you were the prettiest girl I had ever seen, and I thought how beautiful you would be when you grew up."

The Lonely Unicorn | 189

"Oh, don't be so silly, Roland," and she laughed a short, nervous laugh, and tried to draw her hand from his, but he held it firmly, and drew her a little nearer to him, so that he could take her other hand in his. They stood close together, then she raised her face slowly to his and the puzzled, wistful, trusting expression released the flood of sentiment that had been surging within him all the afternoon. His misery was no longer master of itself, and her beauty drew to it the mingled tenderness, hesitation, disappointment of his vexed spirit. She was for him in that moment the composite vision of all he prized most highly in life, of romance, mystery, adventure.

His hands closed upon hers tightly, desperately, as though he would rivet himself to the one thing of which he could be certain, and his confused intense emotion poured forth in a stream of eager avowal:

"But I never thought, Muriel, that you would be anything like what you are; you are wonderful, Muriel; I've been realising it slowly every day. I've said to myself that we were only friends, just friends, but I've known it was more than friendship. I've told myself not to be silly, that you could never care for me—well, I've never realised, not properly, not till this afternoon, Muriel."

She was no longer frightened; his words had soothed her, caressed her, wooed her; and when he paused, the expression of her eyes was fearless.

"Yes, Roland," she said.

"Muriel, Muriel, I love you; I want you to marry me. Will you?"

She blushed prettily. "But, Roland, you know; if father and mother say yes, of course."

In the sudden release of feeling he was uncertain what exactly was expected of a person whose proposal had been accepted. They were on the brink of another embarrassed silence, but Muriel saved them.

"Roland," she said, "you're hurting my fingers awfully!"

With a laugh he dropped her hands, and that laugh restored them to their former intimacy.

"Oh, Roland," she said, "what fun we shall have when we are married."

He asked whether she thought her parents would be pleased, and she was certain that they would.

"They like you so much." Then she insisted on his telling when and how he had first discovered that he was in love with her. "Come along; let's sit on the gate and you shall tell me all about it. Now, when was the first time, the very first time, that you thought you were in love with me?"

"Oh, but I don't know."

"Yes, you do; you must, of course you must, or you'd be nothing of a lover. Come on, or I shall take back my promise."

"Well, then, that evening on the stairs."

Muriel pouted.

"Oh, then!"

"Do you remember it?" he said.

"Of course I do. You frightened me."

"I know, and that's why I thought that one day you might marry me."

"Oh, but how silly!" she protested. "I wasn't a bit in love with you then. In fact, I was very annoyed with you."

"And, besides, I think I've always been in love with you."

"Oh, no, you haven't."

"Don't be too sure. And you?"

She smiled prettily.

"I've often thought what a nice husband you would make."

And then she had taken his hand in her lap and played with it.

"And where shall we live when we are married?" he had asked her, and she had said she did not care.

"Anywhere, as long as there are lots of people to amuse me."

She sat there on the gate, her light hair blowing under the wide brim of her hat, laughing down at him, her face bright with happiness. She was so small, so graceful. Light as heatherdown, she would run a gay motif through the solemn movement of his career.

"You are like a fairy," he said, "like a mischievous little elf. I think I shall call you that—Elfkin."

"Oh, what a pretty name, Roland—Elfkin! How sweet of you!"

They talked so eagerly together of the brilliant future that awaited them that they quite forgot the lateness of the hour, till they heard across the evening the dull boom of the dinner gong. They both gasped and looked at each other as confederates in guilt.

"Heavens!" she said, "what a start. We've got to run!"

It was the nearest approach to a dramatic entrance that Roland ever achieved. Muriel kept level with him during the race across the cricket ground, but she began to fall behind as they reached the long terrace between the rhododendrons.

"Take hold of my hand," said Roland, and he dragged her over the remaining thirty yards. They rushed through the big French windows of the drawing-room at the very moment that the party had assembled there before going down to dinner. They had quite forgotten that there would be an audience. They stopped, and Muriel gave out a horrified gasp of "Oh!"

They certainly were a ridiculous couple as they stood there hand in hand, hot, dishevelled, out of breath, beside that well-groomed company of men and women in evening dress. Mrs Marston hurried forward with the slightly deprecating manner of the hostess whose plans have been disturbed,

"My dear children——" But Muriel had by this time recovered her breath and courage. She raised a peremptory hand.

"One minute. We've got something to tell you all."

"But surely, dear, after dinner," Mrs Marston began.

"No, mother, dear, now," and, with a twinkle in her eye and a sly glance at her embarrassed lover, Muriel made her alarming announcement:

"Roland and I, mother, we're going to be married."

Roland had seen in a French novel a startling incident of domestic revelation recorded by two words: *consternation générale*, and those two words suited the terrible hush that followed Muriel's confession. It was not a hush of anger, or disapproval, but of utter and complete astonishment. For a few minutes no one said anything. The young men of the party either adjusted their collar studs and gazed towards the ceiling, or flicked a speck of dust from their trousers and gazed upon the floor. The young women gazed upon each other. Mrs Marston thought nervously of the condition of the retarded dinner, and Mr Marston tried, without success, to prove adequate to the situation. Only Muriel enjoyed it; she loved a rag, and her eyes passed from one figure to another; not one of them dared look at her.

"Well," she said at last, "we did think you'd want to congratulate us." To Mr Marston some criticism of himself appeared to be implied in this remark. He pulled down his waistcoat, coughed, and went through the preliminaries usual to him when preparing to address the board. And, in a sense, this was a board meeting, a family board meeting.

"My dear Muriel," he began, but he had advanced no further than these three words when the dinner gong sounded for the second time. It was a signal for Mrs Marston to bustle forward.

"Yes, yes, but the dinner'll be getting quite cold if we don't go in at once. Don't trouble to change, Mr Whately, please don't; but, Muriel, you must go up and do your hair, and if you have time change your frock."

"Weren't they lovely?" said Muriel, as she and Roland ran upstairs to wash. "I could have died with laughter."

"You made me feel a pretty complete fool," said Roland.

"Well, you made me feel very silly about three-quarters of an hour ago. I deserved a revenge." And she scampered upstairs ahead of him.

Roland washed quickly and waited for her at the foot of the stairs. He was much too shy to go in alone.

"And they say that women are cowards," said Muriel, when he confessed it to her. "Come along."

The quarter of an hour that had elapsed since the sensational disclosure had given the company time to recover its balance, and when Muriel and Roland entered the room, they found that two empty seats were waiting for them side by side.

"Here they are," said Mr Marston, "and I hope that they're thoroughly ashamed of themselves." He felt himself again after a glass of sherry, and it was an occasion of which a father should make the most. It could only come once and he was prepared to enjoy it to the full. "To think of it, my dear, the difference between this generation and ours. Why, before I got engaged to your mother, Muriel, why, even before I began to court her, I went and asked her father's permission. I can remember now how frightened I felt. We respected our parents in those days. We always asked their opinions first. But to-day—why, in you burst, late for dinner, and announce with calm effrontery that you're going to be married. Why, at this rate, there won't be any engagements at all in a short time; young people will just walk in at the front door and say: 'We're married.'"

"Then we are engaged, father, aren't we?" said Muriel.

"I didn't say so."

"Oh, but you did; didn't he, Roland?"

Roland was, however, too confused to hold any opinion on the subject.

"Well, if you didn't actually say so you implied it. At any rate we shall take it that you did."

"And that, I suppose, settles it?"

"Of course."

Mr Marston made a theatrical gesture of despair.

"These children!" he said.

It was a jolly evening. Roland and Muriel were the centre of congratulations; their healths were drunk; he was called on for a speech, and he fulfilled his duty amid loud applause. Everyone was so pleased, so eager to share their happiness. Beatrice turned to him a smile of surprised congratulation. Only Gerald held back from the general enthusiasm. Once across the table his eyes met Roland's, and there was implied in their glance a question. He was the only one of the party who had heard of April, and never, in all their confidences, had there passed between them one word that might have hinted at a growing love between his sister and his friend; it was this that surprised him. Surely Roland would have told him something about it. Roland was not the sort of fellow who kept things to himself. He always wanted to share his pleasures. Gerald would have indeed expected him to come to him for advice, to say: "Old son, what chance do you think I stand in that direction?"—to entrust him with the delicate mission of sounding Muriel's inclinations. He was surprised and a little hurt.

As they were going towards the drawing-room after dinner he laid his hand on Roland's arm, holding him back for a minute. And as he stood in the doorway waiting for his friend, Roland felt for the first time a twinge of apprehension as to the outcome of this undertaking. But he could see that Gerald was nervous, and this nervousness lent him confidence.

"It's no business of mine, old son," Gerald began, "I'm awfully glad about you and Muriel and all that, but," he paused irresolute; he disliked these theatrical situations and did not know how to meet them. "I mean," he began slowly, then added quietly, anxiously: "It's all right, isn't it, old son?"

"Of course," said Roland. "It's the most wonderful——"

"I know, I know," Gerald interrupted, "but wasn't there, didn't you tell me about——"

"Oh, that's finished a long time ago. Don't worry about that."

"You see," Gerald went on, "I should hate to think——Oh, well, I'm awfully glad about it, and I think you're both fearfully lucky."

Two hours later Roland and Muriel stood on the landing saying good-night to one another. She was leaning towards him, across the banisters, as she had leant that evening three years earlier, but this time he held her hand in his.

"I can't tell you how happy I am," he was saying; "I shall dream of you all night long."

"And so shall I of you."

"We're going to be wonderfully happy, aren't we?"

"Wonderfully."

And in each other's eyes they saw the eager, boundless confidence of youth. They were going to make a great thing of their life together. Roland cast a swift glance over the banisters to see if anyone was in the hall, then stood on tiptoe, raising himself till his face was on the level with Muriel's.

"Muriel," he said.

"Yes."

"I want to whisper something in your ear."

"What is it?"

"Lean over, close to me, and I will tell you."

She bent her head, her cheek brushing against his hair. "Well?" she said.

He placed his mouth close to her ear.

"Muriel, you haven't kissed me yet."

She drew back and smiled.

"Was that all?" she said.

"Isn't it enough?"

She made no answer.

"Aren't you going to?" he said.

"I don't know."

"Please, please do."

"Some day I will."

"But why not now?"

"Someone would see us."

"Oh, no, they wouldn't. And even if they did what would it matter? Muriel! please, please, Muriel!"

He raised himself again on tiptoe; and leaning forward, she rested her hands upon his shoulders. Then she slowly bent her head to his, and their lips met in such a kiss as children exchange for forfeits in the nursery. As she drew back Roland slipped back again on to his heels, but he still held her hand and her fingers closed round his, pressing them, if not with passion, at least with fondness.

"You're rather an old dear, Roland," she said. And there was a note in her voice that made him say quickly and half audibly:

"And you're a darling."

She drew her hand from his gently. "And what was that pretty name you called me?"

"Elfkin."

"Let me be always Elfkin."

Both of them that night were wooed to sleep by the delight of their new-found happiness.

CHAPTER XIX
THE LONELY UNICORN

The lovers went for a walk together on Sunday morning through the woods that lay beyond the village, and they sat on a pile of broken sticks that a charcoal burner had collected for a fire, and they held hands and talked of the future. Her pleasure in this new relationship was a continual fascination to Roland. She regarded love, courtship and marriage as a delightful game.

"What fun it's going to be," she said; "we shall announce our engagement and then everyone will write and congratulate us, and we shall have to answer them, and I shall have to pretend to be so serious and say: 'I am much looking forward to introducing you to my fiancé. I hope you will like each other.'"

"And what sort of a ring am I to get you?"

"The ring! Oh, I had forgotten that. One has to have one, doesn't one? Let's see now. What should I like?" And she paused, her finger raised to her lower lip. She remained for a moment in perplexed consideration, then suddenly shook her head.

"Oh, I don't care, just what you like. Let it be a surprise. But there's one thing, Roland, dear—promise me."

"Yes."

"You will promise, won't you?"

"Of course."

"Well, then, promise me you won't put any writing inside it, because I shall want to show it to my friends and I should feel so silly if they saw it."

After lunch Mr Marston asked him to come into the study for a talk.

"I'm not going to play the heavy father," he said; "in fact, you know yourself how thoroughly pleased we are, both of us, about it all. We couldn't have wished a better husband for Muriel. But there is such a thing as finance, and you've got, I gather, no money apart from what you earn from us."

"No, sir."

"And your salary now is— —?"

"Four hundred a year, sir."

"And how far do you think that will go? You could start a home with it, of course, but do you think you could make Muriel happy with it? She's a dainty little lady, and when she's free from home authority she will want to be going out to dances and theatres. How far do you think four hundred will take her?"

"Not very far, sir."

"Then what do you propose to do? Long engagements are a bad thing."

"Yes, sir."

"Well, then, what do you think of doing?"

Roland, who had expected Mr Marston to make his daughter a generous dress allowance, was uncertain how to answer this question. Indeed, he made no attempt.

"I suppose," said Mr Marston, "that what you were really thinking was that I should make you some allowance."

Roland blushed, and began to stammer that, as a matter of fact, that was exactly what—but he never finished the sentence, for Mr Marston interrupted him.

"Because, if that's what you were thinking, young man, I can disillusion you at once. I don't believe in allowances; they put a young couple under an obligation to their parents. And that's bad. A young couple should be independent. No!" he said, "I'm not going to make Muriel any allowance, but," and here he paused theatrically, so as to make the most of his point, "I am going to give you a good opportunity of making yourself independent. I am going to offer to both you and Gerald junior partnerships in the business."

Roland gave a start; he could scarcely believe what he had heard.

"But, sir— —" he began.

"Yes, a partnership in our business, and I can't say how pleased I shall be to have you there, and how proud I am to have a son-in-law who will want to work and not be content to attend an occasional board meeting and draw large fees for doing so. I know a business man when I meet one. We are jolly lucky to have got you, and as for you and Muriel, well, honestly, I don't know which of you is luckier!"

They were the same words that Gerald had used, and he was convinced of their truth five minutes later when he sat in the drawing-room pouring out this exciting news to Muriel, when he saw her eyes light with enthusiasm, and heard her say on a note of genuine comradeship and admiration: "Roland, I always knew it. You're a wonderful boy!"

This state of rapture lasted till he said good-night to Gerald on Monday evening in the doorway of the office. Then, and then only, did he realise to what a series of complications he had delivered himself. He had fallen into the habit of regarding his life at Hogstead and his life at Hammerton as two separate entities; what happened to him in one life did not affect him in the other. Hogstead had been his dream country. During the week-end he had retreated within his dream, flung up bulwarks, garrisoned himself securely. He had not realised that, when he returned to Hammerton, he would have to deliver an account of himself. So far, what had happened in that dream country had only mattered to himself. His engagement to Muriel, however, involved the fortunes of persons other than himself, and this fact was presented to him acutely as he sat on the top of a bus and drew nearer, minute by minute, to No. 105 Hammerton Villas.

In the course of seventy-two hours he had completely altered the direction of his life. He had left home on Saturday morning with every intention of proposing definitely to April at the first opportunity and of marrying her as soon as the necessary arrangements could be made. Yet here he was on Monday evening returning home the fiancé of Muriel Marston and a junior partner in her father's firm. He could not imagine in what spirit the news would be received. His parents knew little enough of Gerald and his father; they were hardly aware of Muriel's existence. Years earlier he may have said, perhaps, in reply to some casual query: "Oh, yes, he's got a sister, much younger than himself, a jolly kid!" But of late, nothing. He did not see either how he was to introduce the subject. He would be asked hardly any questions about his holiday; he had always been uncommunicative.

"Have you had a nice time, my dear?"

That's what his mother would say, in the same indifferent tone that she would say "Good morning, how do you do?" to a casual acquaintance. She would then proceed to tell him about the visitors they had received on Sunday.

His father would arrive, lay down his evening paper on the table and begin to change his boots.

"So you're back all right, Roland?" That would be his only reference to his son's holidays before he plunged into a commentary on the state of the bus service, the country and the restaurant where he had lunched.

The Lonely Unicorn | 199

"Coming for a walk, Roland?" That would be his next indication that he was conscious of his son's presence, and on the receipt of an affirmation he would trudge upstairs, to reappear ten minutes later in a light grey suit.

"Ready, my son?" And they would walk along the High Street till they reached the corner of Upper College Road. There Mr Whately would pause. "Well, Roland, shall we go in and see April?" And in reality the question would be an assertion. They would have to go into the Curtises'; it would be terrible. He would feel like Judas Iscariot at the Last Supper. He would be received by Mrs Curtis as a future son-in-law. April would smile on him as her betrothed. Whatever he did or said he could not, in her eyes, be anything but perfidious, disloyal, treacherous. He would be unable to make clear to her the inevitable nature of what had happened.

The red roofs and stucco fronts of Donnington had by now receded into the distance; the bus was already clattering down the main street of Lower Hammerton. The lights in the shop windows had just been kindled and lent a touch of wistful poetry to the spectacle of the crowded pavements, black with the dark coats of men returning from their offices, with here and there a splash of gaiety from the dress of some harassed woman hurrying to complete her shopping before her husband's return.

"In three more minutes we shall be at the Town Hall," Roland told himself. "In two minutes from then I shall have reached the corner of Hammerton Villas; 105 is the third house down on the left-hand side. In six minutes, at the outside, I shall be there!"

And it turned out exactly as he had predicted. He found his mother in the drawing-room, turning the handle of the sewing-machine. She smiled as he opened the door and, as he bent his head to kiss her, expressed the hope that he had enjoyed himself. Three minutes later his father arrived.

"A most interesting murder case to-day, my dear; there's a full account of it in *The Globe*. It appears that the fellow was engaged to one girl, but was really in love with the mother of the girl he murdered, and he murdered the girl because she seemed to suspect—no, that's not it. It was the girl he was engaged to who suspected; but at any rate you'll find it all in *The Globe*—a most interesting case." And he opened the paper at the centre page and handed it to his wife. As he did so his arm brushed against Roland, and the forcible reminder of his son's existence inspired him to express the hope that the cricket at Hogstead had reached the high expectations that had been entertained regarding it. This duty accomplished, he proceeded to describe in detail the lunch he had selected at the Spanish café.

"There was a choice of three things: you could either have *hors d'œuvre* or a soup, and then there was either omelette or fish or spaghetti, with veal or chicken or mutton to follow, and, of course, cheese to finish up with. Well, I didn't think the spaghetti at that place was very good, so I was left with a choice of either an omelette or fish."

While he was stating and explaining his choice Mr Whately had found time to divest his feet of his boots.

"Well, and what about a walk, Roland?"

"I suppose so, father."

"Right you are. I'll just run up and change."

Ten minutes later, before Roland had had time to unravel the complicated psychology of the Norfolk murder case, Mr Whately was standing in the doorway in his grey tweed suit and straw hat. "A bit late for a straw, perhaps, but it's lovely weather, almost like spring. One can't believe that summer's over." The repetition of the phrase jarred Roland's conscience. Would it not be better to get it off his chest now, once and for all, before he was taken to see April, before that final act of hypocrisy was forced on him?

"Father," he said, "there's something — —"

But Mr Whately did not like to be kept waiting.

"Come along, Roland, time enough for that when we are out of doors. It'll be dark soon."

And by the time they had reached the foot of the long flight of steps the moment of desperate courage had been followed by a desperate fear. Time enough when he got back to tell them. He made no effort even to discourage his father when, at the corner of Upper College Road, they paused and the old assertive question was asked. Roland nodded his head in meek submission. What was to be gained at this point by discussion? There would be enough turmoil later on.

But he regretted his weakness five minutes later when he sat in the wicker chair by the window-seat. He looked round the room at the unaltered furniture, the unaltered pictures, the unaltered bookshelves, and Mrs Curtis eternal in that setting, her voice droning on as it had droned for him through so many years. There was no change anywhere. Mrs Curtis was sitting beside the fireplace, her knitting on her lap, the bones of her body projecting as awkwardly as ever. His father sat opposite her, his hat held forward before his knees, his head nodding in satisfied agreement, his voice interrupting occasionally the movement of his head with a "Yes, Mrs Curtis," "Certainly, Mrs Curtis." And he and April sat as of old, near and silent, in the window-seat.

As he looked at April, the profile of her face silhouetted against the window, an acute wave of sentiment passed over him, reminding him of the many things they had shared together. The first twenty years of his life belonged to her. It was to her that he had turned in his moment of success; her faith in him had inspired his achievements. She had been proud of him. He remembered how she had flushed with pleasure when he had told her what the school captain had said to him at the end of the season, and when he had been invited to the cricket match at Hogstead it was of her that he had asked soft encouragement, and it was at her feet that he had laid, a few days later, his triumph. How strange that was, that she should have been the first to hear of Hogstead. The wave of tenderness swept away every little difference of environment and personality that had accumulated round their love during the past three years. What a fine thing, after all, they had meant to make of their life together. What a confession of failure was this parting. And when Mr Whately rose to go, and Mrs Curtis followed him to the door, no doubt with the intention of leaving the lovers alone together, Roland put out his arms to April and folded her into them, and for the last time laid his lips on hers in a kiss that expressed for him an infinite kindness for her, and pity, pity for her, for himself, and for the tangle life had made of their ambitions. As he drew back his head from hers she whispered the word "Darling!" on a note of authentic passion, but he could not say anything. His hands closed on her shoulders for a moment, then slackened. He could not bear to look at her. He turned quickly and ran to his father. Was it, he asked himself, the kiss of Iscariot? He did not know. He had buried a part of himself; he had said good-bye to the first twenty years of his life.

He walked home in silence beside his father. He was in no mood for the strain of the exacting situation, the astonishment, the implied reproach that lay in front of him. But he was resigned to it. It had to come; there was no loophole.

He made his announcement quite quietly during a pause in the talk just after dinner. And it was received, as he had anticipated, in a stupefied silence.

"What!" said Mr Whately at last. "Engaged to Muriel Marston!"

"Yes, Muriel Marston, the daughter of my employer, and I'm to become a junior partner in the firm."

"But——" Mr Whately paused. He was not equal to the pressure of the situation. He was not perplexed by the ethics of Roland's action; his critical faculties had only appreciated the first fact, that a plan had been altered, and he was always thrown off his balance by the alteration of any plan. He was accustomed to thinking along grooves; he distrusted sidings. He got no further than the initial "But." His wife, however, had recovered from the shock and was by now able to face the matter squarely. When she spoke her voice was even.

"Now, please, Roland, we want to know all about this. When did you propose to Miss Marston?"

"During the week-end—on Saturday evening."

"And her parents agree to it?"

"Yes, yes," said Roland, a little impatiently. "Didn't I tell you that I've been offered a junior partnership in his business."

"Of course; I forgot. I'm sorry. This is rather difficult for us. Now, you say——"

But at this point her husband, whose thoughts had by now travelled a certain distance along the new groove, interrupted her.

"But how can you talk about being engaged to this Muriel Marston when you've been engaged for nearly three years to April?"

Roland's retort came quickly.

"I've never been engaged to April."

"You know you have! Why!..."

But Mrs Whately had held up her hand.

"Hush, dear," she said. "Roland's quite right. He's never been officially engaged to April."

Roland shivered at the venom that was revealed by the stressing of the word "officially."

"And how long," she went on, "have you been in love with Miss Marston?"

"Oh, I don't know, mother; I can't tell. Please let me alone." And there was genuine misery behind the words. "One doesn't know about a thing like this."

But Mrs Whately would not spare him. She shook her head impatiently.

"Don't be absurd, Roland; you're behaving like a child. Of course one knows these things. You've known Miss Marston for four or five years now. You couldn't suddenly find yourself in love with her."

"I suppose not, mother, but——"

"There's no 'but.' You must have been thinking of her for a long time. On Friday night—Saturday morning, I mean—you must have gone down there with the full intention of proposing to her; didn't you?"

Roland did not answer her. He rose from his seat and walked across to the window.

"It's no good," he said, and his back was turned to them. "It's no good. I can't make you understand. You won't believe what I say. I seem an awful beast to you, I know, but—oh, well, things went that way."

And he stood there, looking out of the window through the chink of the blind towards the long, grey stretch of roofs, the bend of the road, the pools of lamplight, till suddenly, like a caress, he felt his mother's hand upon his shoulder.

"Roland," she said, and for the first time there was sympathy in her voice, "Roland, please tell me this. You're not, are you, marrying this girl for her money?"

He turned and looked her full in the eyes.

"No, mother," he said, "I love Muriel Marston. I love her and I want to marry her." As he spoke he saw the kind light vanish from her eyes, her hand fell from his shoulder and the voice that answered him was metallic.

"Very well, then, if that's so, there's no more to be said. As you've arranged all this yourself, you'll let us know when the marriage will take place."

She turned away. He took a step towards her.

"Mother, please——"

But she only shrugged her shoulders, and when her husband asked what was going to be done about April, she said that she supposed that it was no affair of theirs, and that no doubt Roland would make his own arrangements. She picked up the paper and began to read it. Roland wondered what was going to happen next; the silence oppressed him. He listened to the slow ticking of the clock till he could bear it no longer.

"Oh, please, one of you, won't you say something?"

They both turned their heads in surprise as though they would survey a curiosity, a tortoise that had been granted miraculously the gift of speech.

"But, my dear Roland, what is there to be said?"

"I don't know, I——"

"Your mother's quite right," said Mr Whately. "You're your own master; you've arranged to marry the girl you want. What is there to be said?"

And their heads were again turned from him. He stood looking at them, pondering the wisdom of an appeal to their emotions. He half opened his mouth, took a step forward, but paused; what purpose would it serve? One could not appeal to stone; they were hard, unreceptive, hostile; they would turn cold eyes upon his outburst. He would look ridiculous. It would do no good.

"Oh, very well," he said, and walked out of the room.

As he sat on his bed that night he remembered how, five years ago, he had returned to his study after that tempestuous interview with the Chief and had reflected on the impossibility of one mortal making clear his meaning to another. Life went in a circle: here was the same situation in a different setting. Everything was repetition. Had not the Eastern critic laid it down that in the whole range of literature there could be discovered only seven different stories? He remembered the Chief telling him that; it had stuck in his mind: music had evolved from seven notes, painting from three colours, literature from twenty-four letters, the chronicle of mankind from seven stories. Variety, new clothes, new accents, but at heart the same story, the same song.

One problem, however, that he had not previously considered, had become clear for him during that discussion. How was April to be told? He had imagined that he had only to tell his parents for the matter to be settled. They would do the rest. He had never thought that the responsibility of breaking the news to April would rest with him. And he could not do it; it was no good pretending that he could. He could no more tell April himself than he could murder a man in cold blood. He knew also that if he once saw her he would be unable to carry through the part. She would open the door for him and as soon as they were alone in the hall she would throw her arms about his neck and kiss him, and how should he then find words to tell her? His old love for her would return to him; there would be further complications. Perhaps he might write a letter to her, but he had only to take up pen and paper to realise that this was impossible. He could not express himself in writing; the sentences that stared at him from the paper were cold and stilted; they would wound her cruelly. He was accustomed in times of perplexity to turn for advice to Gerald. But this was hardly an occasion when that was possible. Gerald was, after all, Muriel's brother. There were limits.

The next day brought Roland no nearer to a solution of his immediate problem. Indeed he had not thought of one till, on his way home, he boarded the wrong bus, and on handing threepence and saying "Hammerton Town Hall" was informed that the bus he was on would take him only as far as Donnington before turning off to Richmond. The word "Richmond" gave him his idea. Richmond, that was it, of course that was it! Why had he not thought of it before? He would go round to Ralph at once and send him on an embassy to April. So pleased was he with this inspiration that he was actually shaking hands with Ralph before he realised that the battle was not won yet, and that he had before him a very awkward interview.

"Ralph," he said, "I want a word with you alone. I don't want to be disturbed."

"Shall we go out for a walk then?"

"Right."

Ralph went into the hall, fidgeting his fingers in the umbrella stand in search of his walking stick, did not find it, and paused there indeterminate.

"Now, where did I put that stick?"

"Oh, don't bother, please don't bother; we're only going for a stroll."

"Yes, I know, but if I don't find it now—let me see, perhaps it's in the kitchen." And for the next three minutes everyone seemed to be shouting all over the house: "Mother, have you seen my walking stick?" "Emma, have you seen Mr Ralph's walking stick?" And by the time that the stick was eventually discovered, in the cupboard in Ralph's bedroom, Roland's patience and composure had been shattered.

"Such a fuss about a thing like that," he protested.

"All right, all right; I didn't keep you long. Now, what's it all about?" And there was firmness in his voice which caused Roland a twinge of uneasiness. Ralph had developed since he had gone to Oxford. He was no longer the humble servant of Roland's caprice.

"It's not very easy," said Roland; "I want you to do something for me. I'm going to ask you to do me a great favour. It's about April."

"Why, of course," said Ralph, "I know what it is; you're going to be married at once, and you want me to be your best man—but I shall be delighted."

"Oh, no, no, no," said Roland, "it's not that at all."

Ralph was surprised. "No?"

"No, it's—oh, well, look here. You know how things are; there's been a sort of understanding between us for a long time—three or four years— hasn't there? Well, one alters; one doesn't feel at twenty-three as one does when one's seventeen; we're altering all the time, and perhaps I have altered quicker than most people. I've been abroad a lot." He paused. "You understand, don't you?" he asked.

Ralph nodded, understanding perfectly. Though he did not quite see where he himself came in, he understood that Roland was tired of April. But he was not going to spare him. There should be no short-cuts, no shorthand conversation. Roland would have to tell him the whole story.

"Well?" he said.

Their eyes met, and for the first time in their relationship Roland knew that he was in the weaker position and that Ralph was determined to enjoy his triumph.

"All right," said Roland, "I'll go on, though you know what I've got to tell you. I don't know whose fault it is. I suppose it's mine really, but things have happened this way. I'm not in love with April any more."

Again he paused and again Ralph repeated that one word, "Well?"

"I don't love her any more, and I've fallen in love with someone else and we want to get married."

"Who is it?"

"Muriel Marston."

"The sister of that fellow you play cricket with?"

"Yes, that's it." He paused, hoping that now Ralph would help him out, but Ralph gave him no assistance, and Roland was forced to plunge again into his confession. "Well, you see, April knows nothing about it. I've been a bit of a beast, I suppose. As far as she is concerned the understanding still holds good. She's still in love with me, at least she thinks she is. It's—well, you see how it is."

"Yes, I quite see that. You've been playing that old game of yours, of running two girls in two different places, only this time it's gone less fortunately and you find you've got to marry one of them, and April's the one that's got to go?"

"If you put it that way——"

"Well, how else can I put it?"

"Oh, have it as you like."

"And what part exactly do you expect me to play in this comedy?"

"I want you to break the news to April."

There was a long silence. They walked on, Ralph gazing straight in front of him, and Roland glancing sideways at him from time to time to see how the idea had struck him. But he could learn nothing from the set expression of his companion's face. It was his turn now to employ an interrogatory "Well?" But Ralph did not appear to have heard him. They walked on in silence, till Roland felt some further explanation was demanded of him.

"It's like this, you see— —"

But Ralph cut him short. "I understand quite well; you're afraid to tell her. You're ashamed of yourself and you expect me to do your dirty work!"

"It's not that— —"

"Oh, yes, it is. I know you'll find excuses for yourself, but that's what it amounts to. And I don't see why I should do it."

"I am asking it of you as a favour."

"That's like you. Since you've met these new friends of yours you've dropped your old friends one by one. I've watched you, and now April, she's the last to go. You haven't been to see me for three or four months and now you've only come because you want me to do something for you."

The justice of the remark made Roland wince. He had seen hardly anything of Ralph during the last three years.

"But, Ralph," he pleaded, "how can I go and tell her myself?"

"If one's done a rotten thing one owns up to it. It's the least one can do."

"But, it isn't— —"

"What isn't it? Not a rotten thing to make a girl believe for four years that you're going to marry her and then chuck her! If that isn't a rotten thing I don't know what is!"

Roland was wise enough not to attempt to justify himself. He would only enrage Ralph still further and that was not his game.

"All right," he said. "Granted all that, granted I've done a rotten thing, it's happened; it can't be altered now; something's got to be done. Put yourself in my place. What would you do if you were me?"

"I shouldn't have got myself in such a place"; his voice was stern and official and condemnatory. In spite of the stress of the situation Roland was hard put to it not to kick him for a prig.

"But I have, you see, and— —"

"Even so," Ralph interrupted, "I can't see why you shouldn't go and tell April yourself."

"Because April herself would rather be told by anyone than me."

It was his last appeal and he saw that it had succeeded. Ralph repeated the words over to himself.

"April would rather be told——Oh, but rot! She'd much rather have it out straight."

"Oh, no, she wouldn't; you don't know April as well as I do. She hates scenes; she could discuss it impersonally with you. With me—can't you see how it would hurt her; she wouldn't know how to take it, whether to plead, or just accept it—can't you see?"

He had won, and he knew it, through the appeal to April's feelings. Ralph would do what he wanted, because he would think that he was performing a service for April.

"I expect you're right," he said; "you know her better than I do, but I'm doing it for her, not for you, mind."

"Yes, yes, I understand."

"If it wasn't for her I wouldn't do it. A man should do his own dirty work. And you know what I think of it."

"Oh, yes, I know." He would make no defence. Ralph might be allowed in payment the poor privilege of revenge.

"And you'll tell me what she says?"

"You shall have a full account of the execution."

They walked a little farther in silence. They had nothing more to say to each other, and at the corner of a road they parted. It was finished.

Roland walked home, well satisfied at the successful outcome of a delicate situation—the same Roland who had congratulated himself five years earlier on the diplomacy of the Brewster episode.

CHAPTER XX
THERE'S ROSEMARY ..

Ralph went round to see April on the next morning, shortly after eleven o'clock. She had just been out for a long walk by herself and, on her return, had taken up a novel with which to while away the two hours remaining to lunch-time. She had left school eighteen months earlier, and time often hung heavily on her. She did little things about the house: she tidied her own room, mended her own clothes, did some occasional cooking, but she had many hours of idleness. She wished sometimes that she had trained for some definite work. Women were no longer regarded as household ornaments. Many careers were open to her. But it had not seemed worth while during the last year at school to specialise in any one subject. What was the good of taking up a career that she would have to abandon so soon? The first year in any profession was uninteresting, and by the time she had reached a position where she would be entrusted with responsibilities her marriage day would be approaching. And so, instead of looking for any settled work, she had decided to stay at home and help her mother as much as possible. It was lonely at times, especially when Roland was away; she was, in consequence, much given to daydreams. Her book, on this September morning, had slipped on to her lap, and her thoughts had refused to concentrate on the printed page, and fixed themselves on the time when she and Roland would be married. He had not been to see her at all the day before. But the memory of his last kiss was very actual to her. He had loved her then. She had had her bad moments, when she had wondered whether, after all, he really cared for her, but she was reassured by such a memory. And soon they would be married. She would make him happy. She would be a good wife.

A knock on the front door roused her from her reverie, and, turning her head, she saw Ralph Richmond standing in the doorway. She rose quickly, her hand stretched out in friendly welcome.

"How nice of you to come, Ralph; you're quite a stranger. Come and sit down." And as soon as he was seated she began to talk with fresh enthusiasm about their friends and acquaintances. "I saw Mrs Evans yesterday and she told me that Edward had failed again for his exam. She was awfully disappointed, though she oughtn't really to have expected anything else. Arthur's form master told him once that he couldn't imagine any examination being invented that Edward would be able to pass."

Ralph sat in silence, watching her, wondering what expression those bright features would assume when she had heard what he had to tell her. He dreaded the moment, not for his sake, but for hers. He hardly thought of himself. He loved her and he would have to give her pain. In the end he stumbled awkwardly across her conversation.

"April, I have got some bad news for you."

"Oh, Ralph, what is it? Nothing about your people, is it?"

"No, it's nothing to do with me. It's about Roland."

Although she made no movement, and though the expression of her face did not appear to alter, it seemed to him that, at the mention of Roland's name, her vitality was stilled suddenly.

"Yes?" she said, and waited for his reply.

"He's not hurt, or anything. You needn't be frightened. But he wanted you to know that he has become engaged to Muriel Marston."

She said nothing for a moment, then in a dazed voice:

"Oh, no, you must be mistaken, it can't be true, it can't possibly!"

"But it is, April, really. I'm awfully sorry, but it is."

She rose from her chair, swayed, steadied herself with her left hand, took a half pace to the window and stood still.

"But what am I to do?" she said. She could not bear to contemplate her life without Roland in it. What would her life become? What else had it been, indeed, for the last four years but Roland the whole time? Whenever she had bought a new frock or a new hat she had wondered how Roland would like her in it. When she had heard an amusing story her first thought had been, "Roland will be amused by that." When she had opened the paper in the morning she had turned always to the sports' page first. "Roland will be reading these very words at this very moment." Roland was the measure of her happiness. It was a good day or a bad day in accordance with Roland's humour. She would mark in the calendar the days in red and green and yellow—yellow for the unhappy days, when Roland had not seen her, or when he had been unsympathetic; the green days were ordinary days, when she had seen him, but had not been alone with him; her red days were the happy days, when there had been a letter from him in the morning, or when they had been alone together and he had been nice and kissed her and made love prettily to her. Her whole life was Roland. Whenever she was depressed she would comfort herself with the knowledge that, in a year or so she would be married and with Roland for always. She could not picture to herself what her life would become now without him. She raised her hand to her head, in dazed perplexity.

"What am I to do?" she repeated. "What am I to do?" Then she pulled herself together. There were several questions that she would wish to have answered. She returned to her seat. "Now tell me, when did this happen, Ralph?"

"He told me last night."

"I don't mean that; when did he propose to Miss Marston?"

"During the week-end—on Saturday evening, I think."

"Saturday evening!" she repeated it—"Saturday evening!" Then he had been engaged to this other girl on Monday night when he had kissed her. He had loved her then, he had meant that kiss; she was certain of it. And to April, as earlier to Mrs Whately, this treachery seemed capable of explanation only by a marriage for money. It was unworthy of Roland. She could hardly imagine him doing it. But he might be in debt. People did funny things when they were in debt.

"Is she pretty, this Miss Marston?"

That was her next question, and Ralph replied that he thought she was.

"But you've never seen her?"

"No."

"Roland told you she was pretty. Did he say anything else about her?"

"No, hardly anything."

There was another pause. Then:

"I can't think," she said, "why he didn't come and tell me this himself."

She said nothing more. Ralph saw no reason why he should remain any longer. He rose awkwardly to his feet. As he looked down at her, beaten and dejected, his love for her flamed up in him fiercely, and, with a sudden tenderness, he began to speak to her.

"April," he said, "it's been awful for me having to tell you this. I've hated hurting you—really I have. I know you don't care for me, but if you would look on me as a friend, a real friend; if there's anything I can do for you just now.... I can't explain myself, but if you want anything I'll do it. You'll come to me, won't you?"

She smiled at him, a tired, pathetic smile.

"All right, Ralph, I'll remember."

But the moment he had left the room all thought of him passed from her, and she was confronted with the grey, interminable prospect of a future without Roland. She could not believe that he was lost to her irretrievably. He would return to her. He must love her still. It was only two days since he had kissed her. He was marrying this girl for her money; that was why he had been ashamed to tell her of it himself. He would not have been ashamed if he had really loved this Muriel. Well, if it was money she would win him back. She was not afraid of poverty if Roland was with her; she would fight against it. She would earn money in little ways; she would do without a servant. His debts would be soon paid off. She would tell him this and he would return to her.

That evening she walked towards the Town Hall at the hour when he would be returning from the office. She had often gone to meet him without her mother's knowledge, and they had walked together down the High Street in the winter darkness, his arm through hers. Bus after bus came up, emptied, and he was not there. She watched the people climbing down the stairs. She had decided that as soon as she saw Roland she would walk quietly down the street, as though she had not come purposely to meet him. She would thus take him off his guard. But, somehow, she missed the bus that he was on; perhaps a passing van had obscured her sight of it. And she did not realise that he was there till she saw him suddenly on the other side of the pavement. Their eyes met, Roland smiled, raised his hat and seemed about to come across to her; then he seemed to remember something, for he hurried quickly on and was lost almost at once in the dense, black-coated crowd of men returning from their office. The smile, the raising of the hat, had been an involuntary action. He had not remembered till he had taken that step forward, that he had now no part in her life. He felt she would not want to speak to him now. And this action naturally confirmed April in her belief that Roland was marrying Muriel for her money.

"It is me that he loves really," she told herself, and she felt that if she were a clever woman she would be able to win him back to her.

"But I am not a clever woman," she said. "I was not made for intrigues and diplomacy." She remembered how, four years earlier, she had learnt from a similar experience that she was not destined for a life of action. "All my life," she had told herself, "I shall have to wait, and Romance may come to me, or it may pass me by. But I shall be unable to go in search of it." And it seemed to her that this fate had already been accomplished. Roland still loved her; that she could not doubt. But she had no means by which she might recall him to her. "If I had," she said, "I should be a different woman, and, as likely as not, he would not love me."

On her return home she went straight upstairs to her bedroom and, without waiting to take off her hat, opened the little drawer in her desk in which were stored the letters and the gifts that she had at various times received from Roland. There was the copper ring there that he had slipped on to her finger at the party, the tawdry copper ring that she had kept so bright; there was the score card of a cricket match, the blue and yellow rosette he had worn at the school sports when he had been a steward, a photograph of him in Eton collars. She held them in her hand and her first instinct was to throw them into the fireplace. But she thought better of it. After all he loved her still. Why should she not keep them? Instead, she sat down in the chair and laid the little collection in her lap and, opening the letters, she began to read them through, one by one; by the time she had finished the room had darkened. She would have to put on another dress for the evening and do her hair. Already she could hear her father's voice in the hall, but she felt lazy, incapable of action; her hands dropped into her lap, and her fingers closed round the letters and cards and snapshots. Her thoughts travelled into the past and were lost in vague, wistful recollection. Her mother's voice sounding in the passage woke her from a reverie. It was quite dark; she must light the gas, and she would have to hurry with her dressing. It was getting late. She rose to her feet, walked over to the bureau and put the letters back into the little drawer. Her fingers remained on the handle after she had closed it. And again she asked herself the question to which she could find no answer: "What is going to happen to me now?"

CHAPTER XXI
THE SHEDDING OF THE CHRYSALIS

The official position of fiancé was a new and fascinating experience, in the excitement of which Roland speedily forgot the unpleasantness that its announcement had caused in Hammerton. It was really great fun. Important relatives were asked to meet him, and he was introduced to them by Mr Marston as "my future son-in-law." Muriel insisted on taking him for walks through the village for the pleasure of being able to say to her friends: "This is my fiancé." And when he complained that he was being treated like a prize dog, she asked him what else he thought he was. Muriel had always been a delightful companion and the engagement added to their relationship a charming intimacy. It was jolly to sit with her and hold her hand; and she was not exacting. She did not expect him to be making love to her the whole time. Indeed, he did not make love to her very often. They kissed each other when they were alone, but then kisses were part of the game that they were playing. April had at first been too shy to pronounce the actual word "kiss." She had evaded it, and later, when she had come to use it, it had been for a long while accompanied by a blush. There was no such reserve between Muriel and Roland. Kisses were favours that she would accord to him if he were good. "No," she would say to him sometimes, "I don't think I'm going to let you kiss me this afternoon. You haven't been at all the faithful and dutiful lover. You didn't pay me any attention at lunch; you were talking to father about some silly cricket match and I had to ask you twice to pass me the salt. I oughtn't to have to ask you once. You ought to know what I want. No! I shan't let you kiss me."

And then he would entreat her clemency: he would hold her hand and kneel on the wet grass, an act of devotion to which he would call her notice, and beseech her to be generous, and after a while she would weaken and say—yes, if he was very good he might be allowed one kiss. No more! But when his arms were round her he was not satisfied with one, he would take two, three, four, and she would wriggle in his arms and kick his shins and tell him that he had taken a mean advantage of her; and when he had released her she would vow that as a punishment she would not kiss him again—no, never, not once again, and then would add: "No, not for a whole week!" And he would catch her again in his arms and say: "Make it a minute and I'll agree," and with a laugh she had accepted his amendment.

There were no solemn protestations, no passion, no moments of languid tenderness. They were branches in neighbouring boughs that played merrily in the wind, caring more, perhaps, for the wind than for each other.

They talked exhaustively of the future—of the house they were going to build, the garden they would lay out. "We'll have fowls," he said, "because you'll look so pretty feeding them."

"And we'll have a lawn," she repeated, "because you'll look so hot when you've finished mowing it."

They would discuss endlessly the problem of house decoration. She was very anxious to have bright designs, "with lots of red and blue in it." And he had told her that she could do what she liked with the drawing-room as long as she allowed him a free hand with his own study.

"Which means that you'll have a nasty, plain brown paper, and you'll cover it with ugly photographs of cricket elevens, and it'll be full of horrid arm-chairs and stale tobacco."

One day he took her up to Hammerton to see his parents and his friends. They intrigued her by the difference from the type to which she was accustomed.

"It's awfully interesting," she said. "They are so different from the sort of people that we see—all jammed together in these funny little houses—all furnished just the same."

"Yes, and all doing the same things," said Roland—"going to the office at the same time, coming back at the same time, and if it hadn't been for Gerald that would have been my life. That's what I should have been. I should have done exactly the same things every day of my life except for one fortnight in the year. And it would have been worse for me than for most of them, because I've been at a decent school, because I'd seen that life needn't be like that. These people don't believe it can be different." He spoke with a savage sincerity that surprised Muriel. She had never known him so violent.

"Roland! Roland!" she expostulated. "I've never heard you so fierce about anything before. Your proposal to me was the tamest thing in the world compared with that."

"I'm sorry."

"I should hope so. I believe you hate Hammerton more than you love me."

So the autumn passed, quickly and happily. And by Christmas time they had begun to speak of an April wedding. There was no reason for delay. Roland was now making over seven hundred pounds a year, and the Marstons were too certain of their son-in-law to demand a long engagement. Yet it was on the very evening when the date was fixed that Roland and Muriel had their first brief quarrel. Roland had been tired by the long discussion, and Muriel's keen vitality had exasperated him. She was talking so eagerly of her trousseau, her bridesmaids, the locality of her honeymoon. She seemed to him to be sharing their love, his and hers, with all those other people who had no part in it. He was envious, feeling that their love was no longer theirs. He was still angry when they stood together on the landing to say good-night to each other.

"I don't believe you care for me at all," he said, "that you regard our marriage as anything more than a pantomime, a glorified garden-party!"

A look of hurt amazement crossed her face.

"But, Roland!"

"Oh, you know what I mean, Muriel, you—well, all these others!" He paused, unable to express himself, then caught her quickly, roughly into his arms, and kissed her hungrily. "I don't care," he said, "you'll be mine soon, mine!"

She pushed away from him, her face flushed and frightened.

"Oh, don't, Roland, don't!"

He was instantly apologetic.

"I'm sorry, Elfkin. I'm a beast. Forgive me, but oh, Elfkin, you really are anxious about the marriage for my sake?"

"Of course, silly!"

"I mean you're glad that we're going to be married soon?"

She was surprised and at the same time amused by the look of entreaty in his eyes.

"Don't look so tragic about it, of course I'm glad."

"But...." He got no further, for she had taken his hands and was playing with them, slapping them against his sides.

"Don't be such a silly, Roland, darling; you ought to know how pleased I am. I'm looking forward to it frightfully; and I know you'll be an awful dear to me."

She brought his hands together in one last triumphant smack, and leaning forward imprinted a light kiss upon his forehead. He tried to draw her again into his arms, but she broke from him.

"Oh, no, no, no," she said, and ran lightly up the stairs. She turned at the corner of the landing to blow a kiss to him. "Good-night, darling," and she was gone.

It was not repeated. Doubt, remorse, hesitation were alike forgotten in the excitement of preparation. He had arranged to take over the lease of a small house on the edge of the Marston estate, and the furnishing of it was a new and delightful game. The present tenants did not relinquish possession till the end of February, and during the intervening weeks Muriel and Roland would prowl round the house like animals waiting for their prey. They were finely contemptuous of the existing arrangements. Fancy using that big room as a drawing-room; it faced south-east, and though it would be warm enough during the morning, it would be freezily cold in the afternoon. Of course they would make that the dining-room; it would be glorious for breakfast. And that big room above it should be their bedroom; they would wake with the sunlight streaming through the window.

"You'll see the apple-tree while you brush your hair," he told her. And they both agreed that they would cut down the large walnut-tree in the garden. It was pretty, but it shut out the view of Hogstead. "It'll be much better to be able to look out from the drawing-room window and see the funny old people going up and down the village street." And Roland reminded her how they had looked down on them that day when they had leant against the gate: "Do you remember?" And she had laughed and told him that he was a stupid old sentimentalist, but she had kissed him all the same. And then the great day had come when the tenants began to move; they stood all the afternoon watching the workmen stagger into the garden, bowed with the weight of heavy furniture.

"I can't think how all that stuff ever got in there," Muriel said, and began to wonder whether they themselves would ever have enough. "We've nothing like as much as that."

And Roland had to assure her that they could always buy more, and that anyway the house had been over-furnished.

"You couldn't move for chairs and chesterfields and bureaux."

It was two days before the last van rolled away and Muriel and Roland were able to walk up the garden path "into our own house." But it was a bitter disappointment. The rooms looked mean and small and shabby now that they were unfurnished. The bare boards of the floors and staircases were dirty and covered with the straw of packing cases, the plaster of the wall showing white where the book-shelves had been unfixed. And the paper that had been shielded by pictures from the sunshine struck a vivid contrast to its faded environment. Muriel was on the verge of tears.

"Oh, Roland, what's happened to our pretty house?" she cried. And it took all his skill to persuade her that rooms always did look small till they were furnished, and that carpets and pictures covered many things.

"But our pictures won't fit exactly in those places," Muriel wailed, "and all our small pictures will have haloes."

"Then we'll get new papers," Roland said.

There were moments when it seemed that things could not be possibly finished in time. On the last week of March there was not a carpet on the floor, not a curtain over a window, not a picture on the walls.

"I know what it'll be," said Muriel in despair, "we shall have to go and leave it half-finished, and while we're away mother'll arrange it according to her own ideas, and her ideas are not mine. It'll take us all the rest of our lives getting things out of the places where she has put them. It's going to be awful, Roland, I know it is. We oughtn't to have arranged our marriage till we'd arranged our house."

Muriel was a little difficult during those days, but Roland was very patient and very affectionate.

"You only wait," he said; "it looks pretty awful now, but one good day's shopping'll make a jolly big difference."

And it did. In one week they bought all the carpets, the curtains, the chairs and tables, and Gerald was dispatched with a list that Mrs Marston had drawn up of the uninteresting things—saucepans, frying-pans, crockery—and with a blank cheque. "We can't be bothered with those things," said Roland.

It was a hectic week. They had decided to spend three hundred pounds on furnishing, and every evening, for Roland was staying with the Marstons, the two of them sat down to adjust their accounts, and to Muriel, who had never experienced a moment's anxiety about money, this checking of a balance-sheet was a delightful game. It was such fun pretending to be poor, adding up figures, comparing price-lists, as though each penny mattered. She would sit, her pencil on her lips, her account-book on one side, her price-list on the other, and would look up at Roland with an imploring, helpless glance, and: "Roland, dear, there's such a beautiful wardrobe here; it's fifty pounds, but it'll hold all my things; do you think we can afford it?"

And Roland would assume dire deliberation: "Well," he would say, after an impressive pause, "I think we can, only we'll have to be very careful over the servant's bedroom if we get it." And Muriel would throw her arms round his neck and assure him that he was a darling, and turn again to the price-list.

And all the while the wedding presents were arriving by every post. That, too, was great fun, or rather it had been at the start.

The first parcels were opened with unbounded enthusiasm.

"Oh, Roland, Mrs Boffin has sent us a silver inkstand; isn't it sweet of her?"

"Muriel, come and look at these candlesticks; they are beauties."

And letters of eager thanks were written. After a week or so the game began to lose its fascination. The gifts resembled each other; they began to forget who had given what, and as they wrote the letters of acknowledgment they would shout to each other in despair:

"Oh, Roland, do tell me what Mr Fitzherbert sent us!"

"I can't remember. I'm trying to think who I've got to thank for that butter-dish."

"The butter-dish!—that was Mr Robinson—but Mr Fitzherbert?"

"But the butter-dish wasn't Mr Robinson; he was the clock!"

"Then it was Mrs Evans; and, Roland, do, do think what Mr Fitzherbert gave us."

And so it went on, till at last they began to show a decided preference for cheques.

And there was the honeymoon: that had to be arranged. Muriel would rather like to have gone abroad.

"I've been only twice. We'll see all the foreigners, and sit in cafés, and go to theatres and see if we can understand them."

But Roland was not very anxious to go abroad. He went there too often in the way of business. He might meet people who at other times were charming, but were not on a honeymoon the most comfortable company. There would be the fatigue of long journeys, and besides, he wanted Muriel to himself.

"I don't want to go and see foreigners, I want to see you."

"Well, you'll have seen a good deal of me before you've finished."

"But, Muriel," and the firm note in his voice forced her to capitulate.

"All right, all right, have it as you like."

And so, after much discussion, it was decided that they should get a cyclist map of England, find a Sussex village that was at least three miles from any railway station, and then write to the postmaster and ask whether anyone there would be ready to let them rooms for a month.

"Three miles from anywhere! Heavens! but I shall be bored; still it's as you wish. Go and get your map, Gerald."

And with the map spread on the table they selected, after an hour's argument, to see if anything was doing at Bamfield.

"It should be a good place," said Roland. "It's just under the Downs."

In all this fret and fluster Mr Marston took the most intense interest. It reminded him of his own marriage and, finding his youth again in theirs, he spoke often of his honeymoon.

"Do you remember, dear, when we went out for a picnic in the woods and it came on to rain and we went to that little cottage under the hill?" And again: "Do you remember that view we got of the sea from the top of Eversleigh?" Little incidents of his courtship that he had forgotten a long time were recalled to him, so that he came to feel a genuine tenderness for the wife whom he had neglected for business, for cricket, and his children; from a distance of thirty years the perfume of those scented months had returned to him.

Gerald was alone unmoved. He was annoyed one morning when he found the floor of the billiard-room covered with packing cases, but he retained his hardly won composure. He accepted the duties of best man without enthusiasm. "At any rate it will soon be over," he had said, and had proceeded to give Roland two new white wood bats.

"They won't last long, but you can't help making a few runs with them." And his friend was left to draw from that present what inference he might think fit.

They were hectic days, but at last everything was finished. The house was papered and furnished, rooms had been booked at Bamfield, and in the last week in April Roland returned to Hammerton. He had had scarcely a moment's rest during the last two months. Life had moved at an incredible pace, and only with an enormous struggle had he managed to keep pace with it. He had had no time to think what he was doing. Each morning had presented him with some fresh difficulty, each night had left some piece of work unfinished. And, now that it was over, he felt exhausted. The store of energy that had sustained his vitality at so high a pressure was spent.

The sudden marriage was naturally a disappointment to his parents. Their opinion had not been asked; the arrangements had been made at Hogstead. Roland had just told them that such and such a thing had been decided, and they were hurt. They had known, of course, all along that as soon as their son was married they would lose him, but they had expected to retain his confidence up till then; and, being sentimental, they had often spoken together of the wife that he would choose. They had looked forward to his days of courtship, hoping to have a share in that fresh happiness. But the pleasure had been given to others; they had had no part in it.

In consequence Roland did not find them very responsive. They listened attentively to all he told them, but they asked no questions, and the conversation was not made easy. Roland was piqued by their behaviour; he had intended to arrange a picnic for the three of them on the last day, but now decided that he would not. After all, why should he: it would be no pleasure for any of them, not if they were going to sit glum and silent. Two days before his marriage he went for a walk in the evening with his father, and as Gerald would be coming on the next day to stay the night with them this was the last walk they would have together. But in nothing that they said to each other was implied any appreciation of the fact. When Mr Whately returned from the office he handed the evening paper to his wife, commented on the political situation in Russia and on the economical situation of France, and was, on the whole, of the opinion that Spanish cooking was superior to Italian, "Not quite so much variety," he said, "but there's a flavour about it that one gets nowhere else." He then proceeded to remove his boots: "And what about a walk, Roland?"

Ronald nodded, and Mr Whately went upstairs to change his suit. They walked as usual down the High Street, they turned up the corner of College Road, they crossed by the Public Library into Green Crescent, and completed their circuit by walking down into the High Street through Woolston Avenue. They talked of Fernhurst, of the coming cricket season, of the marriage ceremony, of the arrangements that had been made for meeting the guests at the church, of the train that Roland and Muriel would catch afterwards. But there passed between them not one sentence, question, intonation of the voice that could be called intimate, that could be said to express not remorse, but any attitude at all towards the severing of a long relationship. As they walked up the steps of 105 Hammerton Villas they were discussing the effectiveness of the new pull stroke that in face of prejudice so many great batsmen were practising.

"I think I shall go down to the nets at the Oval to-morrow, father, and see what I can make of it."

It was a bleak morning and the Oval presented a dismal appearance; a few men were pottering about with ladders and paint brushes; a cutting machine was clanking on the grass; the long stone terraces were cold and forbidding; the clock in the pavilion had stopped; far over at the Vauxhall end a couple of bored professionals were bowling to an enthusiastic amateur who had no idea of the game, but demanded instruction after every stroke. Roland stood behind the net and watched for a while an exhibition of cross-bat play that was calculated to make him for ever an advocate of the left shoulder, the left elbow and the left foot. He had a few minutes' chat with one of the groundsmen.

"Yes, sir, it do look pretty dismal, but you wait. April's a funny month; why, to-morrow we shall probably have brilliant sunshine, and there'll be twenty or thirty people down here, and when you go away you'll be thinking about getting out that bat of yours and putting a drop of oil on it." Roland expressed a hope that this prophecy would prove correct.

April was a funny month: it was cold to-day, but within a week the sun would be shining on green grass and new white flannels. Only another week! The fixing of this date, however, reminded Roland that in a week's time he would be in a small village under the Downs, three miles from the nearest station, and this reminder was somewhat of a shock to him. He would miss the first four weeks of the season. By the time he came back everyone else would have found their form; it was rather a nuisance. Still, a honeymoon! Ah, well, one could not have it both ways.

Gerald was not arriving till the afternoon, and the morning passed slowly for Roland. He walked from Kennington over Westminster Bridge and along the Embankment to Charing Cross; he strolled down the Strand, looking into the shop windows and wondering whether he was hungry enough to have his lunch. He decided he was not and continued his walk, but boredom made him reconsider the decision, and he found himself unable to pass a small Italian restaurant at the beginning of Fleet Street; and as he had a long time, with nothing to do in it, he ordered a heavy lunch. When the waiter presented him with his bill he had become fretfully irritable—the usual penalty of overeating.

What on earth should he do with himself for two hours? How slowly the time was passing. It was impossible to realise that in twenty-four hours' time he would be standing beside Muriel before the altar, that in two days' time they would be man and wife. What would it be like? Pondering the question, he walked along to Trafalgar Square, and still pondering it he mounted a bus and travelled on it as far as a sevenpenny ticket would take him. Then he got on to a bus that was going in the opposite direction, and by the time he was back again at Trafalgar Square, Gerald's train from Hogstead was nearly due.

It was not a particularly exciting evening and the atmosphere was distinctly edgy. Mr Whately was bothered about his clothes, and whether he should wear a white or a dark tie; and Mrs Whately was fussing over little things. "Did old Mrs Whately know that she had to change at Waterloo? Had anyone written to tell her? And who was going to meet her at the other end?" It was a relief to Roland when they had gone to bed and he and Gerald were left alone.

"It's a funny thing," Gerald said; "five years ago we didn't know each other; you were nothing to me, nor I to you, and then we meet in Brewster's study, and again at the Oval and, before we know where we are you're a junior partner in the business and engaged to my sister. To think what a difference you've made to all of us!"

"And the funniest thing of all," said Roland, "is to think that if I hadn't caught the three-thirty from Waterloo instead of the four-eighteen, none of this would have happened. I shouldn't have met that blighter Howard, nor gone out with those girls; and, even so, none of it would have happened if I had taken my footer boots down to be mended, as I ought to have done, on a Sunday afternoon instead of loafing in my study. One can't tell what's going to be a blessing till one's done with it. If I hadn't had that row I should never have met you and I should never have met Muriel." And he paused, wondering what would have happened to him if he had caught the four-eighteen and taken his boots down to be mended. He would have stayed on another year at school; he would have been captain of the house; he would have gone up to the 'Varsity. He would have had a good time, no doubt, but where would he be now? Probably an assistant master at a second-rate public school, an ill-paid post that had been given to him because he was good at games. Probably also he would be engaged to April, and he would be making desperate calculations with account-books to discover whether it was possible to marry on one hundred and fifty pounds a year.

"That now," he said, "was the luckiest thing for me that ever happened."

And they sat for a while in silence pondering the strange contradictions of life, pondering also the instability of human schemes. One might plan out the future, pigeon-hole it, have everything arranged as by a machine, and then what happened? Someone caught a train at three-thirty instead of at four-eighteen, or was too lazy to take his football boots down to be mended on a wet afternoon, and the plans that had been built up so elaborately through so many years were capsized, and one had to begin again.

"And it's so funny," Roland said, "to think of the fuss they made at Fernhurst about a thing like that—just taking a girl out for a walk, and you'd think I'd broken the whole ten commandments, and all the talk about my corrupting the pure soul of Brewster."

Gerald broke into a great laugh.

"The pure soul of Brewster!" he said. "My lord! if you'd known what he was like after he'd been in the house a term. He'd have taken a blooming lot of corrupting then. Gawd, but he was a lad!" And Gerald supplied some intriguing anecdotes of Brewster's early life. "He was a lad!" And Brewster's name started a train of associations, and Roland asked Gerald whether he had heard of Baker.

"Baker? Baker?" Gerald repeated. "No. I can't say I ever remember hearing anything about him. He must have been after my time."

Roland got up, walked across to his bureau, and taking a bunch of keys from his hip pocket unlocked a small top drawer. He took the drawer out and, bringing it across, laid it on the table. It was full of photographs, letters, ribbons, dance programmes, and he began to fumble among them: "I think we shall find something about Master Baker here," he said. "Ah, yes, here we are!" And he handed across to Gerald a large house photograph. "There he is, bottom row, fourth from the right."

Gerald scrutinised the photograph, holding it to the light.

"Lord, yes," he said, "that tells its own story; what's happened to him now?"

"He was head of the house two years ago; he's gone up to Selwyn. I believe he's going into the Church."

Gerald smiled. "When we all meet at an old boys' dinner in twenty years' time we shall get one or two shocks. Think of Brewster bald, and Maconochie stout, and Evans the father of a family!"

"My lord!"

And they began to rummage in the drawer, till the table was littered with letters and photographs.

The photographs led them from one reminiscence to another; and in that little series of isolated recollections they lived again through all that had remained vivid to them of their school-days.

"Heavens!" said Gerald, "who's that? You don't mean to say that's Harrison! Why, I remember him when he first came, a ridiculous kid; we used to call him 'Little Belly.' About the first week he was there he showed his gym. belt to someone and said: 'Isn't it small? Haven't I a little belly?'"

"And here's Hardy," said Roland. "Do you remember that innings of his in the final house match, and how we lined up on each side of the pavilion and cheered him when he came out?"

"And do you remember that try of his in the three cock? — two men and the back to beat and only a couple of yards to spare between them and the touch-line. I don't know how he kept his foot inside."

And as the store of Fernhurst photographs became exhausted they found among the notes and hotel bills delightful memories of much that they had in common.

"The Café du Nord, Ghent! My son," said Gerald, "do you remember that top-hole Burgundy? Yes, here it is—two bottles of Volnay, fifty-three francs."

"Wasn't that the night when that ripping little German girl smiled at us across the room?"

"And when I said that another bottle of Volnay was better than any woman in the world."

A torn hotel bill at Cologne recalled a disappointing evening in the company of two German girls whom they had met at a dance and taken out to supper—an evening that had ended, to the surprise of both of them, in a platonic pressure of the hands.

"Do you remember how we stood under the cathedral and watched them pass out of sight behind the turning of the Hohe Strasse, and then you turned to me and said: 'There's no understanding women'?"

And then there was the evening when they had gone to the opera in Bonn and had had supper afterwards in a little restaurant, from the window of which they could see the Rhine flowing beneath them in the moonlight, and its beauty and the tender sentimental melodies of Verdi had produced in both of them a mood of rare appreciation; they had sat in silence and made no attempt to express in talk the sense of wonderment. Much was recalled to them by these pieces of crumpled paper, and when Roland put away the drawer it seemed to Gerald that he was locking away a whole period of his life. And when they said good-night to each other on the stairs Gerald could not help wondering whether, in the evening that had just passed, their friendship had not reached the limit of its tether. Roland was beginning a new life in which he would have no part. As he heard his friend's door shut behind him he could not help feeling that never again would they reach that same point of intimacy.

CHAPTER XXII
AN END AND A BEGINNING

No doubt the groundsman at the Oval rubbed his hands together with satisfaction when he looked out of his bedroom window on the following morning. It was not particularly warm; indeed he must have shivered as he stood with his shaving brush in his hand, looking at the sky instead of at his mirror. But the sky was blue and the sun was shining, and he would, no doubt, be warm enough after he had sent down a couple of overs at the nets. The thoughts of Roland as he surveyed the bright spring morning were not dissimilar. He saw in it a happy augury. Summer was beginning.

They were a silent party at breakfast; each was preoccupied with his own affairs. They had decided to leave Charing Cross at twelve-thirty-five by a train that reached Hogstead at half-past one; the service was fixed for two o'clock. They would not need to leave the house till a quarter to twelve. They had therefore three hours to put in.

"Now, I suggest," said Gerald, "that you should come down with me to the barber's and have a shave."

"But I've shaved already."

"I daresay you have, but on a day like this one can't shave too often."

And Roland, in spite of his protests, was led down to the shop. Once there, Gerald refused to be satisfied with a mere shave.

"This is a big occasion," he said. And he insisted that Roland should be shampooed, that he should have his hair singed, that his face should be oiled and massaged and his finger-nails polished.

"Now you look something like a bridegroom." And in defiance of Roland's blushes he explained to the girl at the counter that his friend had intended to be married unshaven.

"What would you think," he said, "if your fiancé turned up at the altar with his hair unbrushed and chin all over bristles?"

The girl was incapable of any repartee other than a giggle and the suggestion that he should get along with himself. Gerald then announced his intention of buying a pair of gloves, and when he reached the shop he pretended that he was the bridegroom and Roland the best man. He took the shopmen into his confidence and told them that the bride was very particular—"a very finicking young person indeed"—and he must have exactly the shade of yellow that would match her orange blossom. He produced from his waistcoat pocket a piece of flame-coloured silk. "It's got to go with this," he said.

In the same manner he proceeded to acquire a tie, a pair of spats, a silk handkerchief. As he told his father afterwards, he did splendidly, and kept Roland from worrying till it was time for them to dress.

But the journey to the station was, even Gerald confessed, pretty terrible. It was only five minutes' walk and it had never occurred to them to hire a cab. They wished they had, however, as they stepped down the long white steps into the street that divided the even from the odd numbered houses of Hammerton Villas. Everyone they passed turned to stare at them. They were so obviously a wedding party. "Which is it?" they overheard a navvy ask his mate. "Should be the one with the biggest flower in his button-hole."

"Garn, he's much too young!"

Roland hated it, and the half-hour in the train was even worse. As soon as they reached Charing Cross he made a dash for the platform, leaving Gerald to collect the tickets. But his embarrassment was yet to be made complete, for as he stood on the footboard of the carriage he heard a deep booming voice behind him.

"Hullo, bridegroom!" And he turned to face the bulky figure of a maiden aunt and the snigger of a porter. He did not feel safe till he had heard the scream of the driver's whistle, felt the carriage vibrate beneath him and after two jolts pull slowly out of the station.

He talked little on the journey, but sat in a corner of the carriage watching through the window the houses slip past him, till the train reached meadowland and open country. He knew every acre of that hour's journey. He had made it so often with such eager haste. How much, he wondered, would not have happened to him before the time came for him to make it again? He tried to marshal the reflections that should be appropriate to such an occasion, but he could not. Life moved too fast for thought. A fierce rhythm was completing its circle. He sat watching the landmarks fall one by one behind him, appreciating confusedly the nature of the experience to which he was being hurried.

It was the same at the church. He did not feel in the least nervous. He told a couple of good stories to Gerald in the chancel; he settled the account with the verger; he walked down the aisle and began to speak to his friends as they took their places.

"So good of you to come; hope you had a pleasant journey. See you afterwards."

Gerald was amazed: "You're wonderful! Why, you're as calm as if you were at a tea-party!"

Roland smiled, but said nothing. He attributed no credit to himself. How else should he behave? A swiftly spinning top would, at a first glance, appear to be poised unconsciously upon its point. It did not begin to wobble till its pace was lost. And was not he himself a swiftly spinning top.

He did not even feel nervous when a commotion in the porch warned him of the arrival of his bride; he stood firmly, did not fidget, fixed his eyes upon the door till he saw, framed there picture-wise, Muriel, in white and orange, upon her father's arm. He then turned and faced the altar. The organ boomed out its heavy, ponderous notes, but he hardly heard them. His ears were strained for the silken sound that drew nearer to him every moment. He kept his eyes fixed upon the altar, and it was the faint perfume of her hair that told him first that she was beside him.

During the early part of the service he comported himself with a mechanical efficiency. His performance was dignified and correct. When he found a difficulty in putting the ring on to her finger he did not become flustered, but left her to put it on herself. The ceremony had for him a certain emotional significance. Once, as they stood close together, the back of his hand brushed against hers and the cool contact of her fingers reminded him of the serious oath that he was taking and of how he was bringing to it a definite, if vaguely formulated, ideal of tenderness and loyalty. He meant to make of their marriage a reality other than the miserable, dissatisfied compromise that, for the vast majority of men and women, succeeded the first brief enchantment. His lips framed no prayer; it had been for a long while his belief that the moulding of a man's fortunes lay within his own powers. But that desire for happiness was none the less a prayer. It went as quickly as it had come, and he was once again the lay figure whose contortions all these good people had been called together to observe. He remained a lay figure during the rest of the afternoon.

He walked down the aisle proudly with Muriel on his arm; in the carriage he took her hand in his, and when they were out of sight of the church he lifted her veil and imprinted a gentle kiss upon her cheek. He stood beside her in the drawing-room and received each guest with a swift, fluttering smile and a shake of the hand. The majority of them he did not know, or had seen only occasionally. They were the friends and relatives of Muriel. There were only a few in whom Roland was able to take any personal interest. Ralph was there, and April. He had not spoken to April since the evening when he had kissed her, and he momentarily lost his composure when he saw, over the shoulder of an old lady whose hand he was politely shaking, the brown hair and delicate features to which he had been unfaithful. In what manner should he receive her? But he need not have worried. She settled that for him. She walked forward and took his hand in simple comradeship and smiled at him. She looked very pretty in a grey coat and skirt and wide-brimmed claret-coloured hat. He recalled the day when she had worn that hat for the first time and her anxiety that she should be pretty with it. "You do like it, don't you, darling?" But someone else was already waiting with outstretched hand. "You looked so sweet, Muriel, darling," an aged female was saying. "Your husband's a lucky man!" And by the time that was over, the cake was waiting to be cut and champagne bottles had to be opened, and Roland was passing from one group of persons to another, saying the same things, making the same gestures: "Yes, we're spending our honeymoon in England ... Bamfield, a little village under the Downs ... Sussex's so quiet ... such a mistake to try and do too much on a honeymoon."

He had barely time to exchange a couple of remarks with Beatrice. She came towards him, her hand stretched out in simple comradeship.

"Good luck, Roland," she said. "You are going to be awfully happy. I know you are."

"And when we come back you must come and see us; won't you, Beatrice?"

"Of course I shall."

"Often," he urged.

"As often as you ask me."

Before he had time to reply an obscure relative had begun to assure him of his wonderful fortune and of his eternal felicity.

He caught glimpses of Muriel's white dress passing through the ranks of admiration, and then he found himself being led by the arm to the table where the champagne was being opened and a cricket friend of his, a married man, was adjuring him to take as much as possible. "You don't know what you're in for, old man." And then Gerald was telling him that it was time he went upstairs to change, that Muriel had gone already.

"You're really wonderful, old man," Gerald said, when they were alone. "I can't think how you did it. It's cured me of ever wanting to get married."

There were several telegrams lying on his dressing-table; he opened them and tossed them half read upon the floor. "Thank God I haven't got to answer those," he said. And while he changed into a grey tweed suit Gerald continued to perform what he considered to be the functions of a best man. He chattered about the service, the champagne, the wedding-cake, the behaviour of the guests. "And, I say, old son, who was that mighty topping girl in grey, with the large wine-coloured hat?"

"That? Oh, that was April—April Curtis."

"What! the girl that——"

"Yes, that's the one."

Gerald was momentarily overwhelmed. "Well, I must say I'm surprised," he began. Then paused, realising that as Roland had just married his sister it was hardly possible for him to draw any comparison between her and April. He contented himself with a highly coloured compliment:

"A jolly pretty girl," he said, "and she'll be a beautiful woman."

At that moment there was a tap at the door and Mrs Marston's voice was heard inquiring whether Roland had nearly finished.

"Hurry up, old man," said Gerald, "Muriel's ready." And two minutes later he was running, with Muriel on his arm, through a shower of rose leaves and confetti. They both sank back into the cushions, panting, laughing, exhausted. And as the gates of the drive swung behind them they said, almost simultaneously: "Thank heaven, that's over!"

But a moment later Muriel was qualifying her relief with the assertion that it had been "great fun."

"All those serious-faced people came up and wished me good luck. If I'd encouraged them they'd have started taking me into corners and preaching sermons at me."

But Roland did not find it easy to respond to her gaiety. Now that it was all over he felt tired, physically and emotionally. When they reached the station he bought a large collection of papers and magazines, so that their two hours' journey might be passed quietly. But this was not at all in accordance with Muriel's ideas.

"Don't be so dull, Roland!" she complained. "I want to be amused."

He did his best; they talked of all their guests and of how each one of them had behaved.

"Wasn't old Miss Peter ridiculous, dressing up so young?" said Muriel; and Roland asked whether she didn't think that Guy Armstrong had been paying rather marked attention to Miss Latimer.

"Why, he's been doing that for months," said Muriel. "We've all been wondering when he's going to propose. I don't mind betting that at this very moment she's doing her best to make him. She's probably suggested that he should take her home, and she's insisted on going the longest way."

But Roland's conversational energy was soon exhausted, and after a long and slightly embarrassed silence Muriel tossed back her head impatiently and picked up a magazine.

"You are not very interesting, are you?" she said.

Roland considered it wiser to make no response. He settled himself back into his seat, rested his head against his hand, and allowed his thoughts to travel back over the incidents of the afternoon.

It had been a great success; there could be no doubt of that. Everything had gone off splendidly. But he was unaccountably oppressed by a vague sense of apprehension, of impending trouble. He endeavoured to fix his thoughts on reassuring subjects. He recalled his momentary talk with Beatrice, and remembered that that afternoon he had addressed her for the first time by her Christian name. She had shown no displeasure at his use of it, and as she smiled at him he fancied he had read in the soft wavering lustre of her eyes the promise of a surer friendship, of deeper intimacy. He had seen so little of her during the last few months. It would be exciting to meet her on his return, at full liberty, on an assured status, in his own house.

His reverie travelled thence to Gerald's easy good humour, his unflagging energy, his bubbling commentary on the idiosyncrasies of his father's friends, his surprised admiration of April; and the thought of April brought back in a sudden wave the former mood of doubt and apprehension. How little, after all, he and Muriel knew of one another; they were strangers beneath the mask of their light-hearted friendship. He looked at her out of the corner of his eye. Her magazine had fallen forward on to her lap.

Her eyes were fixed dreamily on the opposite wall of the carriage. Her thoughts were, no doubt, loitering pleasantly in a coloured dream among the agreeable episodes of the afternoon—her dress, her bridesmaids, her bouquets, the nice things everyone had said to her. As he looked at her, so calm, so self-possessed, Roland was momentarily appalled by the difficulty of establishing on a new basis their old relationship.

They had been comrades before they had been lovers. In their courtship passion had been so occasional a visitant.

They were both in a subdued state of mind when they stepped up into the dogcart that had been sent to meet them at the station.

"Tired, Elfkin?" he whispered.

"A little," she said.

The air was cold and she snuggled close to him for warmth; he took her hand in his and held it, pressing it tenderly.

They had a three-mile drive through the quiet English countryside.

And it was quite dark when the dogcart eventually drew up before a small cottage and a kindly, plump woman came out to meet them.

"Ah, there you be!" she said. "I was just expecting you. The supper's all laid out, and I've only got to put the eggs on to boil, and there's some hot water in the bedroom."

Roland thanked her, took down the two suitcases, and followed her up the narrow creaking stairs.

"There," she said, opening a door. "There you are. And if you want anything you ring that bell on the table. I'll just run down and get on with the supper."

Roland and Muriel were left alone in a small room, the greater part of which was occupied by a large double bed, over which had been hung, with a singular lack of humour, a Scriptural admonition: "Love one another." The ceiling was low, the window was overhung with ivy. In midsummer it would be a stuffy room. They looked at each other; they were alone for the first time, and they did not know what to do. There was an awkward silence.

"I suppose you'll want to tidy up," said Roland.

"Well, of course," she answered a little petulantly.

"All right, then; I'll go downstairs. Come and tell me when you're ready."

She was standing between him and the door, and as he passed her he made an ill-judged attempt to take her in his arms. She was tired and she was dusty, and she did not want to be kissed just then. She shook herself away from him. And this mistake increased Roland's despondency, accentuated his nervousness, his vague distaste for this summoning of emotion to order, at a fixed date and at a fixed hour.

Supper was not a cheerful meal; at first they attempted to be jovial, but their enthusiasm was forced, and long silences began to drift into their conversation. They grew increasingly embarrassed and tried to prolong the meal as long as possible. Muriel was not fond of coffee and rarely took it, but when Roland asked her if she would like some she welcomed the suggestion: "Oh, yes, do."

Mrs Humphries, however, had no coffee, but when she read the disappointment of the young bride's face she said she would see if she could not borrow some from her neighbour. And while she ran over the village street Muriel and Roland sat opposite each other in silence; her hands were folded in her lap, and she stared straight in front of her; he played with the spoon of the salt cellar, making little pyramids of salt round the edge.

At last the coffee arrived; its warmth momentarily cheered them and they tried to talk, to make fun of their friends, to scheme things for their future. But the brooding sense of embarrassment returned. Roland, in the intervals of occasional remarks, continued to erect his pyramids of salt.

"Oh, don't, don't, don't," said Muriel impatiently; "you get on my nerves with your fidgeting."

Roland apologised, dropped the spoon, and without occupation for his hands felt more uncomfortable than before. They continued a spasmodic conversation till Mrs Humphries came in to tell them that she would be going to bed directly.

"We get up early here," she said. And would they please to remember to blow out the lamp and not to turn down the wick, as her last lodger had done. She wished them a good-night, and said she would bring them a cup of tea when she called them in the morning. They heard her bolt the front door and fasten the shutter across the kitchen window, then tread heavily up the creaking stairs. For a little while they listened to her movements in the room. Then came the heavy creak of a bedstead.

They were alone in the silent house.

"Well, I suppose we must be going up," he said.

"I suppose so."

"Will you go up first and I'll come when you're ready?"

"All right."

He made no attempt to touch her as she passed him. She paused in the doorway. A mocking smile, a last desperate rally fluttered over her lips.

"Don't forget to turn the lamp out, Roland. My last lodger...."

But she never completed the sentence; and their eyes met in such a look as two shipwrecked mariners must exchange when they realise that they can hold out no longer, and that the next wave will dash their numb fingers from the friendly spar.